ONCE
UPON
A BOY
BAND

ONCE UPON A BOY BAND

JENNY PROCTOR

ISBN: 979-8-9893422-5-9

To anyone who has ever loved a boyband.
(Pretty sure that's all of us.)

A NOTE FROM THE AUTHOR

This book contains a few themes that are serious in nature, including the loss of a parent to cancer (in the past), regret, and grief. It is still a romantic comedy, with lots of fun and laughter and swoony moments. But it does have a few chapters that lean a little more serious than my previous books. Naturally, I decided to balance the serious by writing more kisses into this book than I ever have before. You're welcome.

CHAPTER ONE

Laney

FAIR WARNING. THIS STORY ISN'T VERY BELIEVABLE.

Most stories start with *once upon a time.*

Mine? It's more like *once upon a boyband.*

I'm a twenty-six-year-old woman with a mortgage and a car payment and a career as a veterinarian. I have a gynecologist and a weekly shopping list, and last week, the IRS sent me a letter stating I underpaid my taxes and owe them an additional $438. Letters from the IRS mean I'm solidly adulting, doing very normal things, living a very normal life.

That's the point. I'm so normal, I'm practically boring. Which is why you won't believe that I accidentally fell in love with a popstar.

Twice, really. But the first time was completely one-sided, so I'm not sure it counts.

I was fifteen, and the teen boyband Midnight Rush had just dropped their debut album.

I was not a popular teenager by any stretch. I figured myself out in college, but high school was a lot of too-short bangs and social fumblings and watching other people live life while I stood on the sidelines and worried about the chocolate stain on my white shorts.

I muddled my way through the obligatory high school things. Prom. Homecoming. The occasional football game. But mostly I spent a lot of time at home. Alone. Obsessing over Midnight Rush.

Specifically, Deke Driscoll.

He was the quietest of the four-member group. A little shy, which made me think he would appreciate my similarly introverted tendencies. In interviews, he always came across as bashful, like he couldn't quite believe he was an international popstar.

I could believe it, though. His voice was my favorite of the four, plus, he had these enormous blue eyes and light brown hair that did this swoopy thing over his forehead. He was constantly brushing it back, and there were countless compilations on the internet of Deke running his fingers through his hair in just the right way. Because of course there was. He was perfect. Justifiably beloved by millions of teenage girls worldwide.

A year later, when I stood on the front row of a Midnight Rush concert celebrating my sixteenth birthday, I was convinced I would never experience a happier moment.

Once we get to the end of this, you'll laugh at the irony of that statement.

For now, let's just say that when Deke crouched down at the edge of the stage and touched my hand, holding my gaze for the briefest moment, something inside me shifted. I felt seen. Understood, even, which, in retrospect, I realize was a completely ridiculous thought. But somehow, I *knew* that if I had the chance to talk to Deke about my parent's divorce or my brother's struggle to get through college, or the fact that my best friend was moving at the end of the summer, forcing me to face the last two years of high school alone, he would get it.

It wasn't real love. I know that now. But my love for Deke —for all of Midnight Rush—saved me when I really needed saving. It gave me an online community of friends who understood and shared my obsession. It gave me something to focus on when life felt too hard or too scary or too overwhelming.

Rest assured, while I still feel a happy wave of nostalgia whenever a Midnight Rush song comes on the radio and I may crank up my playlist so I can sing along in the shower whenever I need a mood boost, I did eventually get rid of the branded sleep shorts that had images of Deke's face plastered on either butt cheek.

I do have *some* standards.

But I'm getting off track. Where were we?

Right. The second time I fell in love with Deke Driscoll.

Well. Hang on. It's a wild ride.

───────────

"Hey, Laney?" My vet tech, Percy, sticks his head into the break room where I'm currently hiding from anything four-legged and wrapping a bandage around my punctured pointer finger. He frowns when he sees my hand. "Wait. That little demon spawn actually broke the skin?"

"I'm no match for an angry chihuahua's anal glands."

"I swear, one of these days, I'm going to sneak over to Mrs. Finley's house and accidentally leave her door open so Fifi can escape. Maybe we'll get lucky, and a coyote will find him before she does."

"Percy!" I say, biting back a laugh.

"Don't tell me you haven't thought it, too."

"Maybe, but I'll never say it out loud. She's probably still out in reception."

Percy huffs and folds his arms across his broad chest. "It would serve her right to know how we really feel. I swear, she trains that dog to be mean on purpose."

I really *do* think Mrs. Finley has a lot to do with Fifi's terrible behavior, but she's old, and Fifi is old, and teaching old dogs new tricks is even harder than teaching old owners new tricks. "I doubt Fifi will live much longer anyway," I say. "I can brave it until then."

"Your patience is admirable. *And*...deserving of a reward." He singsongs this last part, and I look up, eyebrows raised.

Percy smirks. "Exam Two is ready for you. Your favorite mountain man is here with a new litter of puppies."

I force a deep breath through my nose as I secure my bandage and throw away the trash. I will *not* hurry into Exam Two to see Adam, the owner of Hope Acres Dog Rescue, no matter how Percy baits me. I have more self-control than that.

The fact that Lawson Cove's resident dog rescuer happens to have mysterious blue eyes, sexy broad shoulders, and an endless amount of patience even when he's wrangling a dozen puppies does not justify me acting like I'm in middle school.

"Oh, are you too busy?" Percy says, his voice dripping with sass. "I think your dad just got back from lunch. I can always ask him to cover the appointment."

"Don't do that!" I say, closing the cabinet that holds the office first aid supplies with a loud slam. "I'm coming right now."

Dad would happily cover the appointment. He was the vet for Hope Acres before I was—it was a random scheduling thing that moved Adam and his dogs onto my books instead of Dad's—and he's always spoken highly of Adam's operation. But I'm not about to give Adam up now.

I live in a very small town, and the dating scene is basically nonexistent. My all-business interactions with Adam are the most action I ever get.

The thought gives me pause. I really should get out more. Maybe drive over to Franklin or go even farther and spend the weekend in Asheville. I have a few friends from college who live there now. It might be nice to catch up, maybe meet a few new people?

I follow that train of thought for exactly seven seconds before deciding it's a terrible idea. What would I talk about with friends from college? Fifi's anal glands?

I pause outside the exam room door and adjust my scrubs.

Percy gives me a knowing look as he holds out an iPad.

"Don't look at me like that," I say, yanking it from his hands.

"Look at you like what?" he says, his expression a little too coy.

I purse my lips and look over the digital chart Percy created for seven—no, eight—cocker spaniel puppies born out at Adam's rescue. "Like you know what I'm thinking."

He chuckles. "I'm not blind, honey. I *do* know what you're thinking. I'd be thinking the same thing if I wasn't already sure that man in there is straighter than a Michael Bay movie."

I glare at Percy, eyes wide. "Would you hush?" We've never tested just how much you can hear through the gigantic crack at the bottom of the door, and I'd rather not test it now, when Adam could be listening. But I still can't keep myself from whispering, "But also, what makes you so sure?"

"Oh, that's easy," Percy says, his eyes gleaming. "I've seen the way he looks at *you*."

My heart flutters at the thought, but I can't take Percy seriously. The man is such a hopeless romantic, he sees heart eyes everywhere.

Besides, I've been taking care of the dogs from Hope Acres for the past eight months, and I've never had a reason to believe Adam is even remotely interested in me.

Not that I have a lot of practice when it comes to this sort of thing. I'm happy with who I am, but who I am will never be the woman smiling at men across a restaurant or writing my number on a cocktail napkin at a bar.

I once made this argument to Percy when I was grumbling over my perpetually single status, not liking that meeting men actually requires me to be *social.*

He simply shrugged and said, "Fine. Don't try. But you'll only have yourself to blame if you're single until you're dead."

Which...*fine.* He might have a point there.

But Adam? He is not the man who is going to break me out of my years-long dating dry spell. For the past eight months, I've been seeing him once every few weeks, and not

ONCE UPON A BOYBAND   7

once has he ever looked at me like I am anything but the veterinarian who happens to be taking care of his dogs. I'm a means to an end. A necessary part of his workload. Percy really could have called my dad in to cover the visit, and I don't think Adam would have even noticed.

"Wait a sec," Percy says, reaching over and tugging at my ponytail. "How are your waves today? Can we take this down?"

I duck and shrug away, smacking at his hand. "Stop it. My hair is fine."

Percy is annoyingly broad, his shoulders wide enough to practically fill a doorway, and he's doing an excellent job of keeping me from my next patient. Or *patients,* in this case, since an entire litter of puppies needs to be examined. He folds his arms across his muscled chest. "Your hair is *amazing* when you wear it down," he whisper yells. "Why settle for *fine* when you have all this going for you?"

"It doesn't matter. Adam is not interested in me," I whisper back. "End of discussion." I grip the doorknob, giving Percy one final warning look. "Behave, please."

He gives me a generous side-eye that seems to say he's making *no* promises, then follows me into the room.

Adam is sitting on the opposite side of the exam table, a wagon full of puppies directly beside him. He's wearing jeans and a faded t-shirt, a baseball cap pulled low on his forehead. His beard looks a little longer than it was the last time he was here, but he's just as handsome as always, and my heart picks up speed at the mere sight of him.

Adam may not be for me, but that doesn't mean I can't enjoy the view.

The only thing better than tall, dark, and handsome is tall, dark, and handsome...*with puppies.*

Adam is currently holding two—a coal black one and another brown one with a white nose and white-tipped ears.

"Adam," I say after clearing my throat and willing some degree of normalcy into my voice. "Good to see you."

"Hi, Dr. Lawson," he says, the rumble of his voice sending a shiver up my spine. "How are you?"

"Better now that you've brought me puppies."

He stands and lowers the black one into my arms. It looks up at me with sleepy eyes and yawns.

"Oh, you're perfect, aren't you?" I say, holding the puppy close. "How's the mama?"

"Healthy and well," Adam says. "Everything with the delivery went great, and they're all eating like champs."

"Any adoptions lined up yet?" I ask as I move to the exam table with the first puppy.

"Several inquiries. We're still reviewing applications."

I nod, grateful that Adam requires a thorough application process before anyone can adopt any of his dogs. His rescue has only been in operation a little longer than I've been in Lawson Cove, and he can't be much older than I am, though the beard makes it admittedly hard to tell. Either way, he must have done a lot of research because he runs Hope Acres like a seasoned pro.

"I'm sure they'll go quickly once they're old enough," I say. "With these cute little faces, who wouldn't want one?"

I've never asked Adam if he's the one managing the Hope Acres website and the rescue's social media presence, but whoever is in charge, they do an excellent job.

The website and Instagram account is updated weekly with professional-level photos and tons of videos of the dogs romping around acres and acres of gorgeous mountain farmland. Somehow, he manages to frame even the oldest, ugliest dogs in a way that makes them seem adoptable.

Much to my disappointment, Adam never shows his face in any of the content. But I've heard his voice in a few of the videos, so I know he has to be somewhat involved.

Not that I spend a lot of time on the rescue's Instagram page. These are all just very casual observations made in my capacity as veterinarian for the rescue. It doesn't have anything to do with the way his deep voice makes my skin hum with energy.

I quickly finish my exam of the solid black puppy, who is perfect in every way possible, and hand her back to Adam. "Three and a half pounds," I say, looking over to make sure Percy is updating the chart. "What are we calling this one?"

"That's Diana," Adam says. "And the other three girls are Florence, Mary, and Betty."

I lift my eyebrows, studying his face. "The Supremes?"

Something like admiration crosses over his features. "Good catch."

"And the boys?" I swap Diana for the brown and white puppy Adam is still holding.

"George, Paul, John and Ringo."

"Be still your music-loving heart," Percy says under his breath, and I send an elbow into his ribs.

"I love the theme," I say as I lift my stethoscope to the puppy's chest. His heart sounds strong and healthy. "Which one are you?" I hold him up and look into his big brown eyes. "Are you George?"

"That's Ringo," Adam says.

The puppy leans forward and licks the tip of my nose, and my heart melts a little bit. "Percy, tell me I don't need to adopt a puppy."

"Laney, you definitely need to adopt a puppy," Percy says.

Adam laughs. "I'm inclined to agree. And Ringo has a really sweet personality. He's a snuggler."

An image of Adam lounging on his couch with Ringo asleep on his chest pops into my mind. If snuggling with the puppy meant snuggling with the man, I'd sign the adoption papers this minute.

"Don't tempt me," I say. "I'm afraid my work schedule would leave this little guy alone way too often."

"True," Percy says dryly. "And your father would *never* let you bring him to work with you."

Dad's bloodhound, Juniper, has been coming to work with him as long as she's been alive, and she's close to thirteen.

Adam gives me a knowing look. "Let me know if you change your mind. And you're welcome to come out to the rescue anytime."

I freeze and lift my eyes to his, the invitation catching me by surprise.

"To...visit the puppies?" he says slowly, and I give my head a quick shake.

"Right. Of course. That's—I knew that's what you meant."

Percy clears his throat a little too loudly, and I keep my eyes down as I put Ringo on the scale.

"He's been the biggest since the beginning," Adam says, and I nod.

"He's a good size," I agree. "Three-fourteen."

Percy holds Ringo while I administer a couple of vaccines, then he hands the squirming puppy back to Adam while I retrieve another from the wagon. "So, are you into music, then?" I ask. "Is that what inspired the names?"

"I could ask the same thing of you," Adam says. "The Beatles was a softball, but not everyone would pick up on the first names of the Supremes."

"The *original* Supremes," I say. "There were more than just those four."

Adam holds my gaze. "Right again. You know your Motown."

"She knows *everything*," Percy says. "She's like the Wikipedia of American music."

Adam cocks an eyebrow, his gaze sparking with a new interest. "Do you play anything?"

"Oh, absolutely not," I say. "I'm a dedicated listener, but I'm not musically inclined at all."

"Do you sing?"

"About as well as a cat screeching her way through a flea bath."

"I'll vouch for that," Percy says. "I've heard her try. Never *ever* take this woman to karaoke."

"Okay, listen," I say, holding a finger out at Percy. "I never would have gotten up to sing if Mimi hadn't guilted me into it. She's very convincing."

Adam chuckles. "Mimi?"

"My grandmother," Percy explains. "It was karaoke night at her assisted living facility, and she wouldn't rest until Laney agreed to sing."

"It was painful," I say.

"So painful," Percy agrees.

"But I'd do it again for Mimi." I look at Adam. "What about you? Do you sing? Or play any instruments?"

Adam shrugs noncommittally, almost like the question makes him uncomfortable. "Uh, maybe a little piano and guitar," he finally answers. "But I mostly just mess around. I'm more of a listener, too."

Something about the way he answers the question makes me think this isn't the entire truth, but I'm so happy to be getting this much undivided attention, I'm not about to push for more. We've been through at least a dozen appointments just like this one, but Adam has never looked at me like he's looking at me now. In fact, I've never heard him say this many non-dog-related sentences together *ever*.

"Do you have a favorite band?" I ask as I finish with another puppy, hoping Percy is noticing my efforts. I'm asking questions! Engaging! Not hiding behind my AirPods and a playlist cranked loud enough to make conversation impossible!

Adam takes the puppy from my hands, trading it for the next one, and my entire body flushes with heat when his fingers brush across mine.

"Just one favorite? That's tough. Depends on my mood, my location, whether I want something with words or something more chill."

"Okay, let's make this less complicated," I say. "If you were to pull out your phone right now and play me the last song you listened to, what would it be?"

Adam doesn't even hesitate before pulling out his phone and dropping it onto the counter between us. The puppy Percy is holding in place leans forward to sniff Adam's hand, and he scratches its ears while he pulls up his playlist.

"Bon Jovi," he says, pulling up the last song. "'Living on a Prayer.'"

"A classic," I say. "Good choice."

He nods and repockets his phone. "Okay. Your turn."

My eyes widen as I think back to my drive into work this morning. I normally wouldn't remember a specific song without having to look. The playlist I listen to most frequently has over five hundred songs on it, and I usually just let it play on shuffle. But I remember this morning distinctly because one of my favorite Midnight Rush songs came on, and I refused to get out of the car until I'd finished the entire thing. Percy stood at my window, shaking his head and rolling his eyes as I belted out the last of the lyrics. Badly and entirely off-key. As soon as it ended, I restarted the song just to spite him and would have listened to it all the way through if Dad hadn't climbed out of his truck and looked at me like I was back in high school and making very poor choices.

Adam doesn't exactly strike me as the kind of man who would be familiar with a ten-year-old boyband song though, so I opt for a different favorite. "I don't have my phone on me, so I can't show you, but if I could, it would be 'Just Breathe,' by Pearl Jam," I say.

Percy scoffs from beside me. "Uh, that is not what I—"

I shoot him a look—he's not about to out me as a Midnighter when I'm *finally* having a real conversation with Adam—and he manages to reroute his sentence.

"—what I thought that song was called," Percy says instead, but he doesn't spare me another eye roll.

Adam has to be able to tell I'm not telling the truth, but he doesn't question. He only lifts his eyebrows, giving me an appreciative nod. "Good song."

"Yeah. I think so too."

He holds my gaze for a long moment before reaching down to pick up another puppy.

I take as long as I possibly can to examine this one

because she's the last one, and Adam is *still* asking me questions about music.

How do I feel about U2's *Songs of Surrender*? What was the last concert I attended live? Do I have a favorite Taylor Swift song? Do I agree that Red Renegade is the most underrated band of all time?

(Love it, Coldplay, "Exile," and absolutely not.)

I feel the heat of Percy's gaze as he watches our conversation, but I'm not about to look at him because then I'll blush and then he'll laugh and then Adam will know that to me, the fact that we're talking like this is a very big deal. Percy can tease me about it later when Adam is gone.

I hand the last puppy back to Adam and loop my stethoscope around my neck. "They all look really great," I say. "Healthy and happy."

"Good to hear," Adam says. He lifts the brown and white puppy out of the wagon and holds him out toward me. "Are you sure you don't want me to save Ringo for you?"

I scoop up Ringo and snuggle him under my chin. He leans up and licks my cheek before huffing out a tiny puppy breath and nuzzling into my neck. "Oh my gosh. He really is perfect, isn't he?"

Adam grins. "He seems to feel the same way about you."

"Oh, this is a done deal," Percy says. "It's love at first sight."

It really does feel like love at first sight. This puppy is perfect. I can't explain it, but he totally feels like he's supposed to be mine.

Which is totally unexpected.

I'm so busy. And I don't have a fence in my backyard and...okay, those are the only excuses I have, but they're both good ones. Puppies are a lot of work.

I kiss the top of Ringo's head, then hand him back to Adam. "Don't *not* list him for adoption, but if you get any serious applicants, maybe check with me first?"

"Can do," Adam says. He hesitates another moment, like he might say something else, but then his eyes dart to Percy and he seems to think better of it.

I could easily think of something for Percy to go and do, but usually it's *me* who's leaving at this point and Percy is the one who makes sure Adam has all the paperwork and records he needs on his way out. We've all done this enough times to know that's how things usually go, so to get rid of Percy would be an obvious *move,* and I am not, in any sense, an *obvious move* kind of person.

Adam clears his throat. "All right, well, I guess that's it, then. And they'll have the updated immunization records for me up front?"

"They should," Percy answers for me, shooting me a conspiratorial look. "Actually, let me head that way now, and I'll make sure they've got it all printed for you."

"Great. Thanks, Percy," Adam says. He holds my gaze for one more beat, but he doesn't say anything else even though he looks like he wants to.

Say something, Laney! Just say something!

I try out a couple of sentences in my brain. How do you feel about the evolution of disco and funk music in the seventies? Did you know Elton John had a cocker spaniel named Arthur? But before I can make any of the words actually come out of my mouth, Adam turns and pulls his wagon full of puppies toward the door.

"I'll see you next time, then," he says.

I nod, wishing, not for the first time, that I had the courage to say something witty and bold. Something like, *Or maybe I could see you sooner?* But then the moment passes, and Adam is in the waiting area, following after Percy.

I groan and head the opposite direction into the back room. Patients are already stacking up, so I don't exactly have time to dwell on what I *could* have said, but it's hard not to feel irritated with myself.

Comfortable in my own skin? Sure. But these are the moments I wish I could be a little more extroverted. Once, when I was in college, my roommate made a passing comment about my tendency to always play it safe. She didn't say it like it was a bad thing, just that it was the opposite of her. She always said the flirty thing, and I never said the flirty thing. She always chose bold, and I always chose... *safe.*

Am I truly incapable of taking life by the figurative horns and *making* something happen?

I grab my iPad and pull up the notes for my next appointment.

"*Please* tell me you gave him your number and the two of you are getting together this weekend," Percy says as he pushes into the backroom.

I stare down at the digital chart in my hands and refuse to make eye contact.

"Laney," Percy says.

I don't need to look up to know he's scowling at me, likely with his hands perched on his hips.

"What?" I say. "I'm kind of busy here. I've got another patient to see."

Percy glances at the chart. "Your next patient is still on the scale out front. He isn't ready for you yet, and you know it."

I sigh and look up. "Fine. No. I didn't give Adam my

number. But he didn't ask for it, so I don't know why you're acting like it's my fault."

"Laney! He was waiting for me to leave! He was clearly into you. Did you give him *any* indication you wanted him to ask you out?"

I think of the witty words I didn't say and frown. "I've never been particularly good at that kind of thing."

"But you had the perfect opportunity! And you two were seriously vibing!"

I sigh. I'm plenty irritated with myself. I don't need Percy to make me feel stupid on top of my own self-recrimination. "Why do you care so much anyway? He's just a random guy."

"He is not just a random guy. He's a guy I know you like. And for the first time, he seemed like he might like you back." Percy reaches forward and takes the chart out of my hands, forcing me to look at him. "Laney, you haven't dated anyone in *months*. I'm bored on your behalf, and that man is probably the most eligible bachelor in all of Lawson Cove. Can you blame me for wanting you to shoot your shot?"

"What are we shooting?" Dad says as he comes up behind us. "Am I invited?"

"We're just talking about Laney's dating life," Percy says.

Honestly. Does the man have *no* respect for my privacy?

"Dating? I suppose shooting could be fun on a date. Has someone invited you to go hunting?" Dad asks. "Bear or deer? I hear bear permits were hard to get this year."

"Nobody invited me to go hunting, Dad. Shooting your shot...it's just an expression. Like, taking a chance. Going for it."

"Ah. Not literal shooting, then. I think I'm following. Is there anyone in particular you're thinking about dating?" He lifts his eyebrows suggestively, and I suddenly wonder if he

knows something, if he's somehow observed my slight preoc-
cupation with Adam. But that would be ridiculous. My
father is a brilliant veterinarian and kind to his very core.
But he lives almost entirely inside his own head. He's not
observant about things like this.

When I was young, I thought it was indifference. Mom
definitely thought it was indifference—something that led to
their divorce and Dad's move to Lawson Cove halfway
through my freshman year of high school.

But now, working with Dad, getting to know him as an
adult, I understand more about how his brain works. He
cares deeply. He's just not very good at picking up on
nuance. At reading emotions. He claims it's why he works so
well with animals. Because animals are so much simpler
than humans.

I clear my throat and shrug. "No one in particular."

Percy huffs out a laugh and rolls his eyes, which only
makes Dad grin.

He leans over and kisses the side of my head. "Why don't
you take off for the afternoon?" he says. "I've run out of
patients myself, so I can take care of the rest of yours."

I look at Dad. "But you always leave early on Fridays."

"True. But I don't have anywhere to be right now.
Besides, there's a young man in the parking lot who looks
like he could use some help. I could be wrong, but I think he
might enjoy getting it from *you* more than me."

Percy's eyes widen, and he hurries across the room,
peering through the door that leads out into the lobby where
the mostly glass wall of the office gives a clear view of the
parking lot. "It's Adam!" he says, his voice low. "Why is he
still here?"

"Why are you whispering?" I ask. "It's not like he can hear you."

"What was it you said earlier about shooting your shot?" Dad asks. He tilts his head toward the parking lot. "Now is as good a time as any."

I narrow my eyes. "How long have you known? Did Percy tell you?"

Dad only shrugs. "Tell me what? You should probably hurry, Elena. Adam and his puppies might not be in the parking lot for long."

CHAPTER TWO

Adam

I'M TRYING TO LOOK ON THE BRIGHT SIDE.

I could have locked my keys in my SUV *after* I put the puppies inside. I could be worrying about the temperature inside the locked car, about potential puppy dehydration, about the length of time it will take the locksmith to show up and break in.

Okay, I should probably be concerned about that last one even with the puppies next to me instead of inside the SUV. The puppies are fine—for now—but they still aren't fully weaned, so the faster I get them back to their mom, the better.

I send a second annoyed text to my sister Sarah, who has, so far, been irritatingly unresponsive, then shuttle the squirmiest two puppies over to the strip of grass at the edge of the parking lot for pee breaks.

Where could Sarah even be? She's the only other full-time employee at Hope Acres, so she should be at the farm with access to my spare key and her own car, which she could easily use to drive down and rescue me.

To be fair, half of Hope Acres has terrible cell reception. If she's out in the barn with the dogs, she's too far from the house to use the Wi-Fi, and her phone won't pick up a signal.

I sigh and glance at my watch, feeling ridiculously stupid this even happened in the first place, then scoop up the puppies and drop them back in with their siblings. At least the cocker spaniel puppies are too small to climb out of the foldable wagon I use for transport. If this were a litter of full-sized goldendoodles, they'd be escaping one after the other.

"Adam?"

I spin around to see Dr. Lawson—Dr. *Elena* Lawson— standing on the sidewalk. Her bag is over her arm, like she's going home for the day, and her hair is down, long, light brown waves cascading over her shoulders.

I swallow as my eyes move over her. I've never seen her with her hair down.

"Hey." I pull off my hat and take an awkward step forward, then put the hat back on again.

Dr. Lawson lifts her eyebrows. "Everything okay?"

I look back toward my SUV. "Not really? I seem to have locked my keys inside the car."

"Oh, no," she says. "How did that happen?"

"It happened before the appointment, actually. I just didn't realize it until now. I've called a locksmith. He should be here"—I look at my watch one more time—"in eighty-three more minutes?"

She frowns. "Adam, you can't sit in the parking lot with eight puppies for eighty-three minutes."

"I won't stay in the parking lot. I was just on my way back inside."

She frowns. "Do you have a spare key somewhere?"

I nod. "Back at the rescue."

"Then let me drive you there. We can drop off the puppies, then I'll bring you back to pick up your car."

My mouth goes dry at the thought of spending time alone with Elena Lawson. Especially after the way we connected today. Eight months ago, the first time she walked into the exam room instead of her father, I was immediately struck by how beautiful she was. I was a little distracted because a dog had just thrown up on the lower half of my left pant leg, but I noticed her. *Really* noticed her. And wondered if she might, at some point, be someone I could get to know.

But then she had this very professional vibe about her, like she wanted to keep things strictly business, so I just assumed she was either one, not interested—I did reek of dog barf, after all—or two, already seeing someone else.

Until earlier today, when I overheard her and Percy talking right before they came into the exam room. He was teasing her—teasing her about *me.*

So I pushed a little. Asked her questions about something other than the dogs. She surprised me with how quickly she responded and with how much she knows about music.

I'm still not sure she's interested.

Percy could have been totally off-base, and I'm not particularly good at reading a woman's more nuanced signals.

But I am sure that *I'm* interested.

Dr. Lawson is beautiful in this easy, understated way that

I really appreciate. Minimal makeup—at least not that I can see—and her hair is usually pulled back in a practical ponytail, which makes sense considering what she does for a living. But her eyes are bright, and her smile is wide and friendly, and she has a dusting of freckles across her cheekbones that I notice every time I see her.

Taking up her entire afternoon because I was an idiot and locked my keys inside my car isn't exactly first-date material, but I'm not about to turn down the chance to spend more time with her.

"You're sure you don't mind?" I say. "We could easily hang out in the lobby until the locksmith gets here. Or my sister, Sarah, who works with me at the rescue and will probably get my seventy-two texts any minute."

She laughs as she steps forward, scooping Ringo into her arms. "You *could* do either of those things, but I'm sure the puppies would appreciate some time with their mama after getting their vaccines. And the sooner the better. Just let me help. I promise I don't have anything else to do with my afternoon." She smiles at the puppy, cuddling him close, and a bolt of awareness flushes through my body.

"Okay. If you're sure. I really appreciate it."

She meets my eye. "Yay. More puppy time for me."

We make quick work of wheeling the wagon around the corner of the building to what I assume must be the employee parking lot. We stop beside a black sedan, and I quickly realize the challenge this is going to be. If I could get into my SUV, I would transfer the puppies from the wagon into a smaller travel crate lined with beach towels in the back to keep them safe and mostly immobile for the drive home. I can't just leave them in the wagon because I'll need to break it down for it to fit in Dr. Lawson's trunk, and there's no way I can hold eight squirmy puppies in my lap for the twenty minutes it will take to drive out to the rescue.

Dr. Lawson looks from me to the puppies, then back to me again. "We have a problem, don't we?"

"Looks like it," I say.

She purses her lips to the side, and I'm momentarily distracted by their deep pink color, by the fullness of her bottom lip as she grasps it between her teeth. "Okay, give me a sec. I think we've got some travel crates inside." She hands Ringo over to me, who she's been holding this whole time, and moves toward a side door that I'm guessing is the regular employee entrance.

It's not lost on me that when Dr. Lawson came outside to leave, she came through the front door, and I feel an irrational pulse of joy at the possibility of her having done it on purpose.

Though that could have everything to do with her concern for the puppies and nothing to do with *me*.

While she's gone, I cancel my request for a locksmith, then crouch down to check on my reflection in the side mirror on Dr. Lawson's car. Nose, teeth, everything looks good, so I stand back up and adjust my hat, forcing myself to relax. This is fine. *Easy.* I've got this.

She's back less than a minute later holding two cardboard carriers, one in each hand. "What do you think?" she says, holding them up. "Think we could fit four puppies in each one?"

"Definitely," I say. "Thanks again, Dr. Lawson. This is definitely going above and beyond."

"Call me Laney," she says. "That's what everyone calls me. And I promise, I'm so happy to help."

Five minutes later, the puppies are secure in the back

seat, I'm settled into the passenger seat, and Dr. Lawson—
Laney—is buckling her seatbelt beside me.

The nickname suits her. Also, her car smells amazing, like citrus and cinnamon and something else I can't quite name. I almost ask her how she manages it. She works with animals as much as I do, and I'm constantly battling the smell of musty wet dog that seems to permeate every corner of my SUV. Though, she doesn't take work home with her like I do, so maybe I shouldn't be surprised.

As soon as Laney's phone connects to the car, music blasts through the speakers at high volume, the familiar lyrics of Midnight Rush's first number-one hit filling the space between us.

My gut tightens as Laney's eyes go wide, and she reaches forward to turn it off, plunging us into silence. "Sorry. I had no idea that would be so loud."

I cock my head and lift an eyebrow, ignoring the surprise and embarrassment that washed over me at the sound of my own voice ringing through Laney's speakers. "Pearl Jam, huh?"

She purses her lips. "That was...I must have heard that one *before* this one."

"Right," I say, drawing the word out in a teasing tone. "Should we track back a song just to check?" I reach for her phone, which is sitting on the console between us, like I'm going to do just that, and she swats my hand away.

"You wouldn't dare," she says through a laugh. "I promise there's plenty of Pearl Jam on my playlist. And I *did* hear 'Just Breathe' at some point on my morning drive."

"You seem like you're trying awfully hard to convince me. You sure you aren't hiding a playlist of nothing but Midnight Rush songs?"

Her eyes dart to mine. "Hmm. He knows the group name. Are we sure I'm the *only* fan inside this car right now?"

I pull my hat a little farther down on my face. It's been long enough since anyone has recognized me as *the* Deke Driscoll that I've stopped worrying about it happening. When I walked off the stage at the O2 Arena in London after singing with Midnight Rush for the last time, I was barely eighteen, three inches shorter, and at least thirty pounds lighter. I look nothing like the kid I was back then, but I still haven't quite shaken the weird sense of self-awareness whenever I'm somewhere public and a Midnight Rush song happens to play.

Talking about the group with Laney only intensifies that feeling, as well as triggering a potent sense of dread deep in my gut. My anonymity isn't something I take lightly. I don't *want* to be Deke Driscoll anymore, so protecting my privacy is very important. It's the biggest reason I haven't really done much dating. I can't get serious with someone and *not* tell them about my past.

But that part is also complicated. I never know if people will believe me, and the idea of trying to convince someone just feels entirely too uncomfortable. But more than that, Midnight Rush didn't exactly end on the greatest terms. If people know I used to be Deke, what will keep them from asking questions? From digging into a past I'd much rather leave...well, *in the past*?

I look over at Laney. "So you're saying you *are* a fan?"

"So *you're* avoiding the question?" she fires back.

"I'm in my twenties," I begrudgingly say. "Anyone in their twenties has heard of Midnight Rush."

"True. But you recognized their song in less than three measures. That's saying something."

I recognized the song because I was the one singing it. But I'm not going to split hairs if she isn't.

"I had a girlfriend who was a big fan," I say, because technically, I did. So what if I was only sixteen and was actively in the band at the time. My reason isn't a lie.

Laney huffs out a laugh. "Right. And all those guys singing along at Taylor Swift concerts are *only* there for their girlfriends."

I roll my eyes. "Fine. They had some great music. Is that what you want me to admit?"

She smiles and sits up a little taller. "It is, thank you. Someone who knows as much about music as you do should recognize their greatness. Thanks for being man enough to acknowledge it."

I allow myself a small moment of pride at her words, but I squelch it before it can really take root. The truth is, I was a very small part of what made Midnight Rush great...but a very large part of what made Midnight Rush *end*.

Even eight years later, I still feel conflicted about that.

Laney eases to a stop at a red light right in the middle of Lawson Cove. "Left here? Aren't you out on Highway 23?"

"Yep," I say. "Left here, then right onto the highway. The rescue is six miles out on the right."

She nods and makes the turn, and we pass the sign at the edge of town that reads, "Thanks for Visiting Lawson Cove."

I look over at Laney, suddenly curious. "Are you a Lawson Cove Lawson? Or is that just a coincidence?"

"I am *that* family of Lawsons," she says. "My grandfather's grandfather established the town in 1873, and at least some combination of extended family members has lived here ever since."

Most people who are native to Lawson Cove have a distinct Southern accent, lilting but with a twinge of something I've only heard in the Appalachian mountains. Laney's dad has traces of it, though his is softer than most, but I don't detect much accent from Laney.

"Did you grow up here?"

"Some," she answers. "I lived over in Hendersonville, mostly. But my parents got a divorce when I was fifteen, and my dad moved home—here—to start a new practice. I spent summers and holidays with him from then on."

"I'm sorry," I say. "Divorce can't be fun."

"Honestly, my parents were so much easier to be around once they *did* divorce. We were all happier after. And they get along great now. I know it can cause a lot of scars for some kids, but once I got over the initial shock of all the change happening so fast, I mostly just felt relieved." She turns onto the highway and shoots me a questioning look. "What about you? What brought you to Lawson Cove?"

"How do you know I didn't grow up here?"

"Because Patty made sure we all knew about it when you moved in."

"Patty from the front desk?"

Laney nods. "She worked at the high school for twenty-three years before Dad hired her. She knows every kid who has ever lived in Lawson Cove, and you aren't on that list."

A twinge of something close to regret—maybe more like wistfulness?—washes over me. I like the sound of living somewhere long enough to belong to a community like that. To have people immediately recognize you. *Know you.* I didn't have that growing up.

Mom was on her own with Sarah and me, and we moved around a lot as she shifted from job to job, each one a little better than the last. We went to three different elementary schools and two middle schools before we finally landed somewhere that stuck—in a tiny town just outside of Knoxville, Tennessee. Mom had a steady paycheck, we lived on a nice street a couple of blocks from the high school, and we were only a few minutes away from where Mom had grown up, so even though her parents were both gone, I could tell she felt more settled than she ever had before.

I might have found that sense of community in high school. But then, the summer after my freshman year, I paid my neighbor, who was two years older than me and had a car, a hundred bucks of the money I'd made mowing lawns to drive me over to Nashville so I could audition for Midnight Rush. New Groove Records was on the hunt for a boyband and was holding open auditions to anyone fifteen to eighteen years old with a decent voice.

I had never, in all my fifteen years, thought about being in a boyband. Or being famous. Or singing anywhere but in my own shower.

But Mom had just gotten her cancer diagnosis. Followed by the statement from her insurance company detailing which treatments they would pay for, and which treatments they would not.

It was pretty black and white for me. If I made it, I'd have money. And Mom needed money.

My chest tightens at the familiar sense of sadness, and I look over at Laney if only to distract my brain from going down this same tired road. I can think about everything I'd do differently a million times. But it won't change my reality, so what's the point?

"Patty's right," I answer. "I grew up in Tennessee. It was the rescue that brought me here. Or the land, really. It had the outbuildings I was looking for and a house that was workable, so I bought it three years ago."

"Three years? You've been here that long?"

"Not exactly. It took a year to make the house livable and get everything set up for the rescue. I spent my first night in the house two years ago tomorrow."

"And you didn't care that Lawson Cove is literally in the middle of nowhere?"

I shrug. "I like my privacy."

"Do you like restaurants that close before eight PM? Or driving an hour to find the nearest Target? I mean, don't get me wrong. *I* love it. But outsiders usually don't."

I grin. There's a hint of Southern in her voice that I haven't heard until now.

"Outsiders, huh?" I say with an intentional twang.

She smiles as she looks over at me. "Shut up. The accent tends to surface when I'm talking about Lawson Cove. Where's *your* accent? Tennessee is just as Southern as here."

Mostly drilled out of me during Midnight Rush interview coaching, but I can't give her that explanation, so I just shrug. "I had a slight accent as a kid, but it didn't stick. And I *do* like that Lawson Cove is so small. I do fine with the grocery store we've got in town, and I don't mind the restaurants closing early because I like to cook."

"Wow," she says. "Maybe you'll make it here after all. What about your social life, though? You don't miss having friends? Dating?" She shoots me a quick glance. "Not that I'm assuming you aren't dating. You totally could be. Just because my social life is nonexistent doesn't mean that's true for everyone here. You probably are dating. I mean, look at you. Who *wouldn't* want—you know what? I'm going to stop talking now."

"You sure? You don't want to add anything else? Because this is pretty entertaining for me."

She purses her lips and scowls, but there's a smile playing around her mouth that makes it clear she doesn't mind my teasing.

"I've been pretty focused on the rescue," I say, "so I haven't worried too much about dating. You're saying I shouldn't get my hopes up?"

"Definitely not," she says. "Not unless you—" Her words cut off, and I wonder how she would have finished that sentence, but we're approaching the turnoff to the rescue, so I don't have time to ask.

"Right here on the right," I say as we approach the wooden sign, flanked on either side by stone pillars.

She slows the car and turns onto the winding, tree-lined drive that will take us up to Hope Acres. Twenty-five acres, to be exact, though most of them are wooded and steep. I've managed to cut a few miles of trails along the ridgeline so I can hike with the dogs, but we mostly stay in the five acres of pastureland that surround the house and barn.

I watch Laney as we approach the house, wondering what she thinks of the place. It'll be more beautiful in a month or so, when summer shifts into fall and everything changes color, but even like this, it's near perfect.

This farm has been a labor of love for me. I renovated the house, the barn, added landscaping and hardscaping to make the grounds comfortable and accessible for anyone coming out to visit—something that happens all the time whenever people come out to adopt. But having Laney see it...somehow this feels different. I don't know why her opinion matters so much, but I find myself hoping she likes it—hoping she's impressed with what Hope Acres has become.

She eases to a stop in front of the giant farmhouse I spent way too much to remodel and leans forward, her eyes taking in the house before she turns to face me. "Adam. This place is gorgeous."

I grin and reach for the door handle. "Come on. Let's get the puppies back with their mom, and I'll show you around."

As Laney climbs out of the car, I take in her profile—the slope of her nose, the line of her cheekbone as she tilts her face up toward the late afternoon sun.

Sarah is always telling me I can't live in secret forever. That eventually I'll have to get more comfortable with telling people about my past.

I've always argued that I'll be more than happy to tell the truth when I meet someone who's worth the effort.

Much to my younger sister's dismay, that still hasn't happened.

But I'm beginning to wonder if the person worth the effort has been standing in front of me this whole time.

CHAPTER THREE

Laney

I DON'T KNOW WHAT I EXPECTED.

But I know it wasn't *this*.

Hope Acres is gorgeous. Stunning.

Lawson Cove has some nicer parts of town. Gated neighborhoods with sprawling lawns and backyard pools and those little signs that warn you each house is monitored with its very own security system.

This isn't like that. It isn't opulent, though the farmhouse does look like it's been recently remodeled. It's glowing white in the late afternoon sunshine, and the front porch is covered in pots overflowing with white and blue blooms. On either side of the house, lush green pastureland lined with white split-rail fencing extends in either direction. Off to the right, an enormous red barn with white trim that matches the fence is nestled up against the tree line, the terrain cutting steeply upward to the Blue Ridge Mountains.

I spin around, taking it all in.

As far as I know, Adam doesn't have another job, and there's no way a nonprofit dog rescue could bankroll a place like this.

Family money, maybe? A random lottery win? If he hadn't already told me he grew up in Tennessee, I might assume the land had always been in his family.

Still, there are a lot of ways people wind up with money, and none of them, at least in Adam's case, are any of my business, so I shove the thought aside and crouch down to greet the golden retriever who's wandered over to say hello. She's actually more red than gold, my favorite variation of golden retriever, and her nose is speckled with a healthy dusting of gray.

"That's Marigold," Adam says. "Or just Goldie for short."

"You aren't very golden, Goldie." I scratch the dog under her chin. "But you're still a pretty girl, aren't you?"

Goldie sits and lifts her paw to shake, looking over at Adam like she wants him to see the gesture.

"Look at you!" I say, shaking her paw.

Adam chuckles. "She likes you. And she wants me to know she likes you."

"It didn't take her long to decide." I stand back up, one hand still resting on Goldie's head.

"She's old enough to be a good judge of character. Which tends to stink for people she doesn't like." He opens the back door of my sedan and pulls out the travel crates full of puppies.

I try not to stare at the flex of his forearms as he does so, but it's a losing battle. When he bends over to set the crates on the ground, I have to shift my gaze to the fluffy clouds overhead. It's too soon to be ogling this end of him, isn't it? I already incriminated myself in the car when I talked about him being so datable. The last thing I need is to get caught staring.

He opens both crates, peering inside, I assume to make sure the puppies are all well, then moves toward the porch. "Let me grab the keys to the Gator, and we'll drive them back to the barn. Do you need anything? Water?"

"Water would be great," I say.

He's back outside in a matter of seconds, a cold bottle of water in one hand and a dangling set of keys in the other. We settle into an oversized all-terrain golf cart, the crates of puppies secured on the back, and I try not to be distracted by the warmth of Adam's arm pressed against mine or the subtle woodsy scent that keeps tickling my nose.

It doesn't really seem fair.

A man who has been wrangling puppies all day long shouldn't smell like a pine forest after it rains with a side of heaven and a sprinkling of sexy.

Or maybe that's just pheromones talking?

I have no idea how it's even possible.

Pretty sure I still smell like Fifi's anal glands.

Oh my gosh. Do I still smell like Fifi's anal glands? I hunch my shoulders forward and try to sniff my scrub top, but I can't detect anything. Surely Percy wouldn't have let me leave if I did. I shift my nose over to one shoulder, then the other.

Adam looks over and lifts his eyebrows. "Are you smelling yourself?"

"No!" I answer much too quickly. Then I wince because clearly I was, and clearly he saw me. "Yes?" I admit. "I'm a little concerned I still smell like Fifi."

"Fifi?"

"More specifically, Fifi's *anal glands.*"

Adam barks out a laugh that warms me from the inside out, though, at this point, that could also just be my embarrassment. I nudge Adam with my shoulder. "Stop laughing! He's a very grumpy chihuahua, and it's an absolute ordeal to treat him, and I'm sure you know how much the stench can linger."

"I do know," Adam says, nudging me back. "If it makes you feel better, I haven't picked up on any traces of Fifi." And then, because he clearly wants to make my heart stop right here in the middle of this pasture, he leans over and sniffs my hair. "You smell good, actually. Like..." He pauses, like he wants to get this right, and my skin prickles with anticipation. "Honeysuckle?" he says. "Or Jasmine?"

My cheeks heat as I reach up and tuck a strand of hair behind my ear. "A little of both," I say. "At least that's what it says on the bottle. You've got a good sniffer."

He grins in a way that makes me almost forgive myself for using the word *sniffer*, then we pull up in front of the barn. A chorus of barks cuts through the afternoon stillness, and Adam smiles.

"They know you're coming," I say.

He glances at his watch. "They know it's dinnertime." He parks the Gator and climbs out to retrieve the puppies. I follow him to the large sliding barn door, waiting while he unlocks and opens it.

Again, with the flexing forearms.

I am going to have *so much* to report back to Percy tomorrow.

Inside the barn, everything is clean and functional and spacious, with good lighting and regulated temperatures. A storage room occupies the front of the barn, plus a full grooming station with an oversized sink and hand sprayer.

Dog kennels fill either side of the aisle, extending all the way to the opposite end. It's no wonder Adam's dogs always do so well. This place is state-of-the-art. He has everything he needs to keep his animals clean and happy and healthy.

We make fast work of returning the puppies to their mom, a beautiful black cocker spaniel with silky ears and friendly eyes, tucked into an oversized kennel closest to the door. She stands and stretches—she probably enjoyed a little alone time—then ambles over to her puppies, who immediately start scrambling over and under and around her. She leans down and licks the top of Ringo's head.

"That's a good mama," Adam says. "Good job, Aretha."

My eyes lift to his. "Aretha? As in, Aretha Franklin? Please tell me all of the dogs here have musical names."

Adam's lips lift in a small smile. "If they come with a name, I let them keep it. But if I'm naming them, music tends to be the theme."

"Oh my gosh. I need to meet them all. And how, in all the times you've brought in dogs, have I not made this connection?"

He shrugs and lifts his hat off his head, running a hand through his wavy brown hair. "I don't know. I think you've seen Elvis, Janis, Taylor. And that's just in the last few months."

I suck in a breath. "That's right! I did see Taylor. She's pregnant, right? Is she still here? Why didn't you tell me you named her after Taylor Swift?"

Adam chuckles. "I didn't think it was relevant." He moves down the narrow aisle between stalls. "She's right down here if you want to say hi."

The dogs bark, tails wagging, as we make our way down to where Taylor is lounging on an elevated bed in the corner of her enclosure. She lifts her head, tail thumping, but doesn't bother getting up. "She has, what, a week left?" I guess, based on the look of her. I can't remember exactly when I examined Taylor in the office, but it was early in her pregnancy.

"Closer to two," Adam says. "At least, according to the ultrasound."

"Can I go in and check on her?"

Adam nods. "Of course." He opens the door for me, and I make my way to Taylor, who shifts, sitting up a little taller as I approach.

"Hey, mama," I say as I scratch under her chin. I ease her back onto her side, slowly moving my hands to her belly. Taylor relaxes under my touch, but I'm still careful as I gently palpate her abdomen. She is *full* of puppies. "How many did we find on the ultrasound?" I ask over my shoulder.

"Four," Adam says. "Hey, she's actually had a little bit of a cough the last few days. Should I be worried about that?"

I give Taylor's belly a final pat. "That's not all that uncommon this close to the end. It's probably just a little bit of acid reflux. If it really seems like it's bothering her, we can start her on an antacid until she delivers." I look up at him over my shoulder. "I've got some samples at the office I can give you if you end up needing them."

Adam moves in behind me, crouching down close enough for me to catch his delicious scent one more time, and scratches Taylor's head. "I appreciate that. I'll keep an eye on her."

"Do you have any idea about the breed of the sire?"

"Not a clue," he says. "I picked her up at the county shelter, and she'd been dumped on their doorstep. Probably because of the pregnancy."

"You're going to have your hands full," I say. "Two litters of puppies at once?"

Adam only shrugs. "It's easier out here than it is at the shelter. We have the space. And plenty of volunteers to help socialize them before adoption."

I sink back onto my heels. "Puppy socializing sounds like the perfect way to volunteer."

Adam stands, then holds out a hand, a clear offer to help me to my feet.

I slip my fingers into his, immediately noticing and appreciating his warm, strong grip. No clammy fingers here, ladies. Just add it to the freaking list.

"You're welcome to come socialize puppies anytime you want," Adam says.

I don't know if he *means* it to sound like a very sexy invitation or if I'm reading *way too much* into things, but my heart rate immediately spikes, pumping so hard, I wonder if Adam can see it pounding through my shirt.

Now that I'm fully upright, I'm standing *very* close to him, and I suddenly wish I were wearing something besides scrubs. That I'd given myself more than a cursory glance in the mirror before I hurried out to the parking lot to see if he needed help. That I could muster up even a sliver of confidence now that his bright blue eyes are looking down at me and the heat from his body is washing over me in delicious waves.

I clear my throat. "Did, um...dinner?"

His eyes narrow. "Dinner?"

At first, I can't figure out why he looks so confused. Then it occurs to me that my inability to clearly form a sentence probably just gave him the impression that I'm trying to ask him out. "Dogs!" I shout, loud enough to make Adam wince and trigger another chorus of barks from the kennels surrounding us.

Get a grip, Laney. And quickly.

"Sorry," I manage to say, taking a deep breath before trying again. "I only meant, didn't you say it was dinner time for the dogs?"

"It's close to it," Adam says. "But they can wait if you need to go. I'd love a ride back to my car, and I don't want to make you wait."

"No, no, I don't need to go," I say. "I can help, even. And..." I look around the expansive barn. "Is there more to see? I'd love to see all of Hope Acres."

Adam smiles. "Help would be great."

It's probably too soon to tell him I'd likely help him with *anything,* but I can absolutely confirm: I am suddenly and completely smitten with Adam.

CHAPTER FOUR

Laney

I AM IN AWE OF THE PROCESS ADAM HAS IN PLACE TO FEED THE dogs. Not because the wheeled cart he rolls down the center aisle of the barn is anything fancy. Most of the dogs eat the same thing, and he measures it out, paying attention to whiteboards hooked on the front of each kennel that specify how much each dog gets. The amazing part is how responsive the dogs are. They sit when he needs them to sit, they wait until food is actually in their bowls and Adam has invited them to eat before they approach their kibble. They even seem to wag their tails in happy gratitude. This man is definitely some kind of magic dog whisperer.

"So...you train, too," I say when we finally reach the end of the row.

He shrugs. "Only the basics. But honestly, it's pretty easy with most rescues. They're usually so happy to be safe and fed, once they decide to trust me, they're pretty eager to please." He rubs his hands together. "Ready for the best part?"

It's hard to imagine anything better than just hanging out with him. Being here like this. But I nod anyway. "Absolutely."

Adam walks to the opposite end of the barn and opens a second sliding door identical to the one we came through, then he walks back through the center aisle to where I'm standing next to the food cart. In every kennel, the dogs are waiting by their doors, tails wagging, like they know what's coming next and they are ready for it.

Adam touches a control panel mounted on the wall next to the supply room. It lights up, and he presses a series of buttons, then, with one final tap, opens all the kennel doors at once. Taylor and Aretha and her puppies stay safely inside their enclosures, but everyone else darts into the aisle and heads toward the open door on the opposite side of the barn.

I follow Adam to the end of the aisle where we step out into the late afternoon sunshine.

"Three acres, fully fenced," he says. "They get this three times a day for at least a half-hour, depending on what my schedule allows. They also get leash walks a few times a week—I have volunteers who come out for that—and they get twice weekly visits to the house so we can work on inside behavior and potty training."

I watch as the two dozen dogs in Adam's care romp around the field, some chasing each other, some walking lazily, some rolling around in the grass.

These dogs are the luckiest dogs in the world.

Adam looks over and catches my eye, a smile brightening his face. He loves this. It's written all over his expression.

I look away, forcing my gaze to the tree-covered mountains climbing into the sky. Based on our time together, if I keep staring directly at his very handsome face, the odds of me saying something stupid are enormously high.

The thing is, Adam has built a life for himself that mirrors almost exactly what I would want for myself. Despite my grumbling about my nonexistent dating life in Lawson Cove, I really love living here. I love the mountains, I love being close to my dad, I love running into cousins and aunts and uncles who have known me since I was a kid. And I would love to have property like this—to have all this land. I've always done better when there's room to breathe.

Of course, in all my imaginings, I'm living *with* someone. Raising a family. Building a life. And Lawson Cove really is tough in that regard. It's hard to meet new people when you already know everyone in town.

But then, I already knew Adam, and I'd never even considered the possibility something could happen between us until today. Not that I'm counting any chickens before they hatch. Maybe this is nothing. Maybe I'm just a ride to get a spare key, and he's only showing me his rescue because I'm his vet and he's proud of his work.

He *does* keep making and holding eye contact though. And he sniffed my hair—which, I may not have a ton of dating experience, but he wouldn't do that with just *anybody,* would he?

I can't fight the tiny flower of hope that blooms in my chest. Maybe finding the right guy is less about location and more about timing.

A breeze lifts the hair at the nape of my neck, and I close my eyes as it brushes over my face. It's still a warm breeze, but there's a hint of cool at the end that reminds me of fall. It won't be long now—just another few weeks or so. I bet this place is gorgeous when the leaves change color.

"I could live out here," I say, eyes still closed, more to myself than to Adam.

But he answers me anyway. "It's not too far away from Target?"

I let out a little laugh and open my eyes. "I may grumble sometimes, but I wouldn't give up living in Lawson Cove for Target."

He nods, like this answer doesn't really surprise him, then he drops his gaze, looking up at me through his lashes, his expression suddenly coy. "And a more active dating scene? Would you give up Lawson Cove for that?"

A weird sense of déjà vu washes over me, and I give my head a little shake. There is an intensity to Adam's gaze that feels familiar, but I can't quite figure out why. Whatever it is, it makes my heart pound in my throat and emboldens me to answer his very pointed question.

"I don't really need a whole scene," I say. "One man would do just fine for me."

He studies me for a long moment, and I get the sense that he's filing this information away. Like he isn't just hearing my words, he's thinking about what they mean, what they say about me.

I look away first, because if I don't, I will either explode or possibly ask Adam to marry me, both things that would unequivocally ruin the rest of my day, and train my gaze on the hazy blue-green of the mountains blending into the sky. "So, how much of this belongs to the rescue?"

Thankfully, Adam runs with the subject change. "Most everything you can see from here," he says. "The property line extends to the top of the ridge. Over there, at the edge of the field, there's a trail that skirts the tree line and comes out on the other side of the house. We use that for leash walks."

He talks for a few more minutes about his volunteer staff and his adoption rates and how hard he works to focus on temperament and family dynamics before matching his dogs with new owners.

He's clearly passionate, his face animated as he tells me about a family who brought their kids out every Saturday for a month until they'd spent time with every single dog, then details an email he recently received from a woman who became engaged to a man she met at the dog park—all thanks to the goldendoodle she adopted last summer.

The longer that Adam talks, the more certain I am that he reminds me of someone. I just can't figure out who.

Despite that one tiny distraction, when he finally finishes, I'm fully convinced he is entirely perfect, and I would very much like for *him* to be the *just one man* I need.

"Adam, this whole thing is unbelievable," I say. "All of it. The land, the way you take care of the dogs. It's amazing."

Adam's cheeks turn the lightest shade of pink, just visible at the top of his beard. "Thanks," he says. "Your dad helped a lot. He must have answered a million questions."

"That sounds like Dad. Has he been out here?"

"Quite a few times," Adam says. "Though, mostly right at first when I was trying to set everything up. I hadn't really worked with dogs before I started the rescue, so I had a lot to learn."

"Really?" I ask. "What were you doing before this?"

Adam immediately looks away, his change in body language so dramatic that I can practically see the wall he's thrown up between us. "Not much," he says, eyes looking out at the horizon. "This was...a new start for me."

Okay. Adam does not like to talk about his past. Noted.

"When did you get Goldie?" I ask, hoping that at least his dog won't be off limits. "Was she a rescue?"

His expression warms the slightest bit, but there's still a distance in his eyes. "She was my mom's dog, actually. I've had her for...going on eight years now?"

Was his mom's dog. I bite my lip. "You lost your mom?"

His eyes briefly meet mine before darting away. "Cancer," he says gruffly.

"I'm sorry."

He's quiet for a beat before he says, "Thanks."

He clears his throat once, then turns and walks toward the barn.

At the door, he lifts his fingers to his lips and lets out a loud whistle. Slowly, the dogs head inside, and Adam makes quick work of ushering them into their respective kennels. Together, we check to make sure everyone has plenty of water and looks settled for the evening, then we're back outside and climbing onto the Gator.

Adam hasn't said anything else since we talked about his mom, and the silence is starting to feel awkward, but I'm afraid to say anything for fear of making things *more* awkward.

It's only going to get worse, though, so I finally blurt, "Did I make it weird by asking about your mom? I'm sorry if I did."

Adam sighs and his expression softens. "If anything, I made it weird. There's no reason you *shouldn't* have asked. I'm just...not very good at talking about her."

"I get that," I say. "I don't understand exactly what it must feel like. But I can imagine."

He pulls up in front of the house and cuts the ignition. "I keep waiting for it to get easier. Eight years should feel like a long time, but sometimes, it feels like it just happened." He shakes his head as he climbs out of the Gator. "Sorry. I didn't mean to make things so heavy."

"Don't apologize. I asked, and I'm glad you told me."

I wait outside while Adam runs in to grab his spare key, then we're back in my car heading down the Hope Acres driveway. I worry it might be hard to talk again after the serious turn in our conversation, but Adam starts telling me a story about a stray pit bull he found at the end of his driveway who refused to leave with him until he followed her a quarter mile down the road to her litter of puppies.

That story leads to another, then another, and we talk easily, any lingering awkwardness between us dissipating completely.

My only complaint is the curvy mountain road we're driving on, because it keeps me from looking over at Adam while he talks.

Learning to drive in Hendersonville—much larger, far less remote—was hard enough. But Lawson Cove takes things to a completely new level. There are no shoulders and no curbs, at least not outside of the two square miles that make up downtown. There are often steep grades going up or down the side of the mountain on either side of the road —sometimes both. There are blind curves, random drive-ways, not to mention a magnitude of squirrels and turtles and bears and deer that love to cross the road seconds before you approach.

I grip the steering wheel, eyes on the road as Adam asks me question after question. About my family, my hobbies, my friendship with Percy, what it's like working with my dad. He even asks about karaoke night at Shady Pines.

Somehow, Adam makes me forget that I don't actually like talking about myself. Or even talking in general. He makes me want to open up—at least when it comes to him— and that's not a compliment I give lightly.

I'm just finishing a story about my little sister Sophie and her social media following—she plays covers of popular songs on her violin and has built a decent fan base—when I pull into the parking lot of my office. "So basically, my little sister is the exact opposite of *me*," I say.

"Not looking to be a star, huh?"

"Are you kidding? There are very few things I wouldn't choose to do over intentionally putting myself in front of an audience. Dental surgery. Pap smear."

"Fifi's anal gland expression?" Adam says through a grin.

I shift the car into park and suck in a breath. "Ohhh, now you're making it hard on me. Can it be a very small audience?"

He laughs. "Thanks again for your help today, Laney. Is it weird that I'm really glad I locked my keys in my car?"

I smile. "I hope not, because I'm glad you did too. Really glad. And thanks for showing me around Hope Acres. It was fun to finally see it."

Seized by a sudden idea, I reach into my center console and grab one of my business cards, then retrieve a pen from my purse. "Listen. I don't normally do this, but if you ever need anything after hours, especially when it comes to Taylor and her puppies, please don't hesitate to call me." I scribble my cell number onto the back of the card. "This is my personal number, so it'll come right to me. For real. Anytime, day or night. Even if it's not dog related."

I freeze the moment the words are out of my mouth, the card still in my hand. Did I just tell Adam he can call me in the middle of the night for non-dog-related reasons?

Adam quirks an eyebrow. "That's a generous offer. So you're saying next time I find a mouse in the kitchen at two a.m., I can call you instead of freaking out?"

"Are you admitting you freak out over mice?"

"Like a tiny fearful child," he says without cracking a smile.

I laugh. "In that case, I hope you do call me. Sounds like something I'd like to see."

I hold out the card, and Adam wraps his big hand around mine, squeezing it for a moment before tucking the paper into his palm.

My skin warms from his touch, my heart responding in that same erratic way it did when he helped me stand inside Taylor's kennel. But the reaction also fills me with courage.

Adam has to feel this too—the *zing* of electricity every time we touch. It makes me wonder how we managed to have so many normal interactions before now without figuring this out.

He slides my card into the front pocket of his shirt. "I'm going to remember this conversation," he says. "I've officially got you down for middle-of-the-night pest control. But I can't promise I won't also call you when I need someone to talk to about music stuff that no one else cares about."

"Yeah? Like what?"

He furrows his brow. "How about...Max Martin's melodic math?"

Listen. I'm absolutely a music nerd. I know this about

myself. My obsession with Midnight Rush was just the beginning of a truly satisfying relationship with music of all different kinds. Most people can talk to me about the basics. They know recording artists. Their favorite songs. But most people aren't bringing up songwriters and their approach to creation in casual conversation. He has no idea what he's doing to me.

"I'm hooked already," I say. "I know of Max Martin, but I've never heard of melodic math."

"It's a songwriting technique," Adam explains. "His hits are not accidental—it's pretty interesting when you really look at the science behind the choices he makes."

"Love it. We can definitely talk about that at two a.m." I turn sideways to face him and pull one leg into my seat, wrapping my arms around my knee. "Though I'm beginning to think I deserve something in return for my willingness to be available at all hours."

"I'm open to negotiations," Adam says.

I grin. "I think I should get to name Taylor's puppies."

"Let me guess. Freddie, Leo, Deke, and Jace?"

I gasp. "You know their names! You really are a Midnight Rush fan."

He chuckles. "I walked right into that one, didn't I?"

"Yes, but don't worry. It's a good thing. Makes up for your fear of mice."

He winces dramatically. "Don't talk about them."

"About cute little harmless creatures? With tiny pink noses and big brown eyes?"

He holds up a finger, his expression serious, and I suddenly wonder if Adam is afraid of mice for real. "Stop or I'm cutting your naming privileges by half."

I let out a little giggle because I literally can't help myself.

I haven't had this much fun in ages. "You would make me pick my favorite two? That's cruel."

"Who would you pick if I did?" he asks, sounding genuinely curious. "If Taylor only has one boy, what would you name him?"

"Deke," I say without hesitation. "That's easy. He was always my favorite."

Adam's eyes sparkle. "Not Freddie? Isn't he the famous one?"

"Pretty sure they all still count as famous," I say. "Freddie's solo career is the biggest, but I still stand by my answer. Deke, then Leo, then Freddie, and finally Jace. But only because Jace is blond, and I'm not into blonds."

I honestly have no idea why I'm telling Adam all this. I haven't thought about Midnight Rush this much in years, much less talked about them with a guy I'm only just getting to know.

But then, maybe it's because I've never met anyone who knows as much about music as I do.

Adam smiles at my admission, then makes a show of pulling down the visor and looking into the mirror. He pulls off his hat and runs his fingers through his hair. "Brown," he says with an adorable smirk, and my stomach swoops down to my toes.

"A very nice shade of brown," I say. I bite my bottom lip as heat climbs my cheeks.

We're sitting here talking, flirting, and I'm actually holding my own. Putting myself out there. And somehow, it feels easy. *Natural.*

Adam reaches for his door handle but pauses before getting out of the car. "So I'm definitely going to call you," he says. "In case that wasn't obvious."

I let out a little laugh. "I'm already looking forward to it."

He studies me for a long moment, his blue eyes fixed on mine. "Why haven't we done this before now?"

"Timing?" I say, with a shrug.

He nods. "Well, I'm glad we're doing it now."

CHAPTER FIVE

Adam

LANEY WAVES AS SHE PULLS OUT OF THE PARKING LOT, AND I wave back, but I don't immediately follow her. Instead, I sit still, hands gripping the steering wheel, and wonder what just happened.

Talking to Laney was unexpected. *Incredible.* Easy in ways that talking to a woman never has been before.

I want to see her again.

I want to pull out of the parking lot and chase her down and see her *right now,* but that would make me creepy and possibly obsessive, so I settle for pulling out my phone instead.

I type in her contact info, then start a text.

ADAM

Hi. I know you just left. Too soon?

I just wanted to say thank you one more time.

> Also, I'm sorry (again) that I got weird when my mom came up. Sarah keeps telling me that making myself talk about her will eventually make it easier. So...here goes.

> My mom had metaplastic breast cancer. She was diagnosed when I was fifteen and died when I was eighteen. Since my dad has never been in the picture, it was just me and Sarah after she died. As a result—we're pretty close. Sarah is my best friend as much as she's my sister.

> Even though she drives me crazy.

> Anyway. Talking to you is really easy, and I'm pretty sure had I said all of this in person, you would have listened and understood.

> And now I'm going to stop blowing up your phone and will probably spend the next half hour worrying about whether I should have texted at all.

> Or at least texted so fast.

> But for real. I'm done now. K, bye.

I read back over my text messages and sigh.

I mean. It could be worse.

I stare at the screen for a moment, but I can't really expect Laney to respond. She's driving. I don't *want* her to respond. *And* now I'm worried about her being distracted by my texts when she should be focusing on the road.

ADAM

> Also, I know you're driving. Sorry. Please don't wreck.

I drop my phone onto the center console of my SUV,

then head back to the rescue, thinking about Laney the entire time.

Sarah isn't going to believe I'm actually putting myself out there. Not that I'm getting ahead of myself. I like talking to Laney. But we haven't even been on a date yet. The point is, I haven't even been interested in trying in *years.*

And now I'm interested.

When I make it back to Hope Acres, Sarah's car is still gone, so as soon as I'm out of the car, I pull out my phone.

I quickly check to make sure I didn't miss a text from Laney, then I call Sarah.

She's a grown woman. Mostly responsible. And I've never been strict about making her keep regular work hours. She manages the rescue's finances and handles our website and social media accounts, both things she can largely do from anywhere, so I don't really care if she comes and goes as she pleases.

But who else will keep up with Sarah if I don't?

She finally picks up on the fourth ring, sounding breathless but alive. "Hey! Are you okay? I just saw all your texts. Do you still need me to come get you?"

"I'm fine. Back at the rescue," I say dryly. "Where have you been?"

She hesitates. "Um, on a date, actually."

"In the middle of the day?"

"Why not?"

"Because normal people work in the middle of the day."

"I ran out of things to do," she says. "Everything is caught up at the rescue, and Jake was available for lunch, so I took off. Sorry I missed you, though. I put my phone on silent when we got to the restaurant, and then we just fell into conversation so easily, and anyway, you know how it is. I'm glad you're okay."

I will myself not to worry simply because Sarah spent the entire afternoon with a man I don't know. She goes on lots of dates, though maybe that's part of why I *do* worry. I would love to see my sister settle down with someone nice, someone reliable with steady work, their own apartment, but so far, she's mostly fallen for guys who are the exact opposite.

She calls them mysterious and exciting. *Free spirits.*

I call them irresponsible freeloaders.

We have agreed to disagree on this point.

"Tell me about Jake," I say as I drop onto the front porch step. Goldie gets to her feet, struggling with her hips as she does, then wanders over and drops her head onto my knee. I wince at the reminder of Goldie's age. She isn't getting around as easily these days. "Are you still with him now?"

"I'm home and alone and totally safe," Sarah says with practiced patience. "Not that you would have any reason to worry if we *were* still together. You'd like Jake. He's a doctor."

"Yeah? How did you meet him?"

"You know Mandy, the volunteer who comes out on Thursdays to walk the dogs? He's her cousin. He just finished his residency down in Charleston and moved here to work with his uncle, who owns Lawson Cove Family Practice. He's living in this tiny studio above his uncle's garage, but only because he's building a house and it isn't done yet, so don't you dare hold that against him."

"Why would I hold that against him?"

"Because you have a ridiculously high bar for the men I date. But Adam, I really like this one. Somehow, he manages to check all of my boxes while still being all the boring things *you* want him to be. Like, he plays the guitar, and he took a gap year in between undergrad and med school so he could hike the entire Appalachian Trail, but also, he works hard and has a car that's paid for and he loves his mom."

"He sounds perfect," I say.

She sighs. "I think he might be."

"So it's funny you went out with him today," I say. "Because I actually met someone too."

"Shut up."

"Don't freak out. We just talked."

"Wait. You went to the vet today," Sarah says. "Is it the hot vet? Did you finally ask out the hot vet?"

"The *hot vet* has a name," I say. "It's Elena, or Laney, really, and she's the one who drove me home to pick up my spare key."

"Oh my gosh. I'm a freaking matchmaking genius, and I didn't even know it."

"Somehow I knew you would find a way to take credit for this," I say.

"Of course I'm taking credit," she shoots back. "Had I answered my phone, you never would have asked her to help." She breathes out a happy sigh. "This is so great. You'd better let me speak at your wedding."

"How about we *not* jump all the way to wedding talk?" I say. "But also, who do you think would be your competition if we were assigning speeches?"

"True. You need to make some new friends. So did you ask her out? When will you see her again?"

"I've texted her," I say. "Hopefully, we'll set something up soon. When do you see Jake again?"

"Actually, we're going on a little getaway this weekend. Just down to Atlanta—Jake has concert tickets—so unless you *really* need me tomorrow, I'll probably take the day off so I can do some shopping before Jake gets off work."

"If everything's caught up, you know I don't care."

She lets out a little squeal. "Yay. You're the best." Sarah launches into a detailed play-by-play of their date, and it occurs to me, as she rambles on and on, that I've never heard her talk so freely about *any* of the guys she's dated in the past. She's genuinely excited about this guy in a way she never has been before.

I'm happy for her, but there's an unexpected twinge of sadness laced around the edges of that happiness, too. I was eighteen when Mom died, but Sarah was only seventeen, so she lived in foster care for three months before she aged out of the system. It killed me that she couldn't just live with me, but my departure from Midnight Rush was fresh enough that the family court didn't think I was prepared to give Sarah the stability she needed.

So I moved into Mom's house, got my finances in order, and waited for her birthday.

As soon as we were together, it was us against the world.

We took care of each other. Turned into adults together —a process that was admittedly easier because of the money I'd made with Midnight Rush. I did a lot of hiding in those early years, trying to stay off the grid and out of the public eye, and Sarah is the one who made that possible. She dealt with the real estate agent when we sold Mom's house and moved deeper into the Tennessee mountains. She dealt with bankers and accountants, she fended off curious journalists and paparazzi. She finally convinced my agent that I was, in all seriousness, finished with the music business.

We didn't know anything about being adults.

But we figured it out together.

And I couldn't have done it without her.

Even though I've logically always known our lives wouldn't be this way forever, there's something about hearing her talk about Jake that feels like the rest of her life is about to begin—a life that won't involve nearly as much time with me. I'd like to think I'm moving in a similar direction, but that doesn't make it any less weird.

"Anyway," she finishes, "I totally promised him he could come by the rescue next week to meet all the dogs, so I was thinking that might be a great time for you to meet him."

"Is he looking to adopt?"

"As soon as his house is done. And get this. He says he wants an older dog because *they* deserve good homes too. Isn't that the sweetest? I was thinking Bono would be perfect for him."

"Maybe so."

"Will you be around when he comes by?"

"I'm always around," I say.

"No, I know. I just mean will you be *present* instead of off in the fields somewhere communing with nature and talking to the dogs?"

"I don't..." My words trail off because I *do,* actually, talk to the dogs, and I tend to be much happier out in the mountains than inside. "I'll make an effort," I say instead.

"Yay. Tell me when you officially make plans with Laney?"

"Will do. And please behave this weekend, all right?"

Sarah chuckles. "If I don't, I definitely won't tell you about it."

CHAPTER SIX

Adam

I'm halfway through dinner when my phone lights up with a call from a contact that makes my gut tighten and my fist clench around my fork.

I'm not surprised to see it. Up until last week, I hadn't heard from my former agent in years. But he's called at least a dozen times in the past few days. Texted, too. I know Kevin Spellman well enough to guess he won't give up.

But that doesn't mean I have to pick up.

There would be no point because I can't give him the answer he wants.

Apparently, our former record label is trying to get the members of Midnight Rush together for a one-time reunion concert.

The first time Kevin mentioned it via text, I couldn't eat, couldn't sleep, and was distracted enough that I almost forgot to feed the dogs. It was only Goldie walking to the back door and looking at me like I was an idiot that spurred me into action.

The routine of feeding and caring for the dogs helped clear my head so I could decide, unequivocally, that I'm not even a little bit interested in the idea.

The call from Kevin rings out and goes to voicemail.

It's been a very long time since I've been *Deke*—the stage name assigned to me by a label executive who thought *Adam* was too white-bread for a boyband. Deacon is my middle name, so it's not like he just made something up, but it was only ever a stage name for me. A gimmick. And it always felt that way. Like I was stepping into a role whenever it was time to perform or handle the press.

I didn't truly mind it. I loved making music, and I loved the other guys. It pushed me out of my comfort zone a lot, but logically, I understood that the fans, the attention, were all part of it.

I wouldn't say I thrived under the spotlight, but in retrospect, I wonder if that had more to do with the way our band was managed and less to do with the industry as a whole.

The record label said a lot to make our families feel like we were in good hands. All of us were under eighteen when we signed, so our parents were signing too. And on the surface, everything looked great.

No one was local to Nashville, but we needed to be together, so the label moved us into a house fifteen minutes from their office location with host parents who were supposed to look after us, feed us family-style dinners, and make sure we were doing our homework. We were all enrolled in a distance learning program through a private high school based in Nashville, and tutors dropped by the house a few times a week, but we never attended an actual class. We didn't go to prom or homecoming or football games. We just worked. Sang. Practiced choreography until our feet were bleeding.

Then our first album dropped, and we started our first national tour, and the rest is history. We basically lived on the road for the next three years, expanding the tour to Europe, then Asia, then doing a second leg back in the US before going back to Europe again.

It was a lot of pressure. A lot of work. And a lot of adults who didn't really seem to remember we were just kids. Jace's mom was sometimes on tour with us, and she was the closest thing we had to an actual advocate. But our agent, our tour managers, they all had one goal. And it wasn't to preserve our mental health or give us the breaks we needed.

A notification pops up that Kevin has left a voicemail, then a text immediately follows.

KEVIN

> Come on, man. Just answer the call. If you want me to leave you alone, pick up and give me a firm no.

Seconds later, the phone rings again.

I sigh and swallow my last bite of rigatoni, then answer the call. "Hi, Kevin."

"Deke freaking Driscoll," he says into the phone. "You are one difficult man to catch."

"I'll take that as a compliment."

"You sound different, man," Kevin says, his words lifting and rolling just like they always did. In person, Kevin looked the part of a professional agent, but his voice always sounded more like he just walked out of the Pacific carrying a surfboard than a boardroom. Apparently, that hasn't changed.

"You sound exactly the same," I say. There's an edge to my words that I wish I could take back, but my response to Kevin almost feels involuntary. The last few months before I walked out on Midnight Rush were hell, and he was the one who was pushing me the most. He was the one coaxing me to stay just a little bit longer.

"Thanks for finally answering my call," he says. "Where are you these days?"

"Living in North Carolina."

"Under a rock?" Kevin asks. "Did you know the internet is placing bets on whether you died?"

"Not dead," I say. "But honestly, I'm happy to let people think Deke is."

"Don't say that, man. I know it's been a while, but this concert—"

"You said you needed a firm no," I say, cutting him off. "And now you have it. I'm not interested." I push back from the table and stand, carrying my plate to the sink.

"Look, if this is about how you left things, I've talked to the guys. They aren't mad. They want you to be there. In fact, they don't want to do it without you."

They aren't mad.

Those words make my stomach clench, because how could they not be?

Every couple of months, I spend a few minutes googling the other guys from the band. Tracking where they are, what they're up to. Last I checked, Leo was living in Nashville, running his own recording studio and making a name for himself as a producer. Jace is out in California with his supermodel wife and the kid they had a year or so ago, smiling in the background of all the lifestyle photos she puts on Instagram. He released a solo album a few years ago, but It didn't get a ton of traction outside of the Midnight Rush superfans, and now he seems to be focused on doing the family thing.

Then there's Freddie. He's got a career bigger than anything Midnight Rush ever was. Every song he drops goes straight to the top of the charts. He's been in the top ten of Spotify's global most-listened-to artists for three years running, and he took home three Grammys last year. I'm honestly surprised he's even willing to do a reunion show. A lot might consider it a step down after all he's achieved.

Either way, he has to still be pissed over how I left things. They all have to be.

Because I didn't just turn my back on the band. I turned my back on my friends.

Kevin has to have an agenda here. He proved over and over again that he'll say what he needs to say to get what he wants, no matter whom he hurts in the process, so I have no reason to believe him now.

"You say that, Kevin, but I don't trust you."

"Ouch. Why not, man?"

"You know my answer to that question," I say. This time, I don't care that my words are sharp.

"Nah. That's water under the bridge. What happened a long time ago—let's leave that out of this. Your friends want you there. That's all that matters."

"Then why aren't they calling me instead of you?"

"They're just busy. I promise you," Kevin says. "You can trust me on this. Did I mention the proceeds of the concert will go to charity?"

I turn on the water to rinse my plate. "Charity?"

"The Breast Cancer Foundation. That's what your mom had, isn't it?"

I drop the plate, and it lands on a glass, which immediately shatters from the impact. I swear under my breath and put down my phone, turning on the speaker. "Kevin, what is this really about? Why that charity? Why a concert now, after all this time?"

He's quiet for a beat before he says, "The charity was Freddie's idea, but New Groove loved it. Great PR."

PR. It's one of Kevin's favorite phrases. *Great PR. Bad PR.* It's how he framed everything. I'd be fine if I never heard the words again.

"The label wants to give all the proceeds to charity? I can't imagine Dixon ever agreeing to something so generous."

"Dixon retired," Kevin says. "But you're right. He would have said no if he were still around. But Meryl Hendrix is in charge now, and she thinks it's brilliant."

I have vague memories of Meryl Hendrix. She was always around when Midnight Rush met with New Groove executives, but I don't remember her having much to say.

"Now that New Groove has lost Freddie, they're anxious to get their hands on what he's doing. Their only way to do that is through Midnight Rush."

The contract the four of us signed with New Groove Records is what the industry calls a three-sixty, which, in simple terms, just means they get a cut of everything. Sales, streaming, tours, merch. Any revenue the band generates. For that reason, it makes sense they'd be excited about a reunion show, generally. And if Freddie were still on their roster, I might understand them donating revenue to charity as an investment in *his* career. But without that incentive, it's hard for me to believe.

"When did Freddie leave New Groove?"

"Last fall. Finished out his contract and cut ties."

"Then why would New Groove be willing to bankroll a concert that won't make them any money?" I say. "That makes no sense."

"The PR, man. Don't worry about the details. The details always work out."

The details always work out. Another one of Kevin's catchphrases. And it usually means he's hiding something.

"Deke, man, listen—"

"Adam," I correct.

"Right. Adam. I don't know if you've watched much entertainment news lately, but Freddie has been all over it. He could use a little positive PR right now."

"What happened?" I ask, feeling simultaneously worried for Freddie and relieved that whatever is going on, it doesn't have anything to do with me.

"He didn't do anything wrong," Kevin says. "He was just in the wrong place at the wrong time, and the media turned it into something it wasn't. But his sales have taken a hit, and his new label isn't liking the current landscape. We're thinking a reunion concert would be good for his image. A way to remind people of his wholesome roots."

Street noise filters through the phone, a car horn honking, the beep of a truck backing up, a hurried shout. It's so starkly different from the sounds of Lawson Cove, and it sends a wave of uneasiness washing over me.

"Not to mention the media storm it would create," he continues. "Fans would lose it. It's all people would talk about, and then all this other stuff would get lost in the excitement."

A few years ago, Sarah asked me if I'd ever consider a reunion show, and I told her I didn't think there would be any interest now that we're all so old. She spent the next thirty minutes showing me websites for all the other boybands still actively touring. The Backstreet Boys even do an annual beach vacation thing that includes a concert and VIP meetings with the band. It sells out every year, apparently, so what do I know?

"Your fans all grew up, dummy," Sarah said. "And now they have jobs and money and cars to drive themselves to a show. Even without Freddie's enormously successful career, which definitely doesn't hurt things, you guys could still sell out a whole tour. I guarantee it."

For a split second, I forget how much Kevin irritates me and let myself think about singing with the guys again. We had a lot of fun on stage, but for me, it was more about the music. That's the part I really miss, and I'd almost say yes just for that—for the chance to make music like I used to.

But I can't just remember the good parts of the past and forget everything else.

I can't undo how or why things ended.

I close my eyes, suddenly wishing I'd never decided to pick up the phone. "I'm sure it will eventually die down anyway," I say. "Freddie will be fine. A little bit of bad press isn't going to hurt him."

"Deke, come on," Kevin says.

"Adam," I correct again. Something makes me think he's getting it wrong on purpose.

"Please just think about it. I know it would mean a lot to Freddie."

I turn off the faucet and pinch the bridge of my nose, leaving tiny droplets of water on my forehead.

"Just picture it," Kevin says. "New Year's Eve. Packed house in the Ben King Arena in Nashville. Midnight Rush on stage for the first time in eight years."

A New Year's Eve concert is sooner than I would have guessed, but it's a detail that doesn't matter because I can't say yes. Even if a small part of me wants to.

"I can't do it, Kevin."

"Why?" he says, his voice sharper than it was before. "After everything, man, you won't do this one thing for your friends? For Freddie?"

Unease swirls in my gut. I don't like the direction Kevin is going. He has all the fodder he needs to guilt me into this.

I was the one who walked away.

I was the one who ended the band.

I was the one who dealt with my grief, with my anger over losing my mom, by shutting everyone out.

I can't let Kevin go there, because I won't be able to say no, and I really, *really* need to say no.

I glance around my kitchen as if the solution to my problem is hidden inside my cabinets or behind the paper towel holder. He said a firm no was all he needed, but I should have known better than to believe him.

I opened the door when I answered the call, and he isn't going to let this go.

"I'm just...busy," I say, grappling for something, *anything* I can tell him to make this all go away. My eyes land on the business card Laney gave me when she said goodbye this afternoon, and an idea pops into my head. "With my fiancée," I blurt. "She's going through...a thing."

"Fiancée? You're getting married?"

"Yep," I say, even as alarm bells sound in my brain. *What am I doing? Why am I lying about this?*

"Wow. Congrats, man. Is she all right? What's she going through?" It shouldn't surprise me that Kevin asks. It's his business to know the business of his clients, so prying for personal details is second nature to him. But I'm not his client anymore.

Also, I don't actually *know* any details, so I really wish he'd lay off.

"Yeah, she's good," I manage to say. "It's just...a family thing. With her dad. I can't really talk about it right now. But it's taking up a lot of time and I need to be here to support her."

I drop my forehead into my hands, squeezing my eyes shut.

"I'm sorry to hear that. What's her name?"

My eyes pop open. Really? He needs me to *name* her?

"It's Laney," I say, a little too loudly. "Her name is Laney."

"Hmm," Kevin says. "Is she a fan of Midnight Rush? I bet she'd love to see you perform."

I almost roll my eyes at the irony. If what she'd name Taylor's puppies is any indication, Laney probably *would* love a reunion show.

"It's not going to happen, Kevin. Look, I should really go. But thanks for calling, all right? Tell the guys I won't be offended if they do the concert without me. They *should* do it without me."

I sit in my living room for a long time, phone in hand, even though the screen has long gone black. I feel for Freddie. I do. But I can't go back to that life.

Since moving to Lawson Cove, I've finally felt like I've well and truly put the past behind me. When we left

Tennessee, we left anyone who still knew who I was. We left all the places that reminded me of Mom. We left her gravestone, her childhood home. *Our* childhood home.

Lawson Cove was my new start.

I can't muddy it up now by reconnecting with my past.

My phone vibrates in my hand, and I look down to see a waiting text from Laney.

My *not* fiancée.

It's the perfect distraction.

This is what I want. Why I came to Lawson Cove.

New start. New life. New relationships as *Adam Driscoll.* And no one else.

CHAPTER SEVEN

Laney

"Here. Wear this one." Percy holds out the navy wrap dress I tried on at the start of this pre-date try-on-athon. "It's the best one for your eyes."

"Seriously? You made me try on twelve dresses just so you could go back to the one I wanted to wear in the first place?"

He shakes the dress, and I grab it from him, then step over the enormous pile of clothes on the floor in front of my walk-in closet so I can change outside of Percy's view.

"Listen. I'm surprised you even *have* twelve dresses. Where did you get all these things? I had you pegged as more of a jeans and hoodies kind of girl," Percy says.

I tie the sash on the dress and adjust my boobs so they aren't climbing out of the top. At least not *too much*.

"Mostly from my mother who, despite my insistence that I have nowhere to wear any of these, still dreams of me being a girly girl anyway." I grab a pair of strappy sandals from the back of my closet. I wipe the dust off the straps before sliding them on, then step back into the bedroom. "Okay. Be honest. Is it too much?"

Percy looks me over. "You should be a girly girl. You're rocking this."

I step around him and go to the full-length mirror in the corner of my bedroom. "I don't mind the dresses. I like to get dressed up. If you ask me to put on eyelash extensions or fake nails, we have a problem. But..." I look down at the dress, which does a nice job of accentuating my waist. "This much dressing up I don't mind."

"I think you look gorgeous. And it won't be too much. He's taking you to Olive's. It's the nicest place in Lawson Cove."

It's been a full week since I gave Adam a ride out to Hope Acres and he blew up my phone with an adorable string of texts. We've texted every day since then, and we talked on the phone for over an hour when he called to ask me out. But tonight will be the first time I see him in person in a week.

Usually, when facing social situations, I have to really pump myself up, convince myself it will be worth the effort. My social battery tends to deplete pretty fast, so I'm very picky about where and how frequently I'll hang out with friends. But I need no convincing to spend time with Adam. Weirdly, I don't even feel nervous about tonight.

I apply a thin layer of lip gloss, then turn away from the mirror. "Okay. I'm done. I can't look at myself anymore."

"I promise you're gorgeous," Percy says. "Here. Look at these instead. Mimi just sent them over."

He holds out his phone, and I take it, scrolling through the photos of what looks like his eighty-eight-year-old grandmother at some sort of party. In the last photo, Mimi is holding up a silky nightgown, showing it to her friend, Ethel, whose head is thrown back in laughter. "Wait. Is this...?" I look up at Percy. "Is she at a lingerie shower?"

Percy nods. "Ethel is getting married, and Mimi thought she needed to refresh her wardrobe."

"Isn't Ethel older than Mimi?"

"By two years, and she's still younger than the groom."

It took exactly one visit to the Shady Pines Assisted Living facility for me to decide that Percy's grandmother has a far more interesting social life than I do. The drama is rich, and Mimi always seems to be right in the center of it all.

"Want to come to Bingo night next week? Mimi says she has a new boyfriend, and she asked for you specifically. Said she's anxious to give you all the dirty details." My eyes widen the slightest bit, and he holds up his hands. "Her words, not mine."

I stifle a laugh. "You know I won't miss bingo night. But tell Mimi if I win this time, I'm keeping my prizes. She doesn't get to keep them just because she lives there. That's not how prizes work."

"Tell her yourself," Percy says. "You know I can't say no to Mimi for anything."

Percy's grandmother is the entire reason he's still in Lawson Cove and not down in Atlanta. When she could no longer live on her own, he volunteered to move to Lawson Cove and stay with her. That worked for a few months, but eventually, her needs were more than what Percy could manage on his own, so she moved into Shady Pines. I guess technically Percy could move back to Atlanta now that she has round-the-clock care, but he'll never leave her. He's there

at least three times a week, and I know how much she means
to him.

He likes to minimize the fact that he moved away from a
bustling city and a thriving social life to be close to his
grandmother, but I realize how big it is. Especially considering how *not willing* his mother—Mimi's daughter—was to
do the same thing.

"She's lucky to have you," I say, and Percy's gaze catches
mine, gratitude evident in his expression.

"And I'm lucky to have you," he says.

I scoff. "What? You think I spend all this time at Shady
Pines for you? I want to win myself a foot spa. Those bingo
prizes are legit."

Percy rolls his eyes. "Okay. I'm leaving you to your sexy
dog-whispering lumberjack. Have fun tonight."

"Lumberjack?"

Percy looks at me like my question makes zero sense.
"The flannel? The beard?"

"Wearing flannel doesn't make him a lumberjack," I
argue, though it doesn't take much to imagine Adam
wielding an ax. He's definitely got the build for it.

A knock sounds on my front door, and Percy and I both
freeze.

"He's here!" I whisper-shout to Percy. Forget what I said
about not being nervous. I'm suddenly terrified. "What do I
do? He's actually here!"

"You go answer your door, you dummy," he whisper-
shouts back. "Then you go have dinner, fall in love, and
make dozens of lumberjack babies."

I swat at Percy's arm as I walk past him and into the living
room, where I cross to the entryway. I take a steadying

breath, pressing a hand to my belly, then I swing open the door.

Oh.

Oh my.

Adam is definitely *not* wearing flannel tonight. Or a hat —something I've never seen him without. His hair is a little longer than I thought it was, pushed back and a little to one side, and his beard looks freshly trimmed. He's in light gray dress pants and a pale purple button-down that stretches across his chest in just the right way. It's a simple outfit, but it's still intentional. I doubt he tried on twelve shirts, but it still looks like he cares, like he put a little extra thought into getting ready.

"Hi," I finally say. I'm not sure how long I've been staring, but the tiny smirk playing on Adam's face makes me think it's been more than just a few seconds.

"Hey." He holds out a bouquet of deep purple lilies wrapped in several layers of paper towel. I was so preoccupied with the fit of his shirt, I didn't even notice the flowers until now. "These are for you. Sorry they're not wrapped any better. I cut them right before I left, and this was all I had on hand."

I meet his eye. "You grew these?"

"Yes? I guess? I hate to take credit for them. They were already in the ground when I bought the farm, so the most I've had to do is keep the weeds out of the beds, and they've come up every year. I think they're lilies? Not sure what kind."

"They look like lilies. Come on in. I'll put these in water, then we can go."

Adam steps inside and pulls the door closed, his eyes

lifting to somewhere over my shoulder. His eyebrows lift slightly before he says, "Hi, Percy."

"Hi," Percy says, dragging out the word as he moves toward the door. "And goodbye. I was planning to be out of the house by the time you showed up, so I apologize for being a very awkward third wheel."

As soon as Percy is behind Adam, he turns and looks at me, eyes wide as he silently mouths, "*Oh my gosh!*" He holds his arms up, like he's rocking an invisible baby, and I wave him away.

Adam turns and looks over his shoulder, and Percy immediately drops his arms and smiles, looking every bit as guilty as he should. "You both look absolutely stunning," he says. "Gorgeous couple." He opens the door. "Okay. Bye for real."

The door clicks shut, and Adam and I stand there awkwardly for five, maybe ten seconds before it occurs to me that Adam might be making some weird assumptions about my relationship with Percy. "Hey, you do know Percy is gay, right? He's just a friend. A great friend. But I just realized right this second that if you didn't know, you might think…"

"I knew," Adam says quickly. He runs a hand through his hair, and I get that same sense of déjà vu I had when he was talking outside the barn that first afternoon we spent together. It might be the gesture that feels familiar—the running his hand through his hair. "Actually, I have a little bit of a confession."

"Yeah?" I move into the kitchen. It's open into the living room, a small breakfast table separating the two spaces, so I can still see Adam, but I don't mind that he follows me, leaning his hip against the counter.

I set the flowers next to the sink, then pull an oversized

mason jar off the top shelf of my cabinet—I am not the kind of person who has real vases just sitting around her house—and fill it with water.

"So, last week, right before you came into the exam room to see Aretha's puppies? I overheard you and Percy talking."

I set down the mason jar and furrow my brow. "Talking about...?"

"Me being straighter than a Michael Bay movie?"

I gasp and lift my hand to cover my mouth. "You heard that?" I try to remember the entire conversation—Percy teasing me about Adam being straight, about me *liking* him. "Please tell me you're lying."

"That's how I know Percy is gay," Adam says. "But it's a good thing! It's also how I figured out I might possibly have a shot with you."

The more evidence he provides, the hotter my face gets. "That's why you suddenly wanted to talk to me? After all these months?"

"I assumed you were dating someone," he says. "You never really seemed interested."

"Adam, I'm an introvert. I never seem interested in *anyone.*"

He grins. "Well, takes one to know one, then. But, just for the record, I *am* pretty interested in you."

I lift my hands to my cheeks. I genuinely can't believe this is happening.

"I tried on twelve dresses," I say, because it's the first thing that pops into my head. "Then wound up going back to the first one I put on. Which feels like a stupid thing to tell you, but I just...I'm interested too."

Adam's eyes heat, his gaze warming me from the inside

out. "If it matters, you definitely chose the right dress." He holds out his hand. "Should we go?"

He could be leading me out to a unicycle I have to ride to dinner myself, and I'm pretty sure I'd still say yes.

Olive's is a gorgeous restaurant. Quaint but classy, always busy but never crowded. We settle into our chairs at a table near the window with a nice view of downtown Lawson Cove. Adam orders wine and we pick out an appetizer, and I debate for way too long between pasta and pork, but once the menus are gone and our waiter has left us with a basket of rolls, we fall into easy, effortless conversation. It basically feels like an extension of the text conversation we've been having all week—but better.

When our appetizer arrives, Adam finally explains the basic principles of Max Martin's melodic math and how it impacts his song writing. Then we shift into a breakdown of the music from *Once*—an excellent movie that everyone should see—and rank popular covers against their originals.

We mostly agree, but I love that when we don't, Adam argues about the greatest cover of all time like it's a matter of life and death.

"I'll give you 'Hurt' by Johnny Cash," I say. "But the top five has to include 'R-E-S-P-E-C-T.' Otis Redding said himself that Aretha did the song better than he ever could have."

"But that would knock out Cake's 'I Will Survive,'" he argues.

"Good! It's not even that great of a cover."

He narrows his eyes. "Those are fighting words, Laney."

I grin. "Jeff Buckley's 'Hallelujah'?"

"Okay. That *is* a good one. But that means our list has to be top ten instead of five."

We take a break when our waiter shows up with our dinner, placing a plate of pork tenderloin with raspberry chutney in front of me and a pasta dish with chicken and sun-dried tomato in front of Adam. I feel a tiny pang of regret when I see his plate. It's the dish I *didn't* order, and it looks delicious.

Without saying a word, Adam takes his bread plate and scoops a generous helping of pasta on the plate before sliding it over to me.

"What are you doing?" I ask as I watch him.

He shrugs. "I heard you debating between the two dishes when you were ordering. Now you can try them both."

I think back to when we ordered our entrees. Adam showed the waiter the menu and pointed, something I noticed because I wondered if there was something he couldn't pronounce.

But that's not what was happening. He hid his order because he was ordering what *I* wanted.

There has to be a catch somewhere.

He likes dogs, he brought me flowers, he knows music even better than I do, he loves his sister, *and* he paid attention enough to know what dinner options I was considering?

"Would you have ordered this had you not heard me say it sounded good?" I ask.

"It *did* sound good," he says, mostly avoiding the question. He takes a big bite and closes his eyes as he lets out a little groan. "And it's absolutely delicious." He nudges my plate a little closer toward me. "Try it."

"Adam, just tell me. Do you even like pasta?"

"Who doesn't like pasta?" he says through another bite.

"But I want you to eat what *you* want. Did you order this just for me?"

"I have no idea what you're talking about."

I huff. "You aren't going to tell me, are you?"

"There's nothing to tell! I love pasta. And this dish is delicious."

I pick up my fork, suddenly feeling overwhelmed, maybe even a little emotional. It isn't truly a big deal. There aren't that many things on the menu, so Adam very well could have been considering the pasta. But just the possibility of him making a choice *for me* feels so genuinely kind and considerate, I'm not sure how to process it. A lump forms at the back of my throat, making my first bite of pasta difficult to swallow.

It *is* delicious. Creamy and a little tart but not too heavy. I haven't tried the pork yet, but it's hard to imagine it being better than this.

I've only ever had one serious boyfriend in my life—a guy I dated through most of vet school. Shane was nice. Or... nice-ish, maybe? In retrospect, I realize he was mostly just nice when he wanted something. Attention. Food. Someone to pick up his drycleaning. When he wanted to be sweet, he knew how to turn it on. But when he didn't, he was distracted. Always on his phone—he worked in finance which meant there were always things he said "had to be dealt with immediately"—and I just never got the sense he was fully invested in *me*.

Turns out, he wasn't. He called things off a month before I graduated and was dating a woman he worked with less than three weeks later.

Two years down the drain, just like that.

I'm only halfway through *one* date with Adam, and I could kick myself for having wasted even a single day with Shane. I remember trying so hard to make him *see* me—to care about what I had to say, how I felt about things. Maybe if I wore a little more makeup or wore his favorite color or suggested we eat at *his* favorite restaurant, he might take notice.

It took a few months of post-break-up therapy to realize I had never been the problem. That with the right person, I would never have to *try* to be seen.

I'm not sure I ever understood what my therapist meant until this moment.

"Hey, you okay?" Adam asks. "Do you not like it?"

I look up and meet his eyes. I'm holding my fork over the pasta like I'm debating whether I want to take another bite.

"No, it's delicious. I'm good. Just...thank you," I say simply.

Luckily, the pork is equally delicious, and it's far too much for me to eat, so I end up sliding my plate into the middle of the table so Adam can help me finish it. It adds an intimacy to the meal, sharing a plate like this, fighting over who gets the last bite. Adam wins, and I scowl, but then he holds his fork up to *my* mouth, his eyes on my lips. I take the bite, and a heat curls in my belly that doesn't have anything to do with the food.

"So why a dog rescue?" I ask over the crème brûlée we share for dessert. "What made you decide that's what you wanted to do?"

"It was Goldie, actually," Adam says. "Mom got her from a shelter after a family purchased her from a pet store, kept her for two months before taking her to the vet, then discovered she was heartworm positive. They didn't want to have to deal with treating her, so they dropped her off at the shelter. Apparently, this particular pet store was really awful about puppy mills with terrible breeding conditions and was selling puppies with all kinds of problems. Goldie was actually one of the lucky ones because her heartworms were treatable." He waves his fork as he talks, and a tiny splatter of crème brûlée flies across the table and lands on the side of my lip.

I flinch in surprise when it hits, and Adam freezes. "That was me," he says sheepishly. "I just did that, didn't I?" He reaches over, his hand hovering in the space between us. "May I?"

I lean a little closer, and he slides the pad of his thumb across my bottom lip. I could be making things up, but his hand is moving awfully slowly.

"Got it," he says, his voice low. I expect him to reach for a napkin, but instead, he holds my gaze as he lifts his finger to his mouth and licks it clean.

My heart starts pounding.

Really pounding.

Pounding like Adam just kissed me instead of cleaned off my face.

But his look was so pointed. So *sexy.*

I clear my throat and drop my gaze to the table because if I don't, I will possibly climb across the table and kiss him *for real.*

"So anyway," Adam says loudly, an obvious effort to cut the tension simmering between us. "Mom got really passionate about shutting down puppy mills and did all this research and said that shelter dogs needed better marketing so people would adopt instead of shop, and...yeah. I did it for her."

I did it for her.

It doesn't surprise me at all that Adam made choices for

his mom. It tracks with everything he's shown me about himself so far.

"I love that, Adam." I say. "I'm sure she'd be proud of you."

A flash of pain flits across his expression. He closes his eyes and his jaw flexes, making me wonder if I said something wrong.

But then he stretches his hand across the table, palm up in invitation.

I slide my hand into his, and a heady sense of longing fills me as his fingers wrap around mine.

"Thank you for saying so," he says. "Sometimes I'm not so sure."

I squeeze his hand. "I don't know how she couldn't be."

He nods. "So...speaking of puppies. I was thinking once we leave here, we could go out to the rescue and visit Ringo."

I let out a happy little gasp. "For real?"

He smiles. "If you want."

"Yes, yes, please!" I probably sound twelve, but I don't even care. I don't have to pretend with Adam. One date in, I can already tell. He's being nothing but real with me, and I can do the same.

I can just be me.

CHAPTER EIGHT

Adam

"I'm not sure I made the smartest shoe decision this evening," Laney says, glancing down at her feet.

We're in the driveway at the rescue, and I can't drive the four-by-four I usually use to get around because it has a flat tire I haven't fixed yet.

"Want to just wait on the porch? I'll bring Ringo to you," I say.

Laney frowns and props her hands on her hips. "And see only one puppy when I could see eight?" She shakes her head, then takes hold of my arm, using me to steady herself as she reaches down and pulls off her shoes. "This will work. I'll just walk barefoot."

"You aren't walking barefoot. It's dark, and the grass is in need of a good mowing. You could step on a snake or a tick or get chigger bites."

She holds up her shoes. "Um. These sandals would not protect me against *any* of those things."

"Still. I don't want you to get hurt." I reach for her shoes and set them on the edge of the porch, then crouch down in front of her. "Jump on."

"You're going to piggyback me all the way to the barn?"

"It's not that far."

She huffs, but then she slips her hands onto my shoulders, and jumps. I catch her legs, adjusting until she's comfortably on my hips, her feet dangling on either side. Her toenails are painted light blue, something I hadn't noticed until right now.

"Are you dying?" she asks.

"Totally comfortable." I head off toward the barn. Between the property's floodlights and the moonlight overhead, I can see the grassy path easily enough, but I take it a little slower than normal anyway, just to be safe.

"You don't have to pretend like I'm not heavy," Laney says, her voice close to my ear. "The women in my family are built to last."

I chuckle. "What does that mean?"

"It means we have dense bones. We're quarter horses, not thoroughbreds."

"I don't know anything about horses, but I think I know what you mean?"

"My grandmother, my mom, both of my aunts, me and my sister—none of us have ever broken a bone. And doctors are always surprised by how much we weigh."

I pause and shift Laney a little higher on my back. "That...explains a lot," I say, pretending to strain.

She lets out a gasp and wiggles like she's trying to get down, but I hold on tightly. "I'm kidding! I'm kidding, I promise! You don't feel heavy at all."

She leans forward, laughing as her arms circle a little

more tightly around my neck. I catch the scent of honey-suckle on her hair, and it's all I can do not to breathe in an obvious lungful of Laney-scented air.

"You're very funny, Mr.—" She pauses. "Actually, it just occurred to me that I don't know your last name."

"It isn't in my chart at your office?"

"Probably somewhere, but the main part just lists the rescue."

I force myself to relax, to keep my movements steady as I cross the last few yards to the barn door. Driscoll isn't a super unusual last name, so I'm not normally nervous about telling people what it is. But Laney is a Midnight Rush fan, and Deke was her favorite. I can't be sure she won't notice the commonality.

Not that it will mean anything. A lot of people have the last name Driscoll.

Then again, if she does make the connection, maybe this would be a good time to tell her the truth.

The thought almost makes me queasy.

Tonight has been good. *So good.* We've talked and joked and laughed, and the chemistry has been amazing. We click intellectually, which is possibly the sexiest thing about her, but the physical chemistry is intense too.

I haven't stopped thinking about kissing her since dessert, when, like an idiot, I flung crème brûlée onto her face and then touched her lip to wipe it off. Her skin was soft, and her mouth parted the slightest bit at the contact and...*yeah.* It's bad. And now, carrying her across the lawn, having so much of *her* touching so much of *me* is only making it worse.

I'm hyper aware of every contact point between us. The warm skin on her legs pressing into my palms, the heat of her body against my back, her arms resting loosely across my chest where they're wrapped around my neck. She's comfortable with me—I can tell. Things are easy between us.

What if telling her ruins all that?

It's not that I think she'll care, exactly. But I do think it might make things weird. That it could make *her* nervous or make her overthink things like I'm overthinking now.

I'm positive it will make her ask questions, and I can't think of anything that would ruin the night faster than having to wade through all the drama surrounding my departure from the band. It's the last way I'd like to end our date.

Still. I can't lie to her.

And that thought is more important than all the others.

So I'll tell her. If she brings up the fact that I share a last name with her favorite boyband member, I'll own it. Admit everything.

"It's Driscoll," I say as casually as I can. We reach the barn, and I do a half-squat to lower Laney's feet to the smooth concrete landing outside the door.

"Adam Driscoll," she repeats once she's steady on her feet. "I like that name."

That's it. That's all she says.

I shouldn't feel so relieved, because I *should* tell Laney the truth.

And I will. I absolutely will.

Just not yet.

I make fast work of unlocking the door and sliding it open, then I turn on the interior lights. The puppies are almost entirely weaned at this point, so they're spending good chunks of the day away from their mom, but they're all together at night, in an oversized kennel near the front of the barn.

When I converted the barn into a rescue space, I hoped to keep as much of the original wood as possible, simply converting stalls into kennels. But the more I learned about keeping dogs healthy and safe and clean, the less of a good idea that seemed. Laney's dad was the one who finally convinced me to have new epoxy floors put in and keep the spaces for the dogs as minimalist as possible. There are still wooden rafters overhead, but everything else in the barn is clean and modern and practical.

At least I don't have to worry about Laney's bare feet in here.

But then, something tells me Laney wouldn't care either way.

The minute we're inside the kennel with the puppies, she's sitting on the floor, legs out in front of her and ankles crossed like she doesn't have a care in the world. The puppies are crawling all over her, and she's smiling wide as she reaches for Ringo.

I run to the supply room by the door and grab an old blanket. "Here," I say, unfolding it as I walk back. "At least sit on this."

She dutifully shifts over and lets me spread out the blanket, then scoots so her back is against the wall, Ringo tucked against her chest.

"I love him," she says as he leans up and licks the bottom of her chin.

"Then he's yours," I say.

She bites her lip. "I'll have to put up a fence in my backyard."

"I'll help you build it," I say.

She lifts an eyebrow. "What if my backyard is enormous?"

"I'll...hire a crew to help you build it."

She lets out a laugh. "So there *are* limits to what you can do. I was beginning to think you were perfect."

I sit down beside her and pick up the closest puppy—Diana. "How big of a yard are we talking? I didn't say I *couldn't* build the entire thing. I'm just saying I wouldn't be opposed to a more efficient method."

"It's actually pretty small," she says. She leans her shoulder into mine and settles there, the warmth of her filtering through the thin fabric of my shirt. "Maybe a quarter of an acre? And there's already a fence along one side. It wouldn't take much to fence in the rest."

"I'm all you need, then. I could knock that out in a weekend."

She yawns, and I glance at my watch. It's just after ten, but she probably got up early. I should get her home sooner than later. "Consider yourself hired," she says.

Diana crawls off my lap and sniffs at Laney's toes, then wanders back to the bed, where Aretha is softly snoring. It's actually nice visiting the puppies this late. They're definitely more chill when they're sleepy.

"When are they ready for adoption?" Laney asks. "I can't remember how old they are."

"Eight weeks tomorrow," I say. "But I'm keeping them until they're twelve. My trainers are working on crate and house training over the next couple weeks, plus basic obedience commands. I like to send them home with a good foundation."

"Trainers? On staff? Or just volunteers? That sounds amazing."

"A little of both? There are a couple of trainers in town whom I hire to come out a few times a week. As for volunteers, the ag science program at the high school keeps kids coming on a regular basis. I worked it out with the administration. They get service hours *and* extra credit, and I get a lot of help."

Laney scoops up another puppy—George, I think?—but he's squirmy and won't settle, so she lets him go and he wiggles his way over to me, where he latches onto the cuff of my sleeve with his tiny puppy teeth.

"Okay. Time out for you," I say, picking him up and setting him back on the floor next to his mom.

Laney's quiet for a beat before she asks, "Can I ask you a totally invasive, outrageously personal question that you absolutely don't have to answer unless you want to?"

I will my muscles to relax. "Go for it," I say. "But I'm not telling you how many hair products I use on my beard. Or anything about the cats in the freezer."

"I mean...in my line of work, cats in the freezer aren't entirely unheard of, so if you're looking for shock value, try again."

I tsk with disappointment. "I should have just gone with *bodies* in the freezer."

She laughs. "That might have done it. But for real more than one product on your beard? Or were you making that up too?"

I lift a hand and rub it down my beard. "It takes a lot to keep it this soft."

She reaches over and lifts a hand to my face, sliding it along my jaw.

I lean into her touch without thinking, like there's some kind of gravitational force that triggers whenever we're close.

Just *close* isn't good enough. I want closer. *More.* Anything she'll give me.

"You're right. That *is* pretty soft." Her thumb lingers on the edge of my lip and she tugs it down for a brief second before her hand falls away and she smirks. "Now we're even," she whispers.

I immediately know what she means. I touched her lip the same way at dinner, and the air crackled with the same kind of heat and tension. If this is the game we're playing, teasing, pushing boundaries, trading touches and looks, then send me in, coach.

I swallow and force myself to look in her eyes, but then she licks her lips, pulling my gaze downward, and I start to lose my resolve. It's impossible not to notice the way her teeth are tugging at her bottom lip, or the curve of her neck as it slopes down to her shoulder. There's a tiny chain holding a circle studded with pale blue stones in the hollow of her throat, and it rises and falls with her breathing, which appears to be as shallow and fast paced as mine.

I have never wanted to kiss someone as much as I want to kiss her, but there's something holding me back.

It could be that we're sitting on a cold epoxy floor with nothing but a thin blanket underneath us. But...*dammit.* That's not it.

I need to tell her before I can kiss her.

I need to tell her about Deke.

I don't know why I feel like I do, but it feels important. *Necessary.*

It has never felt important before. I haven't dated a ton in the past few years, and it's only ever been casual. A few dates here and there. I've never been tempted or felt any sort of obligation to come clean about Midnight Rush. A relationship never lasted long enough for it to matter.

But this thing with Laney...it's different. Even one date in, I can already tell.

When I kiss her, everything is going to change.

And I don't want there to be any secrets between us when that happens.

I drop my gaze and lean away so we're no longer touching, forcing a deep breath.

Laney must feel the shift, because she moves too, pulling her arms a little closer around herself.

"So you were going to ask me something?" I say. My voice sounds loud in the stillness, and I suddenly wonder how long we just sat, staring at each other, *not kissing.*

She clears her throat. "Was I?"

"Something outrageously personal?"

"Oh! Right. I was just going to ask how you fund Hope Acres. Most nonprofits like this one are constantly fighting to keep their doors open, but this place is beautiful, and I don't really get the vibe that you're struggling to pay the bills."

It's a valid question with a complicated answer, and it could easily steer us into talking about Midnight Rush, but Laney yawns again at the end of her sentence. I don't want to start this conversation now, and I don't want to have it on a cold floor. So I settle for telling her a partial truth.

"I have some personal investments that have done pretty well," I say simply. "I mostly fund Hope Acres on my own, but we also get donations from people who have adopted and a few businesses around Lawson Cove. Your dad makes a regular donation."

"Does he?" she asks. "He still handles all the financial stuff, so I didn't know that."

"He does. Every quarter."

She yawns again, and this time her head drops onto my shoulder. "My dad's a pretty good guy."

"He is, but I like my current vet better."

When she doesn't respond, just lets out an easy, "Hmm," I decide to call it.

"Okay, sleepy head. Let's get you home."

She snuggles Ringo a little closer. "I don't want to say goodbye to him."

"Trust me. You'll love him more if he's mostly house-broken before you get him. You only have to wait a few more weeks."

She sits up and holds Ringo out to me. "Fair enough."

I move Ringo over to the dog bed, where the rest of his siblings have already curled up with their mom, then offer Laney a hand, pulling her to her feet.

The piggyback ride to the car and then the drive back to her house are mostly quiet, but it's a comfortable silence instead of an awkward one. I think she might even doze a little during the drive.

I like that she's relaxed enough that she can sleep—that she feels safe with me.

"I had a really nice time tonight," she says when we're standing at her door, bathed in the soft yellow glow of her porch light.

"Yeah, me too." I reach for her hand and tug her close, wrapping my arms around her. It's just a hug—or it's just *supposed* to be a hug—but my body ignites at the feel of her against me. Before I realize what I'm doing, my hands are on her face and my forehead is pressed against hers, my heart hammering as I feel the exhale of her breath on my lips.

"Adam, I really want you to kiss me goodnight," she says.

I breathe out a sigh. "I really want to kiss you goodnight. But..."

She leans back and looks up to meet my eye, her expression curious. "But?"

"But I'm not...ready to kiss you yet."

Her mouth opens like she might say something, but then she closes it again, pausing before finally saying, "Oh."

"Trust me. It's not that I don't want to. I do. But...next time, okay?"

She nods, but I can see the confusion in her hazel eyes, mixed with what looks like a little bit of hurt.

"Laney, this has been the best first date I've ever been on. The best date *period*. I promise...there will be a next time."

She offers a hesitant smile. "I would really love that."

I would too.

Which means now, I just have to tell her who I am.

CHAPTER NINE

Laney

It takes four rounds of bingo on Tuesday evening, but I finally win my foot spa.

Mimi looks over from her place on the opposite side of Percy and narrows her brown eyes before raising two fingers and pointing them at her eyes, then shifting them over to me in an *I'm watching you* gesture.

I raise my eyebrows in challenge, and she finally cracks, laughing as she shakes her head and clears her board for the next round.

"You know you're still giving her that foot spa, right?" Percy asks under his breath. "She's trying to lure you into complacency with her charm."

"Fully aware," I say. "And probably I'm going to let her have it."

"Sucker."

"She saved me her Boston cream pie from dinner

because she knew it was my favorite. How can I truly argue with her?"

"You're asking me? The biggest Mimi pushover on the planet?"

"There are worse things to be," Mimi says from beside him, and we both laugh.

We play a few more rounds while I pepper Mimi with questions about Ethel and Roberto's lightning-quick courtship and how she really feels about it, then milk her for the "dirty details" she promised about a certain Mr. Martinson who has been coming to visit her every evening to watch *Wheel of Fortune* and *Jeopardy!*. Apparently, they've come up with a game they play as they watch. Every time one of the contestants guesses an incorrect letter or misses a trivia question, they kiss.

"The more idiots on the show, the better," Mimi says with a twinkle in her eye.

"Oh, good grief," Percy says, but I have to respect Mimi.

"She's getting more action than either of us," I say.

Percy laughs. "Sad, but true."

Another round ends, and we clear our boards for the final round. It's only six forty-five, but bingo at Shady Pines never lasts past seven PM or residents tend to get cranky. At least according to Mimi.

"So when are you seeing the man who isn't ready to kiss you yet?" Percy says. "Did you ever make plans?"

"Don't make me regret telling you what he said," I say as I cover up a square in my *g* column. "And yes. He's coming over to watch a movie tomorrow night."

"Think he'll be ready to kiss you then?"

"He did promise next time," I say. "That's tomorrow night, so I'm assuming he will be."

He'd better be, I think. Because I was more than ready when he dropped me off last Friday night, my body practically vibrating with the need to kiss him. I can't think about it too much, because every time I do, a faint sense of embarrassment washes over me.

I have zero doubts that Adam wanted to kiss me as much as I wanted to kiss him. And we've been texting almost nonstop ever since. I just can't figure out why he wasn't ready.

Maybe he has a no kissing on the first date rule?

Maybe he...was worried about bad breath?

Maybe he has a secret long-distance girlfriend and wanted to break up with her before starting something new?

Oh, gross. I hate that last thought. Adam has been so open with me about everything else, I can't imagine he'd lie about something so big, but women have been duped before. I'm too practical not to acknowledge that if something seems too good to be true, it probably is.

But a bigger part of me wants to believe Adam really is perfect—at least perfect for me.

"I don't know," Percy says. "I still say it's weird."

"It's not weird. He said he wasn't ready. Why aren't we celebrating a man being honest about what he wants and when he wants it?"

"Fine. I'm celebrating. But I'd be celebrating more if he'd slipped you a little tongue."

I swat him in the shoulder, then gasp when Mimi says, "Mr. Martinson could give him some pointers."

Across the room, someone calls out bingo, and I breathe out a sigh of relief. "Finally," I say. "I'm done with you troublemakers."

I clean off my board and start picking up my chips when

my watch vibrates with an incoming call. I glance at it, my heart skipping the tiniest bit when I see Adam's name on the screen. I grab my purse from the back of my chair and nudge Percy. "Adam's calling. Clean up for me? I'll be right back."

He nods as I leave the table and move to the back of the room, where refreshments line the wall, and answer the call.

"Hey!" I say.

"Hey." The deep rumble of even just that one word sends a delicious shiver down my spine. "How are you?"

"I just won bingo at Shady Pines, so I'm absolutely fabulous. How are you?"

"Actually, I'm in a little bit of a predicament, and was hoping you might be free to help me—but only if it won't mess with your evening."

"Not at all. Things shut down early around here, so we're almost done. What can I do? Is Taylor okay?"

"Yeah. She's great. Still no puppies. But none of my regular volunteers are free, and I'm stuck in Asheville traffic with Sarah. I know this is a really big ask, but do you think you could drive out to the rescue and handle the dinner routine for me? They usually eat around five, and we're still an hour and a half away with no sign of any movement on the interstate."

"Does she know I'm your sister?" a voice says somewhere in the background. The call must be on speaker phone or piped through the sound system in Adam's SUV. "I'm his sister, Laney. He's with Sarah who is his *sister*."

"Thank you, Captain Obvious," Adam says. "I've told her you're my sister."

I smile at the irritation in his voice because it's exactly how I talk to my sister when she's driving me crazy.

"Just making sure," Sarah says. "I didn't want her to think you were on a date. You have to be clear about these things."

"I just had dinner with Laney last weekend, and I'm seeing her again tomorrow night. You really think I would date someone else in between?" Adam asks, and his tone is so genuine, I instantly know he would never do something like that.

Sarah tsks. "You poor, innocent man," she says. "Do you know anything about your own species?"

"Do you know anything about *me*?" he shoots back.

"Okay, that's fair," Sarah says. "You would never do that. But I just wanted to make sure *Laney* knew too."

I chuckle at their good-natured back-and-forth. "It's nice to finally talk to you, Sarah. I hope I meet you in person soon."

"Me too!" Sarah says. "I've heard so much about you. Did Adam for real tell you about me already? The man does *not* like talking about his private life."

"He did," I say. "He mentioned you pretty quickly, actually."

"Aww," Sarah says. "That makes me happy. And gives me a very good feeling about you. I bet he tells you *all* his secrets."

"Sarah," Adam says, a slight edge to his voice.

"What? I didn't say *I* was going to tell your secrets." She clears her throat. "Or that you even have any. I was just talking about...hypothetical secrets. And saying that if you did happen to have any, you probably wouldn't share them with just anyone."

"Are you finished?" Adam asks when Sarah's rambling finally stops.

"Completely," she says. "No more secret talk."

Somehow, Sarah's insistence that he does *not* have any secrets only makes me more certain Adam does.

"What do you say, Laney?" Adam asks, ignoring his sister. "Can you help? I'll try my volunteers again if you can't, so no pressure to say yes."

"I'm happy to help," I say. Across the room, Percy and Mimi move to the door, and I step into the hallway, following after them as they head toward Mimi's room. "Can you send me instructions? I don't think I remember enough to do it on my own."

"I'll text over a detailed list of instructions. It's the same one our volunteers use, so it's basically a full play-by-play. That should make it really easy."

"Perfect."

"Be sure to pull it up before you go to the barn though," Sarah adds. "Because the reception is terrible out there. You won't have service."

"Got it," I say. "I'm with Percy right this second, but as soon as I drop him off, I'll head straight there."

It's stupid I'm so excited to do this since Adam won't even be there, but it feels good that he called me. That after just one date, he trusts me to unlock his house and take care of his animals.

"Thanks, Laney," Adam says. "I owe you one for this."

I almost tell him I'll accept payment in kisses, but I don't have the nerve to say it in front of his sister, so I simply say, "Don't worry about it. I'm happy to help."

We say goodbye, and I hurry down the hall to Mimi's room. She's just sitting down in her favorite chair when I step through the door. She looks up and smiles, eyes twinkling. She's had a good day today, her mind clear and sharp.

"I thought you might have left without saying goodbye," she says as she holds out her hand.

"I would never." I take her fingers in mine and crouch down in front of her.

She gives my hand a little squeeze. "Thank you for spending your evening with a bunch of old ladies."

"Are you kidding? I won ten dollars and a new foot spa. This was a perfect way to spend my night."

"Pretty sure you mean *I* won a new foot spa," she says. "But I'll let you keep the ten dollars."

"You're terrible, Mimi," Percy says. "And I love you dearly."

Mimi smiles up at him, warmth in her eyes. He told me once how terrified he'd been to come out to his grandmother, but she'd surprised everyone in the family when she'd patted seventeen-year-old Percy on the cheek with tears in her eyes and said, "Oh, Percy. I already knew, baby. And it doesn't change a thing." Then she'd asked him to make her a tomato sandwich with a side of french onion chips, and that was that.

"I love you too, but get on out of here before Mr. Martinson comes. You'll cramp my style if you're still hovering over me like a bunch of hens when he shows up."

"Understood," Percy says with a laugh.

I lean forward and kiss her on the cheek. "Bye, Mimi. I'll come by next week, okay?"

Percy only grumbles a little when I explain why we can't go get our typical post-bingo dinner like we planned.

"You can always come with me," I say, "then we can go get food after."

"Are you kidding?" he says. "I spend all day taking care of other people's pets, and you want me to spend my evening doing the same thing? Remember, I don't have the same sexy lumberjack incentive that you do. There is nobody who is going to kiss me thank you at the end of the night, so I'll just go home, please and thank you."

"You're still calling him a sexy lumberjack? Even after you saw him when he picked me up on Friday?"

"Until he shaves, he's a sexy lumberjack," he says as I pull into his driveway.

I roll my eyes. "I won't even see him. He's not home. That's why he called me in the first place."

He looks at me like I'm five cards short of a full deck. "So feed the dogs *slowly*," he says. "Make sure you're there when he gets home so your *next time* can be tonight."

I sit up a little taller in my seat. The thought hadn't occurred to me, but now that Percy has suggested it, I realize it's not a terrible idea.

"Yeah," Percy says, clearly reading my expression. "Laney's gonna get her some."

"Stop it. I am not."

But as he climbs out of the car and I back out of his driveway, turning toward Hope Acres, I can't help but hope that maybe Percy is right.

CHAPTER TEN

Laney

Twenty minutes later, I let myself into Adam's house. His absolutely *stunning* house.

Goldie meets me in the entryway, and I follow her into a living room with whitewashed wood floors and simple furniture with clean lines in muted colors.

Just beyond the living room, I can see a spacious sunroom, windows filling every wall, where two desks sit facing each other, making me think this is where Adam runs the rescue. And probably handles the *investments* he mentioned, because *hello*, the man obviously has money.

The kitchen is on the right, opposite a wide staircase with open risers and a modern iron railing. At the back of the living room, a half wall and a few steps down separate what can only be a music room. There's a piano and several guitars hanging on the wall and a record player sitting next to a bookshelf that's packed full of vinyls. I think about Adam telling me he's more of a *listener* when it comes to music. I didn't believe him then, and I definitely don't believe him now.

It's all I can do not to cross the space and sort through the records, but that really would feel like snooping, so I head back through the living room and into the kitchen. The house isn't fancy, but it *is* nice. This is not a space that was cobbled together on a budget using throw pillows from HomeGoods and furniture from Ikea. I know that look because it describes my house perfectly.

This is more elevated than that. Intentional and cohesive in a way that makes the whole house feel inviting. I make my way through the kitchen and find the barn keys exactly where Adam said they would be. Goldie seems ready to go with me, like she knows the routine, so I pull up Adam's instructions, making sure I've got the entire message loaded, then the two of us head out to the barn.

The dogs greet us with a chorus of happy barks, and I talk to them by name as I make my way down the aisle with the rolling food cart Adam used the last time I was here. I give lots of pets and words of love as they each get their dinner, spending an extra-long minute with my sweet Ringo. It takes a lot longer to finish working by myself, but eventually, everyone is fed, and we're ready to go outside. I'm a little nervous about letting them all out at once, but the dogs seem familiar with the routine, and no one gives me any trouble.

I spend the next forty-five minutes lounging in the grass while the late evening sun sinks behind the mountains and eight cocker spaniel puppies crawl all over me. Their mother is stretched out a few yards away, and she occasionally looks over at me, her eyes letting me know just how grateful she is for the break. Ringo spends the entire time curled up on my lap, only shifting when he wants to lean up and lick my nose.

Soon, the field is blanketed in shadows, and a slight chill fills the air. Most of the dogs have wandered back to the barn door like they know as well as I do it's time to go back inside.

Once everyone is secure in their kennels, I check on Taylor, who only went outside long enough to pee before finding her own way back to her bed. She's resting peacefully, and I feel the wiggle of her puppies when I rest a hand on her belly.

"It won't be long now, mama," I say, giving her head a good scratch.

She licks my hand, her tail thumping against her bed.

As I lock up the barn and walk with Goldie back to the house, the first flickers of fireflies appear in the grass beside me. It's full dark now, and I wonder if I've stayed long enough for Adam and Sarah to make it home. And not just because of Percy's kiss comment. I would also love the chance to meet Adam's sister.

Once I'm back inside the house, my phone pings with half a dozen messages. Unsurprising, since Sarah mentioned there wasn't reception out in the barn. There's one message from Dad and five from my little sister, Sophie.

SOPHIE

Hey. I need boy advice. You got a sec?

LANEY. It's a random Tuesday night. I know you're home rewatching Bridgerton.
CALL ME.

What gives? Your phone is going straight to voicemail.

> ARE YOU DEAD? Blink once if you need
> me to rescue you.

> Mom says you're probably just busy or
> whatever, so I'm just going to tell you
> what's up.

I scroll through the next three messages without reading them because they are *long,* and unless I'm going to crash on Adam's couch and hang out for a while, this is not the time or the place to get into a text conversation with Sophie. My little sister can *talk,* especially when she's talking about boys.

When I get to the end of what can only be described as Sophie's monologuing, her last few messages make me laugh.

SOPHIE

> For real if something is actually wrong with
> you, please don't think I'm shallow for
> texting about boy problems when you could
> be bleeding out or something.

> Okay, should I be worried you really are
> bleeding out somewhere? Do I need to
> call Dad?

> I'm calling Dad.

> He says I'm overreacting and you're an
> adult with a life. So just, whatever. Call me
> when you're back in the land of the living.
> Unless you really are dead, and then I'm
> totally telling Dad I told you so.

I send my sister a quick text, assuring her I'm alive and well and promising to call her later, then I stop in Adam's kitchen to wash my hands. The hand soap is my favorite scent from Williams Sonoma, and I wonder if it's something Adam orders for himself or if Sarah helps with stuff like that. Which leads me to wonder if Sarah lives here or has her own place.

I dry my hands on a dish towel sitting on the counter, then glance around the kitchen, looking for anything that might indicate one way or the other.

The kitchen is clean, but it's not so clean that it looks like someone doesn't live here. There's a bowl of fruit on the counter and another bowl by the stove full of onions and shallots and bulbs of fresh garlic. A drawer is slightly ajar, and I pull it out to see the most beautiful spice drawer I've ever seen, full of matching glass jars with hand-written labels. The handwriting is masculine, a little slanted, making me think it's definitely Adam's, not Sarah's.

There's a food scale on the counter next to the gas range and a small notebook with a pen on top, filled with the same handwriting I saw on the spices.

I could be wrong, but I don't think Sarah lives here. It's not so much that the house seems absent of a woman's touch. It's more that the space just really feels like Adam.

I make my way back to the living room, walking slowly past the music room. On the wall just beside the piano, there's a seven-inch LP *Elvis Christmas Album* signed by Elvis Presley himself, framed in a glass case.

I swallow. I don't know a ton about collecting rare records, but I've read about the red vinyl Christmas LP, and it's worth thousands.

And Adam has one.

It's all I can do not to sit on the floor in front of his record shelf and see what else he has, but then I hear footsteps on the porch.

My heart starts pounding. It has to be Adam getting home.

Will he care that I'm still here? Will he be surprised to see me hanging out in his music room? I mean, he'll see my car, but it feels weird to just...*be* here, in his space.

I scramble to my feet and head into the living room. I can at least look like I'm on my way out and not snooping through his house.

Just before I reach the front door, a knock sounds on the other side.

Goldie stands alert, ears perked, and lets out a low *woof.*

Okay, so...maybe it isn't Adam getting home. But who else could it be?

That thought makes me nervous. Hope Acres is remote. There are no other houses in either direction for at least a mile, and I am very much alone.

I move to the front window in the living room and peek onto the porch. There's a man standing in front of the door and a dark sedan in the driveway. The man has shaggy brown hair and is wearing a leather jacket, but from this angle, I can't see his face.

He leans forward and knocks one more time, and I debate my options.

If I stay still and quiet, he'll likely just go away. That's the smartest course of action, right? Then I get to stay safely behind a locked door, and this stranger, whoever he is, can come back another time.

Outside, the man moves to the porch steps and sits down.

I frown. What am I supposed to do now?

I could go out the back door and try to creep over to my car, but there's no way the guy wouldn't see me.

I could call the police, but that feels like an overreaction. The guy could be perfectly nice.

He could also be a serial killer.

But honestly, what are the odds? He's hanging out on Adam's porch, clearly waiting for him to return, which means he must be a friend. Right?

Maybe I could call Adam and ask if he's expecting someone?

Or just go back to the barn and lock myself in with the dogs until Adam returns?

I peek through the window one more time. The man is leaning forward on his elbows, looking at his phone. There's something about his profile that feels vaguely familiar, but I don't think I've ever seen him before.

He *does* look pretty harmless. Lean and lanky. Not like Adam, with all his flexing forearms and biceps. I took a couple of self-defense classes in college, and I still remember a few moves. I could probably take this guy.

When in doubt, go for the eyes or go for the balls.

After one more deep breath, I make a decision, then steel myself and open the front door.

The man turns, then stands, a wide smile stretching across his face, and the air freezes in my lungs.

I *do* know this man. Me and every other woman on the planet.

Freddie Ridgefield is standing on Adam's porch.

The Freddie Ridgefield.

Three-time Grammy-award-winning, formerly of Midnight Rush, top ten artists in the *world* Freddie Ridgefield.

He smiles and stretches out his hand. "Hello. You must be Laney, Deke's fiancée."

CHAPTER ELEVEN

Laney

IN ANY NORMAL CIRCUMSTANCE, COMING FACE TO FACE WITH the world's biggest popstar would be overwhelming all on its own.

But there's something else competing for attention in my brain.

You must be Laney, Deke's fiancée.

I *am* Laney, he got that part right, but...Deke? As in, his former bandmate Deke? Is it just a coincidence that I happen to have the same name as Deke Driscoll's fiancée?

But then, why would Freddie Ridgefield expect her to be *here,* at Adam's house?

Adam...*Driscoll's* house.

Wait.

No.

No, no, no, no, no.

That's not even a little bit possible. Adam Driscoll runs a dog rescue in Lawson freaking Cove. He is not...he can't be...

I picture Adam's face. Bright blue eyes. Strong jaw. Soft beard. Perfect lips.

He can't be Deke. Deke is...*Deke.* Boyish and winsome and definitely *not* six feet of sculpted muscle.

I wobble on my feet a little, and Freddie steps into the doorway to steady me. "Hey, whoa. Why don't you sit down for a sec?" He gently grips my elbow, leading me onto the porch and over to a wide, wooden bench to the left of Adam's front door. He hovers as I sit, like he wants to make sure I make it all the way down without falling over. "Just breathe," he says. "Can I get you anything? Some water, maybe?"

I lift my eyes to his. They are really pretty eyes. Wide and green and full of concern.

"You're Freddie Ridgefield," I say.

He offers me a bemused smile. "I am."

"And you're here to see Deke Driscoll?"

He sits down on the bench beside me, careful to keep a respectable amount of space between us. "Right again," he says. "He probably isn't expecting me, not unless Sarah mentioned that I was coming?"

He says this like it's a question. Like I might be able to confirm or deny and shed light on this whole situation. But I am zero help here. I'm too busy trying to calculate the statistical odds that Adam Driscoll and Deke Driscoll are two different people, both with sisters named Sarah and romantic interests named Laney, and this is all just one hilarious coincidental mix-up.

Because Adam simply cannot be Deke.

I look up at Freddie one more time. "You're really him," I say, like this is all some kind of fantastical dream. "And you came here because Deke lives here. Because you know Deke."

He nods, patiently. "It's the address Sarah gave me, so... yes? Is he...not here?"

I don't answer because I can't answer. I have no idea what I would even say. Instead, I lift my hands to my fiery cheeks and will myself to take several deep breaths. I don't think I've been getting a lot of oxygen into my lungs, because the effort feels really good, and my head clears the slightest bit.

"Good," Freddie says gently. "Just keep breathing. Air is your best friend right now."

I'm sure he thinks I'm overwhelmed because of him. Stuff like this is probably part of his day-to-day. Women fainting in front of him, freaking out badly enough that they forget to breathe. That's not exactly what's happening to me, but I'm happy to let him think it is. I mean, I *am* over-whelmed by his presence, but I'm more overwhelmed by the reality he's presenting.

Adam is Deke Driscoll. *Midnight Rush* Deke Driscoll.

I still can't make it compute.

Adam and I have talked about Midnight Rush. Joked about naming Taylor's puppies after the members of the band. I told him right to his face that my *favorite* band member was Deke, and he didn't say a word.

This *would* explain why he recognized the group's song so quickly, but if it *is* him, why is he living in the middle of nowhere, hiding behind a different name? And why does he look like a completely different person?

I scour my brain for something, *anything,* that might make it make sense. At one point, I knew everything there was to know about *all* of the members of Midnight Rush. Even Deke's full name. I knew birth dates, astrological signs, names of pets, and every other scrap of information the band ever revealed.

I was *that* fan. At least, I was at sixteen.

But then I got older. I went to college, and my brain filled with other more useful things. Essential things. Vet school things.

It's still in there. Somewhere in my head, there has to be a piece of information that would explain all of this.

If I remember correctly, after the band broke up, Deke fell off the map pretty quickly. I was naturally devastated, but I was days away from heading off to college and was, for the first time, preoccupied with something a little bigger, a little more important than my Midnight Rush obsession. Still, I remember talk in entertainment news about family drama, maybe a disagreement between Deke and his management team. Or was it his agent? Both, maybe?

I can't remember any specifics about the breakup, so I dig deeper, reach even farther into the back corners of my mind.

Adam told me he moved to Lawson Cove from Tennessee. Was Deke from Tennessee? Did he have a Southern accent at all?

I think through the names of the band members one by one, trying to trigger a memory.

Freddie Ridgefield from Seattle, Washington.

Leo LeClair from Bridgeport, Connecticut.

Jace Campbell from San Diego, California.

Deke Driscoll from...Knoxville, Tennessee.

Suddenly, the information I need drops into my brain like candy falling out of a vending machine.

Adam Deacon Driscoll. Born in Knoxville, Tennessee, May 27th.

Deacon. *Deke.*

It *is* him.

I have been on a date with my favorite member of Midnight Rush. Held his hand. Almost kissed him.

I lean forward, resting my arms on my knees and take a stuttering breath. "Ohhhh no," I say, staring at the floorboards. "I think I might be sick."

"Keep breathing," Freddie says, his voice growing slightly more alarmed. "I'm going to go inside and grab you some water. Can I do that? Can I go inside?"

I nod numbly. At least if he leaves, I'll have a minute to wrap my head around this new reality. Except...*wait.*

Adam being Deke might explain Freddie's presence on his porch, but it doesn't explain the other part of what he said.

Why does he think I'm Deke's fiancée?

Freddie reappears with a bottle of water, cold from Adam's fridge, and he slips it into my hands, the cap already gone.

I take a slow drink, brain still reeling, as headlights appear at the end of the driveway. It can only be Adam, and sure enough, his white SUV quickly comes into view, the familiar Hope Rescue logo emblazoned on the side.

Beside me, Freddie stands, his hands slipping into his front pockets as he shifts his weight from foot to foot. He almost seems nervous, making me wonder when he last saw Adam.

Or...Deke? I have no idea how to think of him now.

Adam cuts the engine in his SUV, but he doesn't get out. Once he turns off the headlights, reducing the glare, the glow of the porch lights makes it easy to see him through the passenger side window. He's staring forward, his hands gripping the steering wheel, while his sister talks, her hands moving as she does.

"Is he going to get out?" Freddie mutters more to himself than to me. He *is* nervous. I can see it in the tight line of his shoulders, the way his fists are clenched next to his sides.

I stand up beside him, swallowing past the lump in my throat, but there's no hiding the tremble in my voice. "I'm sure he will eventually."

But he doesn't.

Not for another minute, at least. And a minute when you're standing beside Freddie Ridgefield is a very long time.

Finally, Adam climbs out of his car.

He stops at the foot of the stairs and looks up at Freddie. It takes about ten seconds for his usually stoic expression to break, then he's moving forward, and Freddie is rushing down the steps and pulling Adam into a tight embrace.

Adam hugs right back, confirming that he is, actually, Deke Driscoll, and also telling me he hasn't seen his former bandmate in a very long time.

Sarah appears beside me, her eyes wide and her expression full of concern. She has Adam's blue eyes and wavy blond hair that just reaches her shoulders, and I'm momentarily distracted by how beautiful she is. "So this must be pretty overwhelming for you," she says, her voice gentle. "I'm Sarah, by the way."

I nod even as my eyes shift back to her brother. "Right. And he's..."

I don't even have the words to finish the sentence. At least not out loud.

"He's still the same guy you thought he was an hour ago," Sarah says. "I know it's a lot. But...just remember that."

I want to believe Sarah, but nothing about any of this makes sense. How can sweet, affable, introverted Adam also be an international popstar? *Former* international popstar?

An image of Adam running his hands through his hair flashes through my brain, and the weird sense of déjà vu I've had a few times since we've started hanging out suddenly makes sense.

Adam seems familiar because he *is* familiar. I've watched Deke run his hand through his hair a million times. It's the move he was famous for, and Adam does it exactly the same way.

"I met your fiancée," Freddie says as he finally pulls back from the world's longest hug. He claps Adam on the back. "I can't believe I had to hear you were getting married from *Kevin*."

"Wait. What?" Sarah says from beside me. "Fiancée?"

Adam's eyes go wide, and they fill with panic as he looks in my direction.

I should object. Clarify. Say *something*. But my utter and complete brain jumble seems to have filled my mouth with concrete.

I wait for Adam to protest or explain, but he seems just as tongue-tied as I am.

It's Sarah who finally breaks me out of my stupor. "Um, Laney? Are you okay? You look a little pale."

Adam hurries up the stairs and grabs my elbow, his touch sending heat coursing through my veins. "You *do* look pale," he says softly. He tugs me toward the bench where I sat with Freddie just minutes ago. "Here. Sit down."

I do as he asks, even as a completely ridiculous thought makes a giggle rise up inside of me. In the past twenty minutes, two different members of Midnight Rush have sat me down on this same bench. The giggle sounds more like a painful snort when it comes out, and Adam lifts a hand to my back, rubbing his palm up and down in a soothing gesture.

It *is* soothing, and I finally look over to meet his eyes. They are full of concern, a deep furrow creasing his brow, and it's almost enough to anchor me, to make me forget that a hundred miles away in my childhood bedroom, there's still a poster of him hanging beside my bed.

A surge of irrational panic shoots through me.

Or maybe it's embarrassment?

Thinking of Adam as *that* guy—the guy he was when I was in high school—somehow throws my brain back to that same time. When I was awkward and insecure and so uncomfortable with myself. It doesn't make any sense. I'm *not* that girl anymore. But I'm in fight or flight mode, and all I want to do is flee. Hide. Go somewhere else, where I can process without so many eyes watching.

I shrug out from under Adam's touch and stand up again. "I think I need to go."

"Laney, please wait."

Adam catches my hand, holding it with a gentle firmness that brings me slightly back to earth. I let him tug me back to the bench, where he drops my hand and wraps both palms around my shoulders. He's wearing a bright red baseball cap, frayed around the edges, and blue flannel over a white t-shirt. It's how I'm used to him looking. How he's looked all these months he been coming into the office, all the times I've imagined him in my mind.

"This doesn't change anything," he says softly. "I'm still me. I just...have a slightly more complicated job history."

I huff out a laugh. "That's one way to put it."

His lips lift in a tiny half grin that makes my heart pinch, because suddenly, I see it.

I *see* Deke.

Honestly, I have no idea how I didn't see it before. The similarities are so obvious. Those intense blue eyes and thick lashes, his cheekbones and the pronounced curve of his upper lip. I stared at Deke's sixteen-year-old face every day for three years, every time I walked into my room. I can see that face now, or at least a shadow of it, hidden inside this manlier version, but he really does look different.

"It's why you wear the beard," I say, and he nods.

"I like the beard, but yeah. It covers a lot."

The beard *is* a good disguise. And the hats and the flannel and the height, but now that I *know,* there's no denying it's him. I feel ridiculous for missing it. For talking to him all this time without thinking, even once, that he looked like Deke Driscoll. He even told me his last name, and I didn't get suspicious, didn't make any kind of connection.

But then, why would I? Why would it ever occur to me that Deke would be *here,* of all places?

"Can you sit here for one more second?" Adam asks. "Let me take care of Freddie, then we can talk."

When I nod, he quickly stands and runs down the stairs, saying something to Freddie too quiet for me to hear. While I watch, the only thing I can think about is how, when I drove over here, the hope in my heart was that I might be around long enough to see Adam and get the goodbye I wanted at the end of our date. The *next time* he promised.

If Freddie hadn't shown up, I might have.

And then I would have kissed Deke Driscoll.

Adam and Freddie make their way up the stairs together, where Freddie says a quick hello to Sarah and gives her a hug. Over his shoulder, she meets my eye and makes a face like she can't quite believe what's happening.

It's a small thing, but it goes a long way to making me feel better about my own reaction. She's Deke's sister—Adam's sister? I'm not sure how to think of him now—and she's still freaking out? Maybe I can give myself a pass for the number of minutes I've spent mute, staring at the wooden slats of the porch, trying not to throw up.

Freddie offers me a hesitant, "Nice to meet you, Laney," before he disappears inside, then Adam gestures for Sarah to follow.

"No way," she says once the door is closed between us and Freddie. "Not until you explain to me why he thinks Laney is your fiancée."

I raise my hand. "Yes, please. Me too. I would also like to know the answer to that question."

Adam sighs. "I can explain to *you*," he says, looking at me, "but *you* need to go. Either inside with Freddie or out to the barn or anywhere that isn't here." This last part he delivers to Sarah with an older brother firmness that makes her scowl. They stare at each other, some kind of wordless communication passing between them until Sarah finally caves. "Ugh, fine. I think I'll go check on the dogs," she says pointedly. "It will probably take me a very long time."

And then, finally, I'm alone with Adam.

Alone with *Deke.*

The first thought that pops into my head is utterly and completely ridiculous. If, by some miracle, I really do find myself in a position to kiss *the* Adam Deacon Driscoll, I will never—and I mean *never*—admit how many times I kissed his poster first.

CHAPTER TWELVE

Adam

FREAKING FREDDIE RIDGEFIELD.

This is not how I thought Laney would find out about my past.

Now, it looks like I kept it from her, like I didn't want her to know. And the fiancée thing...I did not expect that to come back to bite me. But I should have known. I should have expected Kevin would tell Freddie, at least, if not Leo and Jace.

That doesn't explain how Freddie figured out where I live. Property records? A private investigator? He has the resources, so I wouldn't put it past him.

However he found me, I think I underestimated how important this concert is to him. For him to show up on my doorstep after all this time just to ask me in person? That says something.

The truth is, I wouldn't want anything to do with a friend

who ghosted me as badly as I did Freddie—and the others, too.

When I saw him, when he pulled me in for an embrace, I forgot about all of it. I forgot that I shut him out. Ignored his calls, his texts. I forgot that I walked away from the life he was a part of and promised myself I would never go back.

I still have no clue how I'm going to navigate a conversation with him. How I'm going to say no to his face when he came all this way.

But I do know that, despite everything, I'm actually glad he's here. Even if he did make things complicated with Laney.

She's still waiting for me, sitting on the bench with her back straight, eyes focused somewhere in the darkness beyond the house.

I lower myself down beside her, and she offers me a hesitant smile.

"You okay?" I ask.

"Adam Deacon Driscoll," she says slowly, enunciating each part of my name with careful specificity. "I can't believe I didn't figure it out."

I lean forward, propping my elbows on my knees. "If it matters, it's been a very long time since anyone has recognized me. I would have been surprised if you *had* figured it out."

She glances over at me, but her gaze doesn't hold. Like she's afraid to make eye contact. "Did you...what happened? Where did..." She waves her hand up and down my body, scrunching her face up in a way that makes her nose wrinkle. "All of this come from?"

I chuckle. "I grew three inches the year I turned nineteen. And gained about thirty pounds over the next three."

"Guys can do that? I stopped growing when I was fourteen."

"Some guys do," I say. "I did. But you have to admit, when I was eighteen, I could have told people I was fifteen and they would have believed it."

"That's true," she says. "You always looked younger than the other guys." She falls back into silence, her eyes shifting this way and that, like she can't quite keep up with all the thoughts running through her brain.

I wait, giving her the chance to process, to take this conversation at her own pace.

"I was in your house," she says, but it feels more like she's talking to herself than to me. "I was looking at your record collection, which makes so much more sense now. That Elvis album alone is worth...and this house! And the farm. Of course you can fund Hope Acres. I wondered if you'd won the lottery. Or had family money." She looks over at me one more time, and this time her gaze locks in. "You said you had some investments do well."

"Technically, that's still true. It just so happens that the money for those investments came from Midnight Rush."

She furrows her brow like she's considering a new piece of evidence and isn't sure how or where to sort it in her brain. I can't blame her for the struggle. I'm basically asking her to rewrite everything she thinks she knows about me, to insert a whole new past into her mind view.

"So I was looking at your records," she finally says, restarting her story, "and then Freddie was on the front porch, and he greeted me by name." She lets out a disbelieving laugh. "And then he said that I must be Deke's fiancée. I didn't just open the door and come face to face with Freddie Ridgefield, I listened to him tell me I was engaged to Deke Driscoll. That *you* were Deke Driscoll. I couldn't make up a more improbable scenario if I tried."

"I'm sure it felt like a lot," I say.

"It felt like an ambush," she says. "At least an emotional one."

I resist the urge to reach over and put an arm around her, to offer her physical comfort in some way. I want to, but I don't want to spook her.

"Should I explain about the engagement part first?"

It takes her a moment, but she eventually nods, so I walk her through my phone call with Kevin. Her eyes widen to saucers when I mention the reunion concert, then she frowns when I tell her why I felt compelled to lie about having a fiancée in the first place. Her expressions tell a thousand stories, her emotions playing over her face like she's an open book, words written in twenty-four point font.

"But why me?" she asks when I finally finish. "Why did you choose me to be your fake fiancée?"

It's not a question I expect her to ask, because in my mind, it's more like *of course, you.* "Because I like you," I say simply. "And you'd just come out to the farm for the first time the night Kevin called, so you were on my mind. But also, I thought that would be the end of it. That Kevin would tell everyone I said no, and that would be that."

"But then Kevin told Freddie," she says as she pieces the story together. "And Freddie decided to come see you in person because..."

I sigh. "Because he knows if *he* asks me to do the concert, I'm more likely to cave and say yes."

"Why Freddie?" she asks.

I lean back, letting my head drop against the house, a familiar tightness forming low in my gut. I don't usually talk about this. I am much better at leaving the past in the past, at letting those very messy years stay buried in the back of my mind where they belong. But for the first time in I don't know how long—maybe ever—I *want* to talk about it. I want Laney to understand.

"At the end of Midnight Rush's last tour," I begin, "the band still had one more album on contract with our record label. But then I quit. The group had the option of replacing me or doing an album without me, but they all refused. I think they hoped I might eventually change my mind, but... I'd just lost my mom, and I wasn't in a great place mentally, so they stalled as long as they could. Eventually, the label got tired of waiting, so the rest of the guys decided that what they collectively wanted was to move on, focus on their solo careers. In order to appease New Groove, Freddie negotiated a new deal, putting himself on the line if they would release Midnight Rush from the last album on the contract."

She frowns. "I don't understand why that was doing you a favor. Clearly, it worked out well for Freddie."

"On the surface, yeah. But the label required that the terms of the contract stay the same—identical to what we signed when the group was formed. By that point, Freddie had enough star power he should have been able to get a much better deal. Signing another three-sixty was not in his best interest."

"A three-sixty?"

I give her a thirty-second explanation of what a three-sixty deal entails, and she nods along.

"So the label just gets a much larger piece of the pie."

"Right. Exactly."

"What would have happened if Freddie hadn't signed?" she asks. "If Midnight Rush had just not made the album?"

"The label would have defaulted on our royalties, possibly sued us for breach of contract. Leo and Jace were trying to get their solo careers started too, and that kind of legal battle would have been bad for everyone."

"But if the other guy wanted to go solo too, why was Freddie the one who renegotiated with the label?"

"Because he was the only one who could. In the months while all of this was happening behind the scenes, he was already making music online, growing his following, writing songs and playing them on TikTok to millions of fans. When he finally dropped an album, everyone in the industry knew it would be a guaranteed success. That made him a safer bet for the label than Leo or Jace. Freddie had the star power. And he used it to benefit the rest of us. Me, most of all. I had Sarah to take care of, no parents, and no safety net. I couldn't afford to lose royalties. Freddie is the only one who has any kind of leverage when it comes to convincing me. And I know better than to think he won't use it."

"So Freddie signed the crappy deal so no one else would have to."

"Right. And the other guys signed better deals with different labels."

She's quiet for a beat, like she's letting it all sink in. Then she asks, "Adam, why did you quit?" She moves her hands up and down her bare arms like she's rubbing out the chill. It's still September, so it's plenty hot during the day, but this high in the mountains, it drops down into the sixties, even the upper fifties at night. "Is that too personal a question?"

I shrug off the flannel I'm wearing on top of my t-shirt and drape it over her shoulders. The act of doing something distracts me from the growing discomfort in my chest—the tiny pinpricks of pain that still shoot through me whenever I think about the last few months before I quit. Whenever I think of all those phone calls from my mom, from Sarah, begging me to just come home.

But our European tour was almost over—only a few shows left—and Kevin kept insisting that if I just hung on a little bit longer, I could take a break after the tour and *really* focus on my family.

But then Mom died, and it was too late.

Laney tugs the shirt around her shoulders and smiles. "Thanks," she says. "And for real, you don't have to answer if you don't want to."

"It was just complicated," I say. "With my mom and wanting to be there for Sarah—" My words cut off, and I lift a hand to my chest, rubbing against the tightness spreading across my ribs.

"It was around the same time?" she says. "That your mom died?"

I nod and clear my throat, then blow out a breath like I can somehow dislodge the building discomfort inside me by sheer force of will.

Laney shifts on the bench beside me, turning sideways, one knee pulled under her so she can face me. She reaches over and puts her hand on top of mine, squeezing it gently. "I'm really sorry about your mom, Adam. With everything you were dealing with, the travel, the fame and attention, the pressure—to have to deal with that kind of loss when you're so young is really unfair."

Most of the time, people assume that because of the money that comes with it, fame makes things easier. But I was just a kid, trying to juggle the expectations of so many people, and the adults I had giving me advice, talking to me about my career, my choices, were *all* adults who were financially invested in our success. It *wasn't* fair. I didn't see it then as much as I see it now, and it feels good to have Laney acknowledge it.

"I was planning on telling you tomorrow night," I say.

"About Midnight Rush?"

I nod. "I had it all planned out. I was going to bring—oh, actually—" I reach over and pull out a photo from the front pocket of my shirt and hand it to her. "I was going to bring you this. I had Sarah dig it out of her stuff this morning and bring it to me. I worried you might need convincing since I look so different."

The picture is of me and Sarah and the rest of Midnight Rush, the one time she left Mom and came to Nashville to see us in concert.

Laney shakes her head as her eyes linger on the photo. "This is still really hard for me to believe."

"I'm sure."

"And I still have so many questions."

"Like what?"

She tucks the photo back into the pocket of my shirt. "Like...how long has it been since you've seen Freddie? Are you still friends? Does Freddie being here mean there really will be a reunion concert, and if it does, will you get me tickets?"

This one makes me chuckle, and she gives me a playful grin, then keeps going with her list. "I also want to know if you being Deke had anything to do with you *not* kissing me the other night."

I rub my thumb over the back of her hand, tracing small circles over her knuckles.

"Those are good questions."

"Thank you. I just came up with them myself."

I smile. All things considered, she seems to have recovered from the initial shock pretty well. The fact that we're holding hands, that she's asking about kissing me—those have to be good signs.

"I haven't seen Freddie since the funeral," I say, answering her first question. "Or any of the guys. I'd like to think they still consider me a friend, but I have not been good at staying in touch, so it won't surprise me if they aren't interested in anything but what the concert requires. I have some personal reasons for not wanting to sing with the band again, but I really *do* owe Freddie. If this will help him...I don't know. Maybe with the right boundaries in place? But it would take a lot to convince me." I lift her hand and flip it over so our palms are flush, our fingers entwined. "As for the kiss...that's exactly why I didn't kiss you. I wanted to tell you first. I didn't want to start with secrets between us."

Her eyes fall closed, and she tugs her hand out of mine, lifting her palms to her face where she presses them against her cheeks.

"You okay?" I ask.

She gives her head a little shake. "No? Yes? Adam, I had your poster on my wall. I *kissed* your poster before I went to bed every night." She winces and slides a hand up to cover her eyes. "I swore I wasn't going to tell you that, but it feels like just the thing to demonstrate how surreal this is for me. You're...*you*. And I'm the girl who went to your concert with a mouth full of metal and bad hair and thought her life was changed forever when you crouched down during the show and squeezed my hand."

"I really did that?"

"You did," she says, finally letting her hands fall from her face. "We made eye contact and everything."

"Hard to believe I made eye contact with those eyes and didn't follow you home."

She grins and shakes her head, letting out a little laugh. "I would have died," she says. "I was so awkward and uncomfortable in high school. But you—Midnight Rush in general —you guys made life bearable for me. So to be here with you, joking about kissing—"

"Wait. Stop right there," I say.

She cocks her head. "Why?"

I hold her gaze, then lean toward her and lift a hand to her cheek, brushing my thumb over the curve of her jaw. "Because I'm not joking about wanting to kiss you."

Her eyes flutter closed as I brush my nose against hers, then press a kiss to the corner of her mouth.

She sucks in a stuttering breath. "Ohhh, this does not feel like kissing your poster."

I let out a low chuckle. "I should hope not."

When our lips finally touch, it takes Laney a moment to respond, but then she wakes up, kissing me back, her mouth soft and yielding against mine. I lift a hand to the back of her neck, sliding my fingers into her hair while her hands move to my chest.

I sensed that things would change once I kissed her, that it would feel bigger, more monumental than anything I've experienced before, but even with that expectation, I'm still unprepared for how this feels. How consuming it is to have her this close.

Laney breaks the kiss, hovering in front of me long enough to take one, two, three shallow breaths. Then she smiles as she leans forward and drops her head against my chest.

"This isn't happening," she whispers into my shirt. I can't tell if she means for me to hear her, so I ignore it, but I can't stop myself from pressing one more lingering kiss to her forehead.

"I'm coming back from the barn," Sarah says loudly from somewhere behind us. "I'll be coming up onto the porch any minute. I sure hope I don't interrupt anything."

Laney starts to chuckle. "I like Sarah."

"I'd like her a lot more if she'd stayed in the barn a few more minutes."

"Nah. It's time for me to go. You need to go talk to Freddie anyway."

I pull off my hat and set it on my knee, then run my fingers through my hair with a sigh. "True."

Laney stands and tugs me to my feet, then steps closer, wrapping her arms around my waist and stepping into my embrace. I hook my hands together at the small of her back. She leans up on her toes and presses a quick kiss to my lips. "Sometimes the hardest conversations are the ones most worth having," she says. "You're going to do great."

Sarah is on the porch a few seconds later, eyeing us with unconcealed glee, like she can't quite believe we have our arms around each other. "I know you guys aren't actually engaged," she says, motioning between us, "but can I just say how happy this makes me?"

I roll my eyes at my sister's enthusiasm and have to stifle a groan at the reminder of the lie I still need to fix.

It'll be easy to clear up the engagement thing with Freddie. He's here. I can just tell him, explain why I felt like I needed to lie in the first place. But if Kevin told Freddie, there's no telling who else might already know. Or how he might use the information if he thinks it will serve a purpose. Especially if that purpose begins with a dollar sign and ends in a whole lot of zeros.

"That's right," Laney says. "Freddie thinks we're engaged."

"I'll talk to him," I say to Laney. "Explain what's really going on."

She nods. "Will I still see you tomorrow night?"

"I want to see you, but I have no idea how long Freddie will be here. Can I text you after I talk to him? Maybe you can come here instead? We could all hang out together?"

She reaches up and pats my chest. "Baby steps, Adam. I don't know if I can handle hanging out with fifty percent of Midnight Rush at once."

I'll take baby steps. Because she didn't run away. She didn't get mad. She still kissed me after learning that I'm one fourth of Midnight Rush. She knows, and we're still okay.

I walk Laney to her car, kissing her one more time before saying goodbye and watching her drive away.

I should feel overwhelmed by the looming conversation with Freddie. With the idea of disappointing him. After eight years of relative anonymity, I'm just not sure I can go on stage again. *Sing* again after I swore I never would.

But with Laney's scent still lingering on my skin, lips tingling and warm from the pressure of her kiss, I just can't bring myself to care about anything else.

And I smile all the way to my front door.

CHAPTER THIRTEEN

Adam

SARAH LEAVES TO GO HOME JUST AFTER LANEY, SO BY THE TIME I make it inside to find Freddie sitting at the piano, it's just the two of us and Goldie. He's playing something I've never heard before, but I immediately like it. It's catchy, a little wistful, with a nice melody. He looks up and smiles when he sees me, but he doesn't stop, so I walk toward him, lowering myself into the nearest chair.

Beside the piano, a guitar rack holds three guitars—a classical Yamaha that I've had since I was a kid and two acoustic: a Martin D-28 Sarah found at an estate sale in Knoxville priced for half what it was worth, and my favorite, a 1962 vintage Gibson I splurged on when my latest royalty check from the record label was larger than I expected.

Freddie motions toward the guitars, his fingers still rolling across the keys. "Are you playing?"

"Some. I mostly just mess around." I nod toward the piano. "What is that?"

"Just me messing around. I like the melody, but I can't write a lyric worth anything." His hands fall away, and he turns on the piano bench to face me. "It's good to see you, Deke."

"Adam," I say quickly. "I know you knew me as Deke, but I haven't gone by that name in a really long time."

"No problem." Freddie leans forward, propping his elbows on his knees. "You look good, Adam. Different. Had I just seen you on the street, I'm not sure I'd have recognized you."

It's still hard to believe Freddie's here, after so many years apart. The record label loved to talk up our friendship to the press, but it wasn't just talk. We were always as close as they claimed we were.

Until we weren't anymore.

And that's on me.

"Yeah. I've changed a lot, I guess."

Goldie wanders over to Freddie and drops her head onto his knee. Freddie starts to pet her, and her tail wags before she looks over at me, like she's giving me her approval.

"You're huge, man," Freddie says. "You have to be hitting the gym."

"Yeah. Some."

Freddie, on the other hand, looks almost entirely the same. He's as tall as I am, but he's just as lean and lanky as he was when Midnight Rush was still Midnight Rush. His dark hair is long and a little shaggy, and I can see tattoos visible on one forearm and at the open collar of his shirt. He looks every bit the rockstar he's become, but he still looks like Freddie, too. Like the kid from Seattle who stood next to me in line at the final Midnight Rush audition, smiled with uncanny confidence, and told me it wasn't a question of *if* he was going to be a star. Only a question of when.

A beat of silence passes between us, and a tightness forms in my chest. I'm not sure what to say to Freddie. *How* to say anything at all. It's been eight years since things fell apart, but right now, it feels like we're right back on the lawn outside the funeral home the day after I buried my mother, my three best friends looking at me as I tell them I'm walking away from Midnight Rush for good.

"Jace and Leo say hello," Freddie says. "I just saw Leo in Nashville last week. And Jace has another kid on the way. This will be his second."

"Wow. That's—good for him."

Jace was always the one who seemed the most excited about getting married and having a family, so this doesn't surprise me. He was never big into dating around. Every girl he met, even when he was sixteen, he talked about her like he'd just found his soulmate. There were at least a dozen soulmates in the three years the band was together, but the last one actually stuck. A model from Australia named Jasmine, whom he married on his twenty-second birthday.

At least, according to Sarah, who fills in the gaps between my cursory quarterly searches.

"And now you're getting married," Freddie says. "Laney seems nice."

I clear my throat. "Yeah, about that. Laney and I aren't actually engaged."

Freddie frowns. "No?"

I sigh and run a hand through my hair. "We've been texting. And we had dinner last weekend. But I made up the engagement because Kevin wouldn't stop hounding me about the reunion. That man will not take no for an answer."

Freddie chuckles. "What I love and hate about him the most."

I don't understand how Freddie is still working with Kevin after all these years, but he must see some value in keeping him around. Especially now, when he could have his pick of agents.

"I told him I needed to focus on my fiancée, but I clearly wasn't thinking because I didn't even consider that he'd tell you. But of course he would."

Freddie's quiet for a beat before he says, "I gotta admit. It stung hearing news like that from Kevin instead of you. Even after all the time that's passed, I'd like to think you'd call me if you were getting married for real."

I lean forward, elbows propped on my knees, eyes on the floor. I'm not actually sure I *would* call him, and that realization sends shame washing over me. Cutting ties with all three of them was a matter of survival, the only way I knew how to deal with the guilt and grief surrounding my mother's death. It's been easy to convince myself it was the best way, the only way for me to keep living my life as *Adam* and leave that part of me behind for good.

But now, with Freddie sitting in front of me, looking at me, talking to me just like he did when we were kids, I'm not so sure.

I've missed him. I've *missed* having friends who know me.

"She's a vet," I say. "Laney. That's how we met. She takes care of the dogs for the rescue."

I don't know why I'm telling him this. As if opening up now will somehow negate the many years I didn't reach out. That isn't usually how friendship works. But I also have to remember that Freddie is here for a purpose. He didn't just come as my friend. He came as an artist who wants my help.

"So that's what this place is?" he says. "A dog rescue?"

"Sarah and I run it together."

His expression shifts. "Sarah. Man. She's all grown up."

"And dating someone," I say. "So don't get any ideas."

He smirks. "Noted. Appreciate the heads up."

The silence stretches between us, broken only by Freddie's continued tinkering on the piano. I brace myself for what I know is coming. This is when Freddie is going to ask. Put the pressure on. Remind me he's the reason I was able to walk without losing a ton of money.

But he doesn't say anything like that. He hardly says anything at all. He just stands and moves to the guitar rack on the wall, where he carefully removes the Gibson. He slides a hand over the neck and lets out a low whistle. "It's a sweet instrument." He holds it out to me. "Come on. Let's play something."

I look up, eyebrows furrowed. "Right now?"

"Why not?" Freddie says.

I take the guitar, and he moves back to the piano bench, positioning himself in front of the keys.

"I don't remember much," I lie.

Freddie rolls his eyes. "Yeah, you do. You wouldn't have all this in your living room if you didn't still play." He plays out the first few chords of "Falling Slowly," then looks up at me. "Isn't this the one you used to play all the time? The one from the movie?"

I don't answer him, but I'm already tuning the guitar, my hands thankfully on autopilot because my brain is completely freaking out. I haven't done this in front of anyone aside from Sarah and Goldie in years, but weirdly, I find I actually want to.

Freddie waits until I'm tuned and ready. When I look up

and meet his eye, he nods, his hands hovering over the keys as he waits for me to strum the first chords. He joins in as soon as I do, and then...I sing.

Badly, at first. I'm not even a little warmed up. But the longer I sing, the easier it gets.

Eventually, Freddie comes in with a harmony, and our voices blend as well as they did when we were Midnight Rush. Before long, I'm not thinking about my trembling hands or how weird it is to sing in front of someone who has found as much success as Freddie.

I just let the music roll over me until it's all I can feel.

When the final notes ring out, neither of us moves, the silence settling between us for a beat, then two, before Freddie finally lifts his hands from the keys and laughs. "That was incredible."

I lean the guitar against the couch and stand up, heading for the kitchen without a word, mostly because I don't want Freddie to notice how weirdly emotional I suddenly am. I've played a lot of music over the past eight years. But only for myself. Usually when Sarah is gone, and Goldie is the only one around to listen.

I wouldn't have guessed that playing with someone else would hit me so hard.

I take a deep breath and pull a couple of beers out of the fridge, a double IPA from a microbrewery that just opened up across the ridge. I stand there, staying in the small triangle of light spilling out of the open door until I feel a little more in control, then open the bottles and return to the music room, where I hand one to Freddie.

He holds it up and studies the label.

"It's local. You'll like it."

He takes a long drink before setting it on the floor beside

the piano. "Yeah, that's good." He lifts his hands back to the keys and grins. "What else you got?"

We play for over an hour. My favorite songs. His favorite songs. Even a few Midnight Rush songs—including our debut single, "Curves Like That," the one with lyrics a group of teenage boys never should have been singing.

By the time we get to the end, we're both laughing so hard we're practically crying.

At one point, Freddie grabs the Martin off the wall, and we play a few with both of us on guitar, then he switches over to the Gibson and I move to the piano. I'm not as good as he is, and he claims he's better on bass than guitar, but I don't think he's giving himself enough credit.

He's grown a lot as an artist, settled into a sound that's more mature, more grounded than the Freddie I knew as a teenager. More than once, I find myself listening more than I'm singing, almost in awe of what he can do.

"For real, man. I don't know why you aren't still doing this," Freddie says after we finish playing through a Lewis Capaldi song we both love. "You're singing with a lot more of your chest voice than you used to, and your tone is legit."

"Nah," I say. "I don't know about that."

"I'm serious," he says. "Let's do 'Never Say Never.' You can do Leo's vocals. Actually, hang on. Where's your phone?"

I lift an eyebrow. "Why do you need my phone?"

"Because I want someone else to hear how good you sound."

"Freddie, come on. I don't..." I hesitate, lifting my hands to my head. "No one else has heard me sing in a really long time."

He frowns. "Really? Not even Sarah? Or Laney?"

I huff out a laugh. "Laney didn't even know I was Deke until you showed up on my front porch and told her."

His eyes widen, then understanding dawns. "So that's why she was so freaked out. I thought it was just me, but her reaction did seem a little extreme."

"I was going to tell her, I just hadn't gotten around to it yet."

"Perfect," he says, standing up and holding out his hand. "Even better. Phone, man. Come on."

I have no idea why I pull my phone out of my pocket and hand it over. Probably because he's Freddie Ridgefield. And nobody gets what he wants like Freddie gets what he wants. Call it charm. Or just really good intuition that tells him exactly how and when to push. Either way, the man is unstoppable. When he gets an idea in his head, you either jump on board or get out of the way.

He scrolls through my contacts and pulls up Laney's number. Then he hits *Call.*

Just like that. No warning. No asking for permission.

It's almost eleven PM, and he just *called her.*

My heart starts pounding as Freddie puts the call on speaker, one ring, then two sounding through the phone. Just before the third ring, Laney answers.

"Hello?"

I breathe out a sigh of relief. At least she sounds fully awake and not like we just pulled her from a dead sleep.

"Hi, Laney? It's Freddie. How are you?"

"Oh my gosh," Laney says, then she laughs. "I'm fine, Freddie. How are you?"

"Actually, I'm just sitting here with your man, Adam, and we've been playing some music."

"Yeah? How's it going?" Laney asks.

"Brilliantly. So brilliantly, in fact, that I was thinking you might like to listen in. Can we FaceTime you?"

"Hmm. Can you put Adam on the phone before I answer? And take me off speaker?"

Freddie rolls his eyes dramatically, but then he smiles. "Sure I can. Hang on."

He hands over my phone, and I take it off speaker before lifting the phone to my ear. "Hey."

"Hi," she says. "I just wanted to make sure you weren't being held against your will."

I chuckle. "Nah, I'm good."

"Do you mind if I listen while you sing? Because I would love to, but I would also be happy to fake a headache if you'd rather I not."

Something catches in my chest. It feels profoundly significant that even as much as Laney was—still is?—a Midnight Rush fan, she's still asking me this. Thinking about how I feel rather than how much she might enjoy hearing Freddie Ridgefield sing to her over FaceTime.

Weirdly, the fact that she's prioritizing *me* over the music makes me want to sing for her more.

"I'm good if you'd like to listen. Freddie has a way of getting what he wants anyway."

In front of me, Freddie lifts his arms in triumph. "Face-Time, man. Let's do this."

I initiate the call, and Laney immediately accepts, then it buffers for a second before her face fills the screen.

She looks like she's in bed, wearing a hoodie, with the hood up, glasses on, and her hair in a loose braid hanging in front of her shoulder.

I am very much a fan of this version of Laney.

"Hi," she says, offering me a shy smile. "This was unexpected."

"I hope Freddie didn't wake you up."

"Nope. Just reading."

Freddie gets entirely too close as he leans into the frame. "Hi, Laney. Nice to see you again." He takes the phone out of my hand and walks over to the piano. "Adam tells me I gave you quite the shock when I showed up. I'm sorry I prematurely outed your boyfriend. Though I was sad to learn all that hyperventilating wasn't for me."

I brace myself for Laney's rebuttal, her insistence that I'm not, actually, her boyfriend, but she only laughs. "I was not hyperventilating."

"Come on," Freddie says. "We both know you were close. What do you think? Was it forty percent me, sixty percent Adam? Can I claim forty percent?"

"I'll give you ten," Laney says.

"Just ten? How about twenty?"

"Fifteen and that's my final offer. Were you going to actually sing something? Or did you really just call me to negotiate the measure of your impact on my emotional well-being?"

Freddie looks over his shoulder at me and grins. "I like her." When he looks back at the phone, he says, "We're singing 'Never Say Never.' Were you a Midnight Rush fan, Laney?"

"I was."

"Yeah? Who was your favorite?"

"Adam, by a large margin," she says.

"For real? And now you're dating him? Someone should write a book about this."

Laney yawns, lifting a hand to her face, something I can see from here, even though Freddie has taken the phone all the way across the room.

"Come on, man," I say. "If we're going to sing, let's sing. She's gotta work tomorrow."

"All right, all right," Freddie says. "Let's do it." He gets up and positions the phone on the bookshelf so we're both in the frame, and then we start to sing.

When Midnight Rush toured, we had a five-piece band that accompanied us on guitars, drums, bass, and keys. The four of us were only ever on vocal. We were told we were too young to be trusted with instruments, which, for all of us but Leo, who was a killer pianist from the start, was probably a smart move. It's hard to do both—to sing and play at the same time—and since we were all just fifteen and sixteen when we started, we were infants compared to the seasoned musicians who toured with us.

Tackling the guitar solo in "Never Say Never" was one of the many projects I used to occupy my time in the years right after Mom died, when I spent a lot more time hiding than I did leaving my house. I never thought knowing how to play it would ever come in handy, but as we approach the solo, Freddie glances over, and I nod to let him know I've got this.

It's not quite the same on an acoustic guitar—it was always electric on tour—but it fits the vibe of what we're doing here better anyway.

When I reach the end, Freddie smiles and laughs and says a quiet, "For real, man?" before we start the chorus for the final time.

Laney claps when we finish. "You guys. That was unbelievable. I liked it better than the original."

Freddie's closer to the phone than I am, so he jumps up

and grabs it first. "Right? I swear, it's Adam. The man's a freaking genius on the guitar. And his voice..."

"Okay, my turn," I say, reaching over Freddie's shoulder and taking the phone.

Freddie grins. "Goodnight, Laney. It was nice to see you again."

"I hope we didn't keep you up too late," I say, looking at Laney.

She shakes her head. "Totally worth it."

"Will you be up a little longer?"

She shakes her head. "I wish I could be, but I've got early appointments in the morning. I need my sleep."

"Can I call you tomorrow?"

She smiles. "Please do. And Adam?"

"Yeah?"

"You really did sound amazing. Thanks for singing for me."

We say goodbye, and I pocket my phone, then reach for my Gibson so I can hang it back on the wall. My fingers are raw, and my throat is dry from all the singing, but there's still a warm buzz coursing under my skin that I haven't felt in years.

"Well, I think it's safe to say if she wasn't in love with you before, she's definitely in love with you after that performance," Freddie says.

"Stop. No one is in love with anyone." I gather up our empty beer bottles and carry them into the kitchen. The brewery owes me a thank you, because Freddie liked the beer enough that halfway through the evening, he posted a photo of himself holding up a bottle on his Instagram page. Hope they enjoy the free publicity.

"I'm serious." Freddie follows me into the kitchen and

leans against the doorframe. "*I'm* practically in love with you after that song."

There are a lot of words Freddie isn't saying. He isn't asking about the concert. He isn't pressuring me into saying yes. But he *is* telling me all the reasons why I *should* say yes. We're having a conversation without having the *actual* conversation.

And I'm not even sure Freddie realizes he's doing it.

"So, what do you say? You got a place for me to sleep around here?" Freddie asks.

"What would you do if I said no?"

"No clue, honestly. I've never been so far in the middle of nowhere. I have no idea where I'd go."

It takes a few more minutes for Freddie to retrieve a giant duffle from the trunk of his car. It's so huge that I think, one, he has no idea how to pack an overnight bag, or two, he's planning on staying for the next three months.

"Wasn't sure what I might need," he says as he lugs it up the stairs to the guest room. "So I grabbed a little of everything."

So we're going with option one, then.

"Hey," he says before I can head back down the stairs.

I turn and hold his gaze.

"Thanks for having me, man. It really is good to see you."

I nod. "Yeah. You too."

I know better than to think Freddie only showed up so we could have a jam session and tomorrow he'll be on his way. I'm even willing to acknowledge this was probably all a part of his plan—a way to remind me of how much I like making music in the first place so I'm more willing to say yes when he finally mentions the concert.

But I still can't be mad about it.

It felt good to sing. It felt particularly good to sing for Laney.

If nothing else, that alone will make tonight worth it.

CHAPTER FOURTEEN

Laney

WHEN I WAKE UP THE NEXT MORNING, I'VE FORGOTTEN everything that happened the night before. But the moment I reach for my phone to turn off my alarm, it all comes rushing back.

Adam is Deke. Adam kissed me last night. And Freddie Ridgefield FaceTimed me so I could hear them play together.

Of all the impossible, unbelievable things I could imagine, I'm not sure I would have put this one on the list.

A wave of trembly nervous energy washes over me as I drop back onto my pillow.

I pull out my phone and open my browser, typing in words I haven't searched in a very long time. *Years,* probably.

Midnight Rush—where are they now?

Freddie is the first one every site mentions, which makes sense because he has the biggest career. Leo and Jace come up with about the same frequency, usually with links to Leo's recording studio—he's producing now—and Jace's latest album. Though, it seems like Jace gets more attention via his wife's Instagram than he does through his music.

What I don't find at all are any mentions of Deke. Lots of speculation. One Reddit post written by someone claiming she attended his funeral after he was killed in a dirt bike accident. A second by someone who said they'd gone to high school together and last she heard, he was in rehab for drug addiction. But nothing that sounds like his current life in Lawson Cove.

I find plenty of pictures of the other band members, but the only ones of Adam go all the way back to their last tour. There's *nothing* of him in the past eight years. The man really did just go dark and disappear.

It's honestly pretty impressive that he managed to do it. The transformation with the muscles and the beard definitely didn't hurt. He's lucky in that regard.

Freddie never would have been able to hide so easily.

I pull up a press photo from the last Midnight Rush tour and zoom in on Adam's face.

I've kissed this man.

The thought is so completely ridiculous, I start to laugh.

I have *kissed* a member of Midnight Rush.

I grab my pillow and squeeze it over my face, squealing as I pick up my feet and bounce them on the bed. In two minutes, I will get up and shower and put on my scrubs and go to work like a responsible adult woman.

But right now, I can't help it. I kissed my teenage crush. My teenage *fantasy.*

If there is ever a moment I should get to squeal, it's this one.

I text Percy over breakfast and tell him I have *big* news, and he'd better brace himself.

Instead of responding, he shows up on my doorstep ten minutes later.

"What are you doing here?" I ask around a bite of cereal.

"What do you mean what am I doing here? You said you had big news."

"That I can tell you at work. You didn't have to drive all the way over."

He moves into my kitchen and helps himself to a mug of coffee. "You live five minutes down the road, and you're on my way to work. Plus, you make better coffee than what we have at the office." He holds up his mug to demonstrate. "Don't feel special, just spill the tea."

I prop my hands on my hips. "Okay, but I think you might need to sit down first."

His eyes widen. "Laney, are you pregnant?" He lets out a little gasp. "Are you moving? I swear, if you're moving, I will never forgive you."

"I say big news, and these are the possibilities you come up with? I'm either pregnant or moving?"

He takes a long sip of coffee, like he is fully justified in his assumptions. "What else could it be? Your life isn't exactly a hotbed of excitement."

I sigh. He's right. I hate that he's right, but he's right.

But not anymore.

"You're going to eat those words in about thirty seconds," I say. "Now sit."

He complies, but he rolls his eyes with extra emphasis as he does so, like he thinks I'm totally ridiculous for making him do it.

I sit down across from him, fighting a smile only because

I don't want to give away too much too soon. "Okay, I'm going to tell you something else first, and it's very exciting, but it's not the big news, it's just something else you need to know. For context."

He nods and motions for me to continue.

I press both palms flat against the table. "Adam kissed me last night."

"Okay. Now we're getting somewhere. How was it? Was there tongue?"

"Percy."

"What? Mimi will want to know."

"And you're comfortable discussing my kissing habits with your eighty-eight-year-old grandmother?"

He shrugs. "If you can't beat them, join them?"

I wave a dismissive hand. "We're getting off topic. Just keep that in your mind when I tell you this next part?"

"Okay. It's in there. Laney. Kissing. Lots of tongue."

"Percy!"

He presses his lips together and lifts his hand, sliding his fingers across his lips like he's zipping them closed.

"Are you ready to take me seriously?"

He nods but doesn't say anything, which I take as the gesture of support I am sure it is meant to be.

I take a deep breath, realizing on the exhale that I'm actually trembling a little.

Percy must notice too, because his eyes narrow, and he immediately breaks his self-imposed silence. "Are you for real freaking out over there? Girl, what is going on?"

I let out a shaky laugh. "Percy, Adam's full name is Adam *Deacon* Driscoll."

He frowns. "I don't get it."

"As in...Adam *Deke* Driscoll."

"Adam Deke…" he repeats. Then he gasps. "No."

"Yes."

"Your Adam—he's…and you kissed…" He stands up. "Laney! Are you for real right now?" He leans toward me, hands pushed into the table, and I quickly slide his coffee mug out of the way. "Are you telling me that Deke Driscoll of Midnight Rush lives in our tiny town? And that you *kissed* him?"

"That is exactly what I'm telling you."

"But he looks so different. How? I mean, I guess with the beard, but no. Are you sure? Maybe he just looks like him."

"I'm sure. Because last night, Freddie Ridgefield showed up at Adam's house."

Percy lifts his hands in the air. "Oh, no. Now you've gone too far. You cannot tell me lies like this."

"I'm not lying, Percy. I swear. Adam *does* look different with a beard, but now that I know, I can totally see it. And Freddie is…Freddie. All the tattoos. The big green eyes. There was no mistaking him."

"Oh my word," Percy says, pressing a hand to his stomach. He starts to laugh, head tilted back. "Oh my word!" He pulls me up off my chair and wraps me in an enormous hug. "I am so happy for you," he says. "It's not a wonder he knows so much about music."

"I know. And you should see his record collection. He has a signed Elvis Christmas album. The red 7-inch LP. Do you know how much those things are worth?"

"I did not understand a word you just said, but I'm sure it's amazing." He turns and retrieves his coffee, then glances at his watch.

We're both going to be late if we don't leave soon, so I

carry my abandoned cereal bowl over to the sink and rinse it out.

Percy follows me to my entryway, where I pull on my shoes and grab my purse. "Last night, on FaceTime, he and Freddie sang 'Never Say Never' for me. Like, just the two of them, singing *just* for me."

"I would have literally peed my pants," Percy says.

"I know. I almost did."

When we get outside, Percy moves to the passenger side of my car. "What are you doing?" I ask.

"I'm riding to work with you. There are too many details you haven't given me yet."

It's only a ten-minute drive to the office, but Percy takes advantage of every minute. He asks question after question, and I end up telling him almost everything, minus the possibility of a reunion concert, only because that doesn't feel like my news to tell. As far as I explain it, Adam and Freddie remained friends, and Freddie has simply come into town to visit.

Which is true enough. I won't betray Adam's privacy to share more.

Our conversation stops short when we get to work and find Dad crouched in front of the main entrance, working on untying a dog leash from the door handle.

Percy sighs. "I guess it was about time. It's been a while."

It happens a few times a year that one of us will show up to work only to find a cat or dog abandoned on the office's doorstep. Dad had security cameras installed because it's illegal to dump your pets at a vet's office or anywhere else, and that helped cut down on how frequently it happens. But some people either don't care or they're desperate enough to take the risk anyway.

I hate it when anyone dumps an animal. But I like to think the people who dump them here at least *want* to do the right thing for their pet.

Dad finally frees the leash, and the chocolate lab on the other end of it looks at him with big brown eyes and an expression that makes me think she's been through something.

"Poor thing," Dad says. He hands the leash over to me. "Want to take her inside and check for a microchip? I'll pull up the security cameras."

Unfortunately, whoever dumped the dog did so wearing dark clothing and a ski mask, so there isn't much we can do to discover who it was, but Dad sends the footage over to the Lawson Cove police station anyway. The dog isn't microchipped, and she hasn't been spayed, but otherwise, she seems to be in good health.

"I just called the county," Percy says. "They don't have room for her."

"I'm not surprised. They were slam full last week." I pull my phone out of my pocket. "I'll just text Adam and see if he can take her."

"You'll just text Adam," Percy says. "Aren't we fancy."

"What are you talking about? We communicate with Hope Acres all the time."

He grins. "No, *I* used to communicate with Hope Acres all the time by calling the business number and talking to Adam as a representative of this office. Now you're shooting DMs right into his pocket. It's not the same thing."

I send the message then put my phone face-down on the counter and cross my arms. "Are you done teasing me?"

"Yes," Percy says. "But please tell Adam if he comes by today, he should absolutely bring Freddie with him."

"You want me to just casually slip that in there, huh?"

Percy shrugs. "Maybe Freddie would be interested in seeing the kind of work Adam does."

I chuckle. "I see straight through you, Percy Hamilton."

He leaves me with the chocolate lab to check in our first patient. "I have no idea what you're talking about," he calls over his shoulder.

Adam responds almost immediately, saying he'd love to meet the dog, and he'll try to stop by this afternoon.

I send him a thumbs up, then throw myself into work, doing my best to ignore my growing anticipation at the thought of seeing him again.

I don't do a very good job.

After I forget patient names twice and completely zone out while a pet owner is walking me through the admittedly very long history of her cat's urinary health, I find my dad and beg him to take over for the morning. He isn't seeing patients today, just working on business accounts, so he's more than happy for a reason to abandon his desk and cover my last two appointments before lunch.

I know my brain will eventually get used to this.

To Adam being someone I can text. *Kiss.* While also being *the* Deke Driscoll. But right now, I can't even think about it without wanting to laugh. Or possibly cry? Probably both, honestly. It feels like there's a magic eight ball lodged right between my ribs, shaking itself up every few minutes to give me a new emotion. Disbelief, joy, excitement, fear, happiness. It's all there, and I never know what I'm going to get next.

Just after lunch, Percy comes flying into the backroom, one hand pressed to his chest as he waves a hand in the general direction of the lobby.

"He's out there!" Percy whispers. "Adam is in the parking lot, and he has Freddie with him!"

I take a steadying breath. "Perfect. Go out and say hello, and I'll bring out the dog in just a second." I pat myself on the back for sounding so remarkably calm.

Am I thrilled that Adam decided to stop by? Yes.

Am I going to lose my cool and freak out like I'm still in middle school?

Okay, also *yes*. But only on the inside.

CHAPTER FIFTEEN

Adam

FREDDIE UNBUCKLES HIS SEATBELT LIKE HE HAS EVERY intention of coming inside with me. I gave him a hat and a flannel to put on over his t-shirt before we left the house, hoping it would make him look slightly less like a rockstar, but I'm not sure it's doing any good.

Lawson Cove might be a small town, but it still has the internet, and Freddie has been drawing attention all morning. Still, I couldn't say no when he wanted to run errands with me. He seemed so excited about it, like there was nothing he would enjoy more than picking up a supply order and swinging by Laney's office to meet a dog.

"Wait. Hold up," I say, reaching over to stop him before he gets out. "Laney works with her father, and I have no idea if she's had the chance to tell anyone who I am."

Freddie nods. "Got it. So if they recognize me that's fine, but don't out you?" He pulls on the Appies Hockey hat he borrowed, positioning it low on his forehead. "Can we tell them I'm your cousin?"

I laugh because honestly, I have no idea how else to handle Freddie. "Sure. You're my cousin."

"Excellent." He climbs out and slams his door closed. "Can we go to a grocery store next?"

I look at him over my shoulder as we approach the Lawson Cove Veterinary entrance. "I'm not taking your face into a grocery store."

Freddie has also requested a trip through a drive thru. And he already made me stop at a gas station so he could pump gas. I had three-quarters of a tank, but I stopped anyway, not wanting to squelch his enthusiasm.

I get the impression Freddie hasn't traveled without security in a very long time.

I get it. The year after Mom died, when I was trying to figure out normal life and doing my best to fade into obscurity, I had a few moments like this—when it felt exhilarating to just do completely normal stuff on my own. The kind of stuff I'd had people doing for me for the past three years.

After Midnight Rush broke up, the opposite happened for Freddie. His career only got bigger and bigger. He went from a completely insane life as a teenager, to a probably more insane life as an adult. I wouldn't be surprised if he's *never* had to buy his own milk.

"A drive thru, then?" he asks for a second time. "I'll buy."

The lobby inside the vet's office is fortunately empty, but Patty greets us with wide eyes, so I'm pretty sure she recognizes Freddie despite the borrowed shirt and hat.

I lean on the counter and offer a friendly smile. "Hi, Patty. How are you?"

She nods. "Good," she manages to squeak out, her eyes darting from me, to Freddie, then back again.

"This is my cousin, Fred," I say. "He's here visiting for a few days."

Beside me, Freddie clears his throat, and I fight a smirk. He used to hate it when we called him Fred, even though that's exactly what's on his birth certificate. Not Frederick. Just *Fred.*

To Patty's credit, she seems to have reined in her initial shock. "Nice to meet you, Fred. Welcome to Lawson Cove."

"Laney texted me about a dog that needs to be picked up," I say. "Do you know anything about that?"

"Holy freaking fudgesicles."

We turn to see Percy standing in the middle of the lobby, eyes locked on Freddie.

"Fudgesicles?" Freddie asks under his breath.

"We aren't allowed to swear at work," Patty whisper-yells from behind us.

"Hi, Percy," I say. "Good to see you."

He makes a noise that might have been a word, but I can't really tell. He clears his throat and tries again, but only fares slightly better. "I'll, um...let me just...I'll be right back."

I look back at Patty. "Will Percy be okay?"

"I think he knows that your *cousin* is famous," Patty says. She puts *cousin* in air quotes, then leans forward, lifting her hand to shield her mouth like she wants to say something without Freddie hearing. "Did you know he was a part of Midnight Rush?"

I nod knowingly at Patty. "I did know that."

"I didn't listen to them," she goes on, her Southern accent soft and rolling and, based on his expression, highly entertaining for Freddie. He's pretending not to listen, since

Patty clearly doesn't want him to, but she's whispering loud enough for the entire room to hear so I doubt he's missing a word. "But my granddaughter went crazy over those boys. Is he really your cousin?" She leans even closer. "I read on the internet that he has seventeen tattoos."

"Eighteen," Freddie says, finally turning to face her. "But one's a secret."

"Hey," Laney says, Percy trailing behind her with a chocolate lab on a leash. "You're here."

She's wearing navy blue scrubs today with little white paw prints embroidered on the front pocket, and she has a stethoscope draped around her neck. She looks perfect. Beautiful. Sexy because she looks so professional.

I am captivated by Laney's eyes and her hair and the way her bottom lip is a little fuller than the one on top. But if my reaction to her right now is any indication, I am also super into her brain.

My eyes drop to her lips, and I'm suddenly overwhelmed with a desire to kiss her hello.

Can we do that yet?

Is there a certain number of dates we're supposed to go on before we can?

I miss my chance because now Laney is introducing Freddie to Percy, and Freddie is saying hello to the dog, and it would be weird to just kiss her in the middle of all this.

I settle for reaching over and squeezing her hand. "How was your morning?"

"Good. Easy appointments." She pauses, her mouth lifting into a playful grin, before she adds, "I'd tell you all about a successful neutering, but I don't have the balls."

"No, you did not make that joke in front of regular people," Percy says. "Laney! Vet humor is only funny to us!"

I laugh. "I thought it was funny."

"You run a dog rescue," Percy argues. "You *are* one of us."

The words are casual. Said in jest more than anything else. But they still trigger something unexpected right between my ribs.

We moved around a lot when I was a kid. Mom was always looking for a better job. One that paid a little bit more than the last one. We changed schools three different times before I was out of elementary school. Things finally got a little more stable in middle school, and she bought the house she lived in until she died. But not long after we moved in, I was in Midnight Rush, always moving, never settling.

I've never really felt like I *belong* anywhere.

And this throw-away comment from Percy about me *belonging*...I want that. I want a community.

I look down at Laney, who is watching me, her expression thoughtful.

I want a community, and I want Laney to be right in the middle of it.

The dog at Percy's feet, who is the entire reason I'm here in the first place, wanders over to sniff my shoe. She sits right in front of me, tail thumping against the floor as she looks up with wide, soulful eyes.

I crouch down in front of her. "Hey, girl. Why wouldn't someone want you, huh?"

"She seems pretty sweet," Laney says. "Makes me sad that someone abandoned her."

I stand back up but keep a hand on the dog's head. "Has she been spayed?"

"No, so we would do that before you take her. We'd just..." She hesitates.

"Need the funding," I finish. "Got it. Go ahead and schedule it. We'll cover it, and I'll come back for her as soon as she's ready."

Laney smiles. "Yay. That means you get to name her."

I look down at the dog one more time. There's something about her eyes that remind me of Goldie, which makes me think of my mom. An idea pops into my head. "Let's call her Dolly."

Laney smiles. She's thinking of Dolly Parton, which is absolutely applicable. My mom, whose name was Dahlia, always asked her closest friends to call her Dolly—a nickname she chose largely because of how much she loved the country music singer. I haven't used the name for any of my rescue dogs yet, and I'm not sure what made me decide to use it now.

But it feels fitting. And when Laney crouches down and calls Dolly by name, she seems to approve, her tail wagging with a little extra enthusiasm.

If it were up to me, I'd spend the rest of my afternoon standing in the lobby of Laney's office talking, but I've got to be back at the rescue at two, and I promised Freddie a trip through the drive thru.

I look over at Freddie. "We should get going."

He nods and shakes Percy's hand. "Hey, nice to meet you, man."

Percy fumbles his way through saying goodbye and asking for a photo while I think, for a second time, about leaning down and kissing Laney, goodbye this time, instead of hello.

"Okay, well," Laney says, shuffling her feet before leaning toward me. At first, I think she's coming in for a kiss, so I bend down to meet her, but then her arms open like what she's looking for is a hug, and we end up just bumping into each other, an awkward tangle of misdirected limbs and overcorrections as we both try to figure out what the other is aiming for.

Finally, Laney backs up a step and holds out her hand. "You know what? Let's just do it this way."

This way. She wants to just...shake my hand?

Embarrassment washes over me, made only worse by Freddie and Percy, who are watching like this is the most entertaining thing they've seen all day.

"Right," I say, taking her hand in mine and giving it three firm shakes. "Probably better. It was good to see you."

As soon as we're outside, Freddie looks over at me like I am the stupidest man who ever lived.

"Seriously?" he says. "That's how you're going to say goodbye to her?"

"It's not like you helped with all the staring."

"Who cares if I was staring? Do you like this woman or not?"

I stop on the sidewalk. He's right. What am I doing?

I turn on my heel and walk back into the office.

"Laney," I say, catching her just before she disappears into the back.

She turns and waits while I walk toward her. As soon as I reach her, I lift my hands to her face, cradling her jaw as I press a long kiss to her lips.

She sucks in a breath of surprise, but she doesn't stop me, instead lifting her hands to my shoulders as she leans into the kiss.

"Sorry I didn't do that earlier," I say, still close enough to feel her breath fanning over my cheek.

She smiles and bites her lip. "I can't believe I shook your hand."

"We'll get better at this," I say. "And we won't always have a captive audience." I glance over her shoulder to Percy, who coughs awkwardly into his fist, then disappears into the back, mumbling something about test results he needs to check.

I lean down and kiss Laney one more time. "I'll text you?"

"Yes, please," she whispers.

Freddie is leaning against the SUV clapping for me when I make it back to the parking lot.

"Much better," he says. "For real, man. I was worried about your game for a second. I mean, the FaceTime serenading probably scored a lot of points, but I'm not always going to be around to be your wingman. Should we practice a few things before I leave town?"

I roll my eyes. "Shut up and get in the car."

"I know you said the engagement wasn't real," Freddie says as I pull out of the parking lot. "But you know that's where you're headed, right?"

I grip the steering wheel a little tighter. "We just started dating."

"Who cares? When you know, you know."

"Says the man who's had how many serious relationships?"

"I'm not claiming I'm an expert," he says, lifting his hands. "I'm just saying. It looks like you've found something real."

I think about his words as we drive toward one of only two fast food places in Lawson Cove.

I'm trying not to get too far ahead of myself, but this thing with Laney *does* feel real. And that feels big.

As we drive down Main Street, Freddie peppers me with question after question. He can't be so sheltered that he's never driven through a small town, but his fascination seems to have less to do with life in Lawson Cove *generally,* and more to do with life in Lawson Cove...*for me.*

"So you can just drive around like normal? And no one knows who you are? That's insane."

"It's how most people live, Freddie," I say.

"No, I know. But you aren't most people." He points out the window. "Look. Right there. There's a girl with a Midnight Rush t-shirt on. That's your face, man. And you can just drive right past her like it's no big deal. I envy that."

I roll my eyes. "No, you don't. You love the attention. You always have."

He tilts his head, like he's really considering. "Okay, I do love it. Still. I wouldn't mind a little more obscurity every once in a while. Plus, this is fun. Just doing stuff. *Normal* stuff."

"You *really* don't get out much, do you?"

"You have no idea," he says.

I eye him suspiciously. "I'm surprised you don't have any security with you. Isn't that pretty routine these days?"

Freddie turns his face away from me, but I don't miss the way his jaw twitches before he does.

"Freddie," I say slowly. "Do your people know where you are? Are you *supposed* to have security with you right now?"

"It's fine," Freddie says. "It's not a big deal."

"Dude, I don't want to get in trouble. And I don't want *you* to get in trouble either."

Freddie holds out his hands. "No one is getting in trouble. Ivy knows where I am. She's my assistant, and she's amazing, and she'll handle things. I *do* usually travel with security, but I didn't want to freak you out showing up with a whole entourage. Besides, what could possibly happen in a town this small?"

I ease to a stop at the next light, and Freddie glances over to the car next to us. There's a woman in a minivan studying us with her eyes narrowed. Freddie turns away, lifting his arm to block her view, and I scowl at him.

"What was that you were saying?"

At the drive thru, Freddie is as fascinated with the Southern accent of the teenager working the window as he was with Patty's, and he asks her to repeat herself twice just so he can listen to her say "french fries" over and over again.

"I freaking love this place," he says as we pull around to the window. "The way everyone talks—it sounds like music."

If this were anyone but Freddie, I might think he was making fun of the South. But Freddie is one of the most genuine people I know. He experiences everything with a level of joy and intensity turned a few notches above what most people feel. He's always been like that, and I envy him for it. For being so good at simply *seeing good.*

When the girl at the window hands us our food, Freddie lifts his sunglasses and smiles at her. "Thanks so much," he says. "Have a great day."

She gasps, eyes going wide, and I gun it, tires practically squealing as I pull out of the parking lot.

I huff out a laugh. "You really can't resist, can you? You hate *not* being Freddie Ridgefield."

He grins. "I mean, he's a pretty charming guy."

I shake my head as I pull into an empty bank parking lot buffeted by a line of sprawling oak trees and pull to a stop in the shade that covers the back half. "I can't imagine," I say, as I reach for the bag of food sitting in Freddie's lap. "I couldn't get away from all that attention fast enough."

Freddie shrugs, then takes a long drink of his soda. "Sometimes it gets annoying. But it means I get to do what I love. Do you not miss that part of it? The music?"

"I still make music," I say.

"But no one ever hears you," Freddie says. "What's the point if other people can't enjoy the music you're making?"

I take an enormous bite of burger, chewing slowly as I consider how to answer. On the surface, it's pretty simple. Freddie lives for the attention; he's an extrovert in the extreme while I'm the opposite. But I know it's more than that.

For good or bad, my feelings about performing are all tied up with my feelings about Mom. No matter how good it felt to sing with him last night, I'm not sure I know how to untangle them. Singing in my living room is one thing, but going back on stage? Performing for an arena full of people? Hot shame claws at my throat every time I think about it, tightening around my vocal cords like a vise.

"I just don't think I'm built for it," I say. "Not like you are."

Freddie studies me, the hand holding his half-eaten burger resting on his knee. I don't miss the hope hovering in his eyes.

I lift a shoulder in a shrug I hope looks casual, even though my gut is already tensing, anticipating the direction our conversation is headed. "Besides, why do they need to listen to me when they've got you?"

He huffs out a sardonic laugh. "Yeah, well, they aren't listening to me as much these days."

I grab a few fries, accepting the inevitable. I know

Freddie didn't come all the way out here to eat fast food burgers and hang out. We might as well get it over with now. "Yeah, Kevin said something about that. What happened?"

"I didn't *do* anything. That's what so stupid about all of this. Well, I did have a small scuffle with this guy at a bar, but he was way out of line, putting hands all over Ivy—"

"Your assistant?" I ask, and Freddie nods.

"They'd been talking at the bar, and she seemed into it, but then he started grabbing at her, really violating her space, and he wouldn't let her get away. So I stepped in and shoved him back, and enough people got *that* part of the altercation on film that entertainment news went wild, throwing around terms like drunk and disorderly conduct, talking about rehab. Which is stupid because I hadn't even been drinking when it happened."

He rubs a hand across his face, then keeps going.

"Just when all that started to die down, I was visiting my parents in Connecticut, and we drove down to New York to have dinner at their favorite restaurant. This woman approached our table with her daughter, wanting selfies and signatures, and they kept asking all these questions, but I really just wanted to focus on my family, so I said no. When they kept asking, Wayne, my security guy, escorted them out, and the owner of the restaurant stepped in and wouldn't let them finish their dinner, which totally pissed her off. Turns out she was some big influencer on Instagram and was hoping to get content for her page. Which...she did. The kind that made me look like an egotistical jerk too famous to care about his fans."

"That really sucks," I say.

"Yeah. The new label isn't happy. The album is supposed

to drop next month, but they're pushing it out, worried this is going to impact sales."

"Come on, man," I say. "You're Freddie Ridgefield. Your concerts sell out in minutes. A few grumpy fans aren't going to mess with that."

"They're already messing with it," he says. "The Instagram lady started a petition, asking people to boycott my music to help me learn some manners, and it's gotten something like five-hundred thousand signatures already."

"Isn't that a form of slander? Can you sue?"

"Yeah. 'Cause that will really help my reputation." He crams a handful of fries into his mouth. "My publicist thinks if we can put something else out there to grab people's attention, it will be a lot easier to make this lady and her false claims disappear."

I sigh. There it is.

"Something like a Midnight Rush reunion concert," I say.

He hesitates, like he senses the weight of our conversation as much as I do. "You have to admit, it's a solid plan."

I run a hand through my hair. "Freddie, I can't do it. I meant it when I told Kevin no. I feel for you. You know I do. But when I walked away, I walked away for good. That hasn't changed."

"It's one show, man. One night. They want to have it in Nashville, so it wouldn't even be that big of a trip for you."

"You know stuff like this is never just one night. There will be promo interviews, photoshoots. You've done this a lot more than I have, Freddie. You know I'm right."

He holds my gaze for a beat before he finally caves. "Fine. You're right. It would be more than just one night. But we can't do it without you, and I really need this to happen."

"You can do it without me," I say. "You should."

"Nah," Freddie quickly says. "We aren't Midnight Rush without you."

He just doesn't understand. He can't know what it felt like. How gutting it was to have everything pulled out from under me in one night.

"This is about your mom, isn't it?" Freddie says. "She's why you don't want to do it."

I slam the truck into gear and back out of the parking lot, turning us around so quickly, Freddie has to grab his drink to keep it from tipping over. I don't know how we got here so quickly when two minutes ago we were talking normally and everything was fine. But suddenly, I can't get away from Freddie fast enough.

This is the worst kind of emotional whiplash, and I just want it to stop.

"You don't know anything about my mom," I say.

"Huh. Wonder why that is," Freddie shoots back. "Not because I wasn't willing to listen."

I grind my teeth together, my hands gripping the steering wheel hard enough to make my knuckles white.

Freddie might have been willing to listen, but he wouldn't have been objective. None of the guys would have been.

Nobody wanted Midnight Rush to end. Any listening they did, any encouragement they offered, it was all colored by the hope everyone had that the band would stay together.

But I couldn't do it. I couldn't keep singing with Mom in the ground. I couldn't keep making all that money, not when it felt like blood money.

I ease my SUV to a stop at the turnoff onto Highway 23 and look over at Freddie. "I didn't see her for thirteen months," I say. "Thirteen months, and then she died."

He swallows. "I know."

"Do you know how many times she asked me to come home? Do you know how many times I ignored that request?"

He sighs and runs a hand across his face. "Adam, I know. But she wouldn't want—"

I lift a hand, cutting him off. "No. You don't get to talk to me about what she would or wouldn't want when the only reason you're here is because the concert would save your ass."

"Isn't that a good enough reason?" Freddie says, anger growing in his voice. "Friendship isn't a good enough reason? I didn't want to say this, but..." He shrugs and sighs, lifting his hands into the air as if to emphasize his point. "You know you owe me, man. I took the fall for you. Signed a bad contract so you could walk and still keep your cut. If you won't do it for Midnight Rush, do it for me. One concert. That's all I'm asking."

A wave of guilt roars through me, making my stomach queasy and my skin prickle with uncomfortable heat. Even knowing it was coming, I'm still not prepared for the impact of Freddie's words.

The hardest part is that I don't disagree with him. After walking away like I did, shutting him and the rest of the guys out no matter their attempts to reach me, to *help,* I do owe them this much.

"I never asked you to do that," I say gruffly, my eyes on the road. "And I think the three of you are doing just fine."

I turn down the drive to Hope Acres, grateful we're almost home. I need to be out of this car, away from Freddie. I need sun and sky and air and a minute to just breathe.

"How would you know?" Freddie says. "Do you know

anything about Leo's studio? About how hard he's having to work to keep the doors open? Do you have any clue whether Jace's last album did even half as well as it should have? Unlike you, the rest of us actually *want* to stay in the music business. And this concert would really help with that."

I park in the driveway and climb out, slamming the car door, but Freddie is right behind me. I skip the porch steps, knowing Sarah is probably inside, and head around the side of the house toward the barn instead.

"Adam, please," Freddie says, stalking after me. "Just tell me why. If you're saying no, at least have the decency to tell me the real reason."

I stop in my tracks and rest my hands on top of my head, a dozen different reasons flitting through my brain. But all of them are excuses except one.

I can't do it because I stood on my mother's grave and swore that I never would. I would never go back to the life that took me away from her.

"I know you love the music, man," Freddie says, the fire in his voice fully tempered. "I heard it last night. Nobody sounds that good if they don't love what they're doing."

My jaw clenches, my hands moving to rest on my hips.

It doesn't matter if those words are true. Loving the music won't bring Mom back. Loving it doesn't justify what I did.

I turn my back on one of the best friends I've ever known and walk toward the ridgeline behind the barn.

This time, Freddie doesn't follow.

CHAPTER SIXTEEN

Laney

I'M HALFWAY THROUGH AN EVENING YOGA CLASS IN MY neighbor's outdoor studio, doing my best to *not* think about kissing Adam long enough to actually relax for a minute, when my smartwatch buzzes with an incoming call. I don't know if the calibration is off or if I somehow screwed up the settings, but the vibration sounds more like a carpenter bee stuck inside a mason jar than the subtle buzz it's supposed to be.

The woman on the mat next to me looks over and frowns and I immediately silence the call, offering a mouthed *sorry* before resuming my downward dog.

But then the buzzing starts *again.*

I study the number more closely this time. I don't recognize it, but the area code is the same as Adam's, so I jump off my mat and grab my phone from the bench at the back of the pavilion.

"Sorry, sorry," I whisper over and over again as I hurry

around the group and to the far corner of the yard where I can talk without disrupting everyone.

"Hello?" I finally answer.

"Laney?" a voice says as soon as I say hello. "It's Sarah. I'm so glad you answered."

"Hey," I say, not liking the trepidation filling her voice. "Is everything okay?"

"I think so?" she says. "The thing is, I'm pretty sure Taylor is in labor and I don't know anything about how this works and Adam isn't here and I have no idea where he is and I know this is a lot to ask but are you busy?" Her words tumble out of her, one sentence running into the next, leaving me with at least a dozen questions, mostly ones having to do with her missing brother. But that doesn't seem to be Sarah's main concern.

"Wow. That's a lot," I say.

"I know. I'm sorry. Is it bad that I called?"

"No, no. Not at all. I'm glad you did. Why don't you start by telling me about Taylor?"

"Right. Yes. I was just out at the barn, and she was pacing around, panting really heavily. She seems agitated, anxious. That's labor, right?"

"It sounds like it," I say. "And that's all totally normal behavior. Most dogs do this without any human assistance, so as long as she has a warm, comfortable space separate from the other dogs, she's very likely going to be just fine."

"Good. That's good," Sarah says. "She is separate, and Adam has her enclosure all prepared. But, I don't know, Laney. Do I need to stay with her? I get super squeamish around blood, so I just don't think I'm the right person for this job."

"*Is* there blood?"

"Not that I've seen, but there will be, right? When the puppies are born?"

Across the lawn, the class shifts into a standing tree pose. "And you said Adam isn't around?" I ask Sarah.

She lets out a little huff. "He does this sometimes. He'll be back, but maybe not for a while. Do you think you could come over? I would feel so much better knowing Taylor has someone experienced looking out for her."

"I can come," I say, swallowing the urge to ask what Sarah means by Adam *does this sometimes*.

Does what, exactly? Goes on a bender at the local bar? Flies to Vegas and gambles away his sorrows? Maybe he's just off somewhere with Freddie? Or off somewhere...*hiding* from Freddie?

Wherever he is, Taylor does deserve to have someone watching out for her. "I'm at a yoga class now, but I can be there in...half an hour, maybe?"

"Thanks, Laney," Sarah says. "I appreciate it."

I get to Hope Acres in twenty minutes, both because I ignored all but the most essential traffic laws and because I didn't stop to change out of my yoga clothes, opting to throw on a cropped hoodie over my leggings and sports bra and call it good. It's not like Taylor is going to care what I'm wearing.

Adam's SUV is parked in front of the house when I pull up at the rescue, and Freddie's car is there too, which gives me some hope. Does that mean Adam is back?

But then Sarah hurries down the porch steps, concern etched across her brow. I climb out and meet her in the driveway, and she tugs me toward the barn. It has to mean Adam *isn't* actually back, which is equal parts disappointing and concerning. I take comfort in the fact that

Sarah is clearly more worried about Taylor than she is her missing brother, so I follow her lead and swallow my own concerns.

Adam is a grown man. Wherever he is, whatever he's doing, I'm sure he's fine.

At least, I hope he's fine.

Taylor still hasn't delivered by the time we reach the barn, but I can tell she's close. Sarah stays with me for a few minutes, but Taylor seems distracted by her nervous energy, so I gently suggest she head back to the house, and Sarah breathes out a sigh of relief. "Are you sure?" she asks, but she's already moving toward the door.

"Absolutely," I say. "I'll be fine. But..."

She pauses and looks back.

"Did you say you don't know where Adam is?"

She rolls her eyes and motions toward the mountains behind the barn. "Out there somewhere, probably. This is what he does when he needs to think. And I guess he and Freddie got into it this afternoon, so he clearly had some stuff to think about."

"You're not concerned that it's basically dark?" I say, looking over her shoulder into the late evening light.

"Nah. He knows these mountains. If he isn't home in another couple hours, I might start to worry, but I'm not worried yet."

Once she's gone, the other dogs settle down and the barn is quiet, filled only with sleepy snorts and snuffles. There isn't much I can do but watch and wait, so I pull out my phone and use my Kindle app to read, periodically checking on Taylor's progress.

It's hard to focus, though, because my brain keeps going back to whatever happened with Freddie and Adam this afternoon. They seemed good when they stopped by the office. What happened after?

Maybe they finally talked about the concert and saying no didn't go quite as well as Adam hoped? A low ache forms right between my ribs. I rub at the spot, but I don't think it's going to go anywhere until I know Adam is okay.

An hour later, Taylor delivers her fourth and final puppy. She handled the delivery like a pro and probably would have been fine on her own, but I'm not sorry I was here for it. I'll never get tired of attending deliveries—especially the ones when everything goes well.

I'm just standing up and closing the door of Taylor's enclosure when the barn door slides open and Adam steps inside.

Wherever he's been, he looks like he's been through something.

He's visibly sweaty, there's a rip on the sleeve of his shirt, and he has a smudge of dirt across his forehead. Tiny red scratches cover his forearms and the tops of his hands. He looks like someone dropped him in the middle of a briar patch and made him crawl a mile to safety.

"I saw your car. Is everything okay? Is Taylor okay?" Adam asks.

"She's fine," I say. "Sarah called me because she was concerned, but everything went great."

His eyes widen the slightest bit. "It's over?"

"She just had the last one not ten minutes ago." I look down at the smallest of the litter, squirming under its mother's dutiful ministrations. "They're beautiful puppies."

He wipes his sleeve across his forehead and walks over, stopping beside me to look down at the new litter. "I'm sorry I wasn't here for it."

He's close enough now that I can see a scratch down the side of his cheek. I hesitate a beat before asking, "Adam, where have you been? Are you okay?"

He breathes out a sigh and lifts his hands to his head, then pulls them away and looks at them. "I lost my hat," he says.

The totally random comment makes me worry he's still a little out of it. Not quite in shock, but a little dazed? I mean, the man does seem to love his hats, but considering his current condition, I'm not sure he should be worried about it now.

There's a gash down the underside of his left arm that I didn't see before, this one deeper and bloodier than the smaller scratches on the top.

"Whoa," I say, stepping toward him. "That looks really deep."

Adam looks at his arm like he didn't even realize the injury was there. I glance back at the puppies. Three are already nursing, and Taylor is nudging the fourth one into position, nuzzling and licking it gently. Feeling like Taylor's got things under control, I reach for Adam's arm. "Can I take a look?"

Adam nods and lets me lead him toward the supply room at the front of the barn. I familiarized myself with everything on the shelves when I first showed up, wanting to know what my resources were should anything go wrong with Taylor's delivery. I can't do much with what's here, but I can at least clean him up a little.

He drops onto a stool, and I grab a clean rag off the shelf, crossing to the sink at the grooming station to get it wet. When I return, Adam is a picture of defeat, his shoulders slumped, his expression dejected.

I reach for his arm, and he lets me take it, flinching the slightest bit when I press the warm rag to his skin. "Did you get lost?" I ask as I wipe the dirt and debris away from the wound.

He lets out a grunt. "Something like that."

I work in silence a few minutes more, cleaning up his arms, making sure he's only dealing with superficial wounds. I'm doing a crap job, honestly. He needs a shower and an antiseptic wash and some butterfly bandages to close the largest cut, but this is better than nothing.

Adam lifts a hand to the curve of my waist. With how he's sitting on a stool and I'm standing in front of him, his head is about eye level with my ribs, and he leans forward the slightest bit, resting his head on my side, his fingertips pressing into the exposed skin at the top of my leggings.

A flutter of emotions spread through my chest and out to my fingertips, making me tingle all over.

This man.

How does he make me feel so much?

I squeeze a little water over a skinned spot on Adam's elbow then brush away a tiny stone lodged in his skin. "You really should clean up with something other than just water," I say. "Nothing looks deep enough for stitches, but your dirt smudges have dirt smudges. You'll risk an infection if you don't."

"My dirt smudges have dirt smudges," he repeats.

"Shut up. I'm a vet, not a poet. What did you do, anyway? Fight a bear?"

"I fell into a ravine," Adam says. "Only about twenty-five feet, but the mountain let me know who's boss." He lifts his shirt the slightest bit, revealing another swath of cuts and scrapes moving up his ribcage. "Got me here, too."

"Adam! What were you trying to do out there?" I return to the sink and rinse the rag, then soak it in warm water one more time. When I'm back in front of Adam, I crouch down in front of him and gesture to his side. "Come on. Let me see."

He leans back, lifting his t-shirt all the way up. *Oh. Oh, this is not fair.* I force my gaze away from the expanse of exposed skin on Adam's chest, the dusting of hair that trails down his chest and disappears into the waistband of his jeans. I have a purpose here, and it has nothing to do with the curve of Adam's pectoral muscles.

When I press the rag to his side, he flinches away, but not like it's painful. More like he's ticklish. He swallows a laugh, pressing his lips together as I squeeze water over the cuts to clean away the worst of the debris. I don't know why it feels like such a big deal to know that Adam is ticklish. It shouldn't be. Lots of people are. Maybe just because it feels like such an intimate thing to know about someone. And now I know it about Deke Driscoll. Except, that's not really it. Sitting with Adam like this, touching him, feeling his gaze on me, I'm not thinking of him as Deke.

He's just...*Adam.*

"Okay. I think that's as good as I can do. I stand up and gesture to his face. "Do you mind?"

He shakes his head and looks up, his blue eyes fixed on mine as I tilt his chin up even further and press the rag to the cut on his cheek.

"Thank you," he says softly.

"Don't worry about it," I say. "It's nothing."

He lifts a hand, curving it around mine, the calluses on his palms rough against the skin on the back of my hand. "It's not nothing."

His thumb brushes across my knuckles, then he lifts my palm and presses a kiss to the pad at the base of my thumb.

I toss the rag into the sink, then step closer, wrapping my arms around his shoulders as Adam pulls me into a hug. There's a leaf clinging to his hair, and I reach up and tug it away. When he leans into the touch, I slide my fingers through his hair as he closes his eyes, letting out a low groan of pleasure.

"Do you want to talk about it?"

He breathes out a sigh and leans into me, his face only inches away from my stomach. The tickle of his breath sends a wave of goosebumps across the inch of exposed midriff at the hem of my hoodie.

"Do we have to?" he asks.

I let out a little chuckle. "Not at all." The last thing he needs is another person pressuring him. "I'm just saying, I'm happy to listen if you need it."

He's quiet for a beat, his breathing steady until he finally says, "I think I have to say yes to Freddie."

My hands still as the idea of Adam on stage with Midnight Rush settles into my mind. This moment is not about me, and I would never be excited about something that isn't good for Adam, but I can't entirely shut down the super fan inside of me that is screaming at the thought of seeing the band back together again. Even just for one night.

"How are you feeling about it?" I ask.

"I don't know. Scared? I think. Really uncertain." He takes a long, deep breath, and I can almost see the thoughts cycling through his brain.

I press the pads of my fingers into his scalp, intensifying the massage. "I can hear you thinking," I say gently.

He chuckles. "Yeah, I bet."

"Try saying the thoughts out loud," I say. "Sometimes, they're not as scary once you hear yourself say them."

He licks his lips and lifts his unbelievably blue eyes to mine. "It's just that I wasn't a very good friend," he says. "They tried to be there for me after Mom died, but I was so torn up, I couldn't..." He shakes his head, his jaw tensing. "I felt guilty when I was with them because before she died, I was with them when I should have been with *her*."

My heart aches. I can't begin to imagine the pain of losing a parent.

"The only way I knew how to deal with that guilt was to push them away. Shut all of it out," Adam says. "So the thought of going back on stage, facing them, I just..." He sighs.

"That's a lot to unpack," I say.

"Yeah. But it's time. I need to do this for Freddie. For all of them."

Behind us, the barn door opens, and Sarah and Freddie step inside.

I'm still wrapped up in Adam's arms, and I tense like I'm going to step away from him, but his grip around me tightens, so I stay put.

"Oh, thank goodness," Sarah says, lifting a hand to her chest. "I was literally ten minutes away from calling the sheriff and demanding he organize a search party." She looks him up and down. "Geez, what happened to you?"

"I fought a mountain lion," Adam deadpans.

I stifle a chuckle as Sarah's eyes widen. "Are you serious?"

"No," he says, and she rolls her eyes.

"Adam. That's not funny."

"I fell into a ravine," he says. "Up above the spring on the east ridge. But I'm fine. Laney checked me over. Nothing's broken."

"Are you sure?" Sarah says. "Jake just left, but I can call him back to take a look."

Adam shakes his head. "I'm sure. Laney's a doctor, too."

"Um, not that kind of doctor. I'd do better with the mountain lion," I say.

"You did great," Adam says. "And I'm fine. Just a little scraped up."

Sarah puts her hands on her hips. "Well, in that case, you're an idiot for running off and missing Jake but also I'm glad you aren't dead and I love you and I hope you're okay."

Adam finally stands, and I shift to the side, making room for him to walk over to his sister. He pulls her into a one-armed hug. "I'm sorry I disappeared *and* that I missed Jake," He says. His eyes shift over to Freddie, who has been standing behind Sarah watching their conversation with a curious expression. "I just had some thinking to do."

"And?" Freddie asks.

It's a long moment before Adam answers.

He and Freddie just stare at each other across the five feet or so of space between them, the tension ratcheting up with every passing second.

"One concert," Adam finally says. "But only one."

Sarah lets out a little squeal, clapping her hands in front of her as Freddie moves to Adam and pulls him into a hug, pounding him on the back hard enough to make Adam flinch.

"You won't regret this, man," he says. "It's going to be amazing."

It *will* be amazing. How could a Midnight Rush reunion show be anything but amazing?

Despite Adam's initial hesitations, maybe this could be a good thing for him. To reconnect with his friends, reconnect with his music. But who am I to have an opinion? We've been on one date.

As a fan? It isn't hard to conjure up how excited I would be if I'd never met Adam and simply found out about the concert like everyone else. I would lose my mind. Then I would force Percy to buy tickets with me, and I would go and sit in the nosebleed cheap seats because who can afford the expensive ones and also pay a mortgage, and I would watch the show with all the enthusiasm a twenty-six-year-old woman can reasonably express without losing her dignity.

But now...watching Adam on stage, knowing I might be the one he kisses after the show?

That's a dream too fantastical to even consider.

Not that any of this is about me.

It's absolutely not.

Still.

To quote Percy: Holy freaking fudgesicles.

CHAPTER SEVENTEEN

Laney

THE NEXT COUPLE OF WEEKS PASS BY IN A BLUR OF DATING BLISS and moments when I want to pinch myself because...is this really my life?

And only part of that has anything to do with Midnight Rush.

Adam is thoughtful and generous and a good cook and he loves to talk about what I love to talk about and we get along so well. We click in a way that I have never clicked with anyone before, and that's all I need to feel like I'm living in some sort of fantasy.

When I think about the fact that Adam is also in the process of preparing for a reunion concert with Midnight Rush, it feels like my head might explode.

When we're having dinner at his house and he gets a text requesting his measurements for a wardrobe fitting.

When we're on our way to a movie and Freddie Face-Times to ask Adam's opinion about the set list.

And right now, when we're spending a Saturday afternoon at the rescue playing with puppies, and Freddie's assistant texts over a rehearsal location and schedule.

All *pinch me* moments.

"Have you ever heard of Stonebrook Farm?" Adam asks, scrolling through his phone.

I sit up from where I've been lounging on a blanket in Adam's backyard and try to untangle my hair from the jaws of one of Aretha's puppies. Paul, I think? Or it might be George. "The one over in Silver Creek?" The puppy tugs a little harder, and I let out a grunt. This is not a game of tug-of-war I'd like to lose.

Adam picks up the puppy and successfully frees me. "Yeah, you know it?"

"A little. It's not far from where I grew up. We went to their Harvest Festival every fall when I was a kid."

"Apparently, that's where we're meeting to start rehearsals."

"Not at a studio somewhere?" I ask.

"I guess they want to keep the concert a surprise for a little longer, so we're going somewhere remote, where no one will notice we're together."

"I guess that's convenient for you. It's, what, three hours away?"

He leans back, stretching out on his side and propping himself up on his elbow. "Convenient if it means I get to drive home to see you."

I lean down and press a quick kiss to his lips. "When do you have to be there?"

"Monday."

"That's less than a week."

He nods. "Yeah. It's starting to feel real."

I'm not quite in the *this feels real* stage yet. I haven't even told anyone besides Percy that Adam and Deke are the same person. My family knows I'm dating *Adam,* but at some point, I'm going to have to mention the fact that he's a former member of my favorite boyband.

I should probably get used to talking about it. Because once the concert happens, people in Lawson Cove are going to figure out who he is.

The thought leaves a low-key discomfort simmering in the back of my mind. I am not an attention seeker. I am so far the opposite that back in high school, when I bought tickets to see Midnight Rush in concert, I didn't enter the fan lottery to win backstage passes because I couldn't think of anything more mortifying than actually *meeting* the band. I was happy to admire them from the front row where I wouldn't be required to converse. I'm not a public speaker. A performer of any kind.

It's not like dating Adam means *I* would have to perform. But it does mean a little of his spotlight might sometimes catch glimpses of me. And I have no idea how to feel about that.

Adam and I spend as much time together as possible over the next week. He's busy getting everything at the rescue ready for his absence, but we still manage to see each other almost every day. Which means when he heads to Silver Creek on Monday morning, there is a giant Adam-sized hole in my day-to-day life. We text a lot. And he calls me every night, telling me all about the work they're doing to elevate the Midnight Rush setlist. Apparently, not everything that works for a group of teenage boys translates when those boys are now full-grown men. They also aren't doing as much dancing—Adam is *so happy* about that—and for the first time, they're playing their own instruments, at least for some songs.

The more I hear him talk about everything, the more excited I become about seeing the concert and not just because I'm a fan. Adam seems *happy*. Like the creative work he's doing has woken him up somehow. It's fun to see—or at least *hear*—whenever he calls.

On Thursday morning, I'm on my way into the office when Adam calls. It's unexpected, mostly because we were up until almost midnight talking, so I'm not expecting to hear from him again until tonight.

"Did I catch you before you got to work?" Adam asks as soon as I answer.

"Just barely. Is everything okay?"

"Yes?" he says, like he's debating how much to tell me. "Maybe?"

"What's going on?"

He breathes out a sigh. "I don't know. We just got briefed on everything that's happening the next few days as they prepare to drop the concert news. Photoshoots. Media coaching. Stylists and wardrobe stuff. We've just been focusing on the music and the creative parts of the actual show, and that's been amazing. But now we're getting into all the marketing stuff."

"And that's not your favorite."

"Not at all," he says. "I'm fine. It's part of it. I get it. I just don't like it." There's a slight edge to his voice that makes my gut tighten. The last time Adam did anything like this, he was weeks away from going through a pretty traumatic loss. This can't be easy for him, and the realization makes me want to get in my car and drive down to Silver Creek right now.

"Yeah, I'm sure," I say. "And they're probably trying to cram a lot of planning into a very small amount of time. It has to be overwhelming."

The concert is only three months out, which was totally surprising to me when I first found out. I have no idea how long it usually takes to plan and execute something of this scope, but I'm guessing this isn't the norm.

With enough money to grease the wheels, probably anything is possible. And if Freddie needs a PR boost *now*, I'm sure everyone is highly motivated to make things happen. But it has to feel like a lot. Especially to Adam, who has been out of the industry for so long.

"It has been, which has me thinking about what might make it easier."

My ears perk up.

"*Who* might make it easier," he says. "Like, maybe there's this person who really makes me happy and would probably distract me from stressing about stuff I have to do that I don't *want* to do."

I lean against the wall outside the office and watch a tiny green lizard crawl up the siding, my heart rate climbing. Is Adam suggesting what I think he's suggesting?

"Adam," I say slowly. "What are you trying to say?"

He waits for a beat, then says, "Are you busy this weekend? And also all of next week?"

I laugh. "An entire week?"

"I know it's a lot to ask. But...I miss you. And so much is happening. They're going to make me shave my beard, Laney. I'm fine—I'll probably be fine—I just find myself wishing you were here. You ground me, I think. And I could use some grounding."

I close my eyes. What is happening right now? Adam and

I have only been officially dating a few weeks. We've kissed and texted and talked and watched movies and eaten dinners together, but it still feels pretty new. To go spend a week with him at a Midnight Rush rehearsal?

I fight to stifle the giggle rising up my chest. We're having a conversation about *Midnight Rush* rehearsals. What even is my life?

Because I knew Adam before I knew he was Deke, when we are hanging out at the rescue or at my house, it's easy to forget his boyband history. He's just Adam. Even knowing the New Year's concert is looming, so far, it's only been a thing we talk about.

But if I drive down to Silver Creek to crash his rehearsal, it'll be a lot more than talk. We'll be living a very different reality than the one I live in Lawson Cove.

Also, and probably most importantly, I have a job.

Though, the truth is, most days, we don't really *need* two vets at the office. Dad has been semi-retired since he hired me on, talking about slowly phasing himself out as he turns the practice over to me. But he's a lot better at that in theory than he is in practice. Sometimes he comes to the office just to be there, even when he doesn't have any patients scheduled. And he's been begging me for months to take a vacation—something I haven't done since he hired me over a year ago—if only to give him the chance to see patients again full time.

He'd be just fine without me.

My heart starts pounding. This is wild. Completely wild. But...*I'm going to say yes.*

If only Percy could see me now.

"Let me talk to Dad," I say. "See if I can make it happen."

"For real?" Adam says, his voice so full of hope it makes my heart squeeze.

I laugh. "This is crazy, Adam. But yes. For real."

"In that case, there's something else I need to tell you," he says. "Everyone here except Freddie still thinks you're my fiancée."

CHAPTER EIGHTEEN

Adam

BEHIND ME, THE HEAVY WOODEN DOOR OF THE STONEBROOK
Farm farmhouse swings open, and Freddie, Leo, and Jace file
out, spreading out across the porch.

Leo sits down on the steps beside me and hands me a
bottle of water while Jace and Freddie take the rocking
chairs on either side of the door.

We just spent two hours working through "Curves Like
That," relearning the choreography. It's our most dance-
heavy song, with a series of moves fans will expect to see in
the show. Fortunately, Jace still knew it all—he was always
the best dancer out of the four of us—and took us through it,
filling in the gaps when the rest of us couldn't remember.

We were never NSYNC level dancers, which suited me
just fine. I could always follow the choreography, but I wasn't
out front like Jace and was just as happy standing still at a
microphone letting my voice do all the work.

"How are you feeling?" Leo says, glancing over.

I take a swig of water. "Out of practice," I say.

"It's all right, man," Jace says. "We never held the dancing bar very high for you."

Freddie chuckles, and I turn to face him. "What are you guys doing out here, anyway?"

We're all on break, but I'm waiting for Laney, and it might be overwhelming for her to see all four of us sitting here like a welcome committee.

I still can't believe she's coming.

When I asked her, it was more of a pipe dream. I didn't think she'd actually be able to make it work, but now she's almost here, and I can't wait to see her.

And I'd rather not have our hello after more than a week apart be witnessed by the rest of the guys.

"You looked lonely," Leo says.

"I just followed Leo," Jace says.

"What are *you* doing out here?" Freddie asks.

I look at him over my shoulder and rub a hand through my hair. "I'm waiting for Laney."

"How come we had to rehearse somewhere close enough for Adam's girlfriend to visit, but not mine?" Leo says.

"Do you even have a girlfriend?" Jace asks.

Leo frowns. "That's not the point. If I *did*, she wouldn't live in North Carolina."

"Girlfriends or wives or fiancées were not factored into the decision," Freddie says. "This place belongs to Flint's family. I told him we needed somewhere remote and private, he suggested we use it, it was available, end of story."

"Flint, is it?" Leo says on a laugh. "You're on a first-name basis now? It's fine, Freddie. We know you're the biggest star. You don't have to name-drop A-list actors to impress us."

Freddie rolls his eyes. "He's a legit friend. I'm not just name dropping."

"I'm not sure I believe you," Jace deadpans. "But let me just call up my bestie Beyoncé real quick and see if *she* knows Flint Hawthorne."

There's an aspect of our conversation that feels familiar, but it doesn't have anything to do with the words anyone is saying. It's more the vibe. The fact that for three years, we were together every single day. We talked about everything. Teased each other. Bickered and complained and annoyed each other. But we also cared for and supported each other.

I did not expect to fall back into this so easily. I expected awkwardness, maybe even judgment. I at least expected Leo and Jace to demand an explanation as good as the one I gave Freddie.

But we haven't talked about how things ended. We just started back up like it never did.

It could be Freddie's doing. I can easily imagine him convincing the other guys to go easy on me if only to keep me around long enough for the concert to actually happen. Kevin made it clear I was the holdout. If they all think I'm a flight risk, it makes sense they would tread lightly.

Or maybe I'm not giving any of these guys enough credit.

I pull out my phone, checking for the millionth time to see if Laney has texted with an updated ETA. There's nothing there from Laney, but I do have a text from Sarah.

And it's one that makes dread pool in my gut.

SARAH

Oh, hi. You're on the internet.

After her text, she sends a link to a *TMZ* article with a

headline that reads: Inside source reveals: Deke Driscoll is alive, well, and getting married.

Freaking Kevin Spellman.

I quickly scan the article. It basically says nothing. It doesn't mention Laney by name or give any significant information. It just rehashes the headline three different ways. I turn and toss the phone to Freddie.

"Check out what your asshole agent just did," I say.

Freddie catches it and looks over the article. "Well, at least he didn't share her name."

Before I can respond, Freddie's assistant, Ivy, comes barreling out the front door. She looks at the phone in Freddie's hand. "Ohhh, so you've already seen it. I was just coming to show you."

Freddie hands my phone back to me. "Do you think this was Kevin?" he asks Ivy.

"Absolutely yes," she says. "We aren't ready to announce the concert yet, but that doesn't mean he can't get people talking about Midnight Rush. And what better way to do that than stir up interest in the one member of the band who fell off the map? Deke will get people talking again. Generate excitement. Then right when the fervor is at its peak? Concert news drops. It's a pretty genius plan. I mean, *evil* genius, because *Kevin*. But still. I recognize his strategy."

I scoff. "Great. So happy my personal life could serve such a valuable purpose."

"Welcome back to showbiz," Jace says. "You know that's how it always is."

"Sure. But that's not how it is for me." I pause, debating whether I should just come clean. I'd rather not be lying to Leo and Jace, especially since Freddie already knows. "I'm not even really engaged," I say.

"You're not?" Leo asks. "Kevin said you were."

"Because I told Kevin I was. But I was lying to try to get him off my back. I didn't think he would tell anyone. I definitely didn't think he would release the news to freaking *TMZ*."

"Um, do you *know* Kevin?" Ivy asks dryly. "Because of course he would."

"Why is he still your agent?" Jace asks Freddie. "Because he's kind of the worst."

"He is," Freddie says. "Unequivocally. But he can negotiate the hell out of a contract. I don't need to like the guy to admit he's good at what he does."

"There are other agents who are also good at what they do," Ivy says, and I get the sense they've had this argument before. "They just also have integrity."

Freddie waves a dismissive hand. "I can't be manipulated by a man I know as well as I know Kevin. I know his tells. I get what you're saying, but he's harmless. At least, he is to me."

"Is this harmless to me?" I say, holding up my phone. "The fact that he just broadcasted my engagement to the whole world when I'm not actually engaged?"

"Except you are now," Jace says. "At least until after the concert. You're engaged, and I'm happily married, Leo's studio is not close to declaring bankruptcy, and Freddie did not swear at the Instagram influencer with the annoying kid no matter what she claims to the contrary. Because that's what will sell tickets. All of us happy, living our lives with no drama, no lies, and no need for privacy whatsoever. You might have forgotten, but that's the way this business works."

My blood runs hot as I think about Jace's words. It sucks to see my name back in a headline again, but it's not like he said anything I didn't already know. It was naive of me to think Kevin wouldn't use the news of my engagement—*fake engagement*—to his advantage.

Even more naive if I thought I could agree to do the concert and *not* be exposed to this side of the business.

Ivy drops onto the step beside me. "Are you okay?" she asks.

"It's a little bit of a wake-up call," I say, "but it's fine. The article barely says anything."

"It doesn't," she says, "but that doesn't mean someone won't try to leak something else." She glances over her shoulder at Freddie, then scoots a little closer. "Listen. I don't trust Kevin like Freddie does, and I wouldn't put it past him to have someone here, someone working on the concert, try to sneak a photo of you or your fiancée. Kevin doesn't want scandal, so he won't make you look *bad*. But he does want you in the spotlight, so if you're worried about your privacy, I'd keep a close eye out. Especially once Laney gets here."

My gut tightens at the thought of telling Laney we've been outed on the internet. She seemed willing enough to keep up the charade when we talked on the phone yesterday, but the way I framed it, it was more about keeping things chill *here*. At least ten different people congratulated me on my engagement within an hour of arriving at the farm. Or, more within an hour of people figuring out who I was. Either way, I got tired of trying to explain because then people assumed I'd experienced a breakup and getting sympathy for that was even worse than the congratulations.

But this—an article on *TMZ*—this is a bigger deal.

This also puts Laney's privacy at risk.

If her name were to be leaked somehow, she'd have

family members, friends, co-workers who would all believe something about her that isn't true.

That's a lot to ask of her. A lot to expect.

As soon as Kevin gets here, it's going to be hard not to punch him in the nose.

A car appears in the distance, slowly making its way toward the farmhouse, and I stand up. I recognize Laney's black Honda from here.

For now, I pocket my phone and push the TMZ article from my mind. I'll tell her about it as soon as I get her alone.

Laney jumps into my arms as soon as she's out of the car, and I spin her around before lowering her back to the ground and pressing my lips to hers.

Behind me, the guys break out in a chorus of whistles and catcalls.

I chuckle as I drop my forehead to hers. "Hi. Thanks for coming. Sorry about them," I say, tilting my head to the house behind us.

Laney finally looks up, and her eyes widen as her gaze moves from one band member to the next. She clears her throat with a sound that's somewhere in between a gulp and a yelp. "It's gonna take me a minute to get used to seeing you all together."

"If it makes you feel any better, I'm still getting used to it, too," I say. "Come on. I'll introduce you."

She lifts her hands and presses them to her cheeks. They're flushed pink, the same color as her lips, and I resist the urge to lean down and kiss her one more time.

"Oh, hey, that's a ring on your finger," I say, noticing the diamond on her left hand.

She holds it out for me to see. "It's beautiful, right? It was Percy's idea. He borrowed it from Mimi, who promised it is absolutely not real and if I lose it, she will still love me." She lifts her gaze to mine. "Do you mind? Since we're running with the engagement story, I thought it would be easier than explaining why I don't have one."

I swallow. The sight of a ring on her finger is impacting me in ways I can't fully process. I haven't even thought about proposing so far. We're nowhere near that point. But the idea of her walking around wearing a ring that tells everyone she belongs with me—I do not mind it even a little.

Then there's the fact that she's willing to do this in the first place. To borrow a ring, to drive all this way. It's so much more than I deserve.

"It *is* beautiful," I say. "Thanks for thinking of it."

We make our way over to the porch, and the guys come down the stairs to say hello. Ivy must have already gone back inside because she's nowhere to be seen, so it only takes a moment to introduce Leo and Jace. They each shake her hand, then Freddie pulls her into an enormous hug. "Good to see you again, Laney," he says.

"You too." She smiles wide, then turns to Leo and Jace. "And it's nice to meet both of you. I'm a big fan of your work." She delivers this line, then looks at me and grins, eyes wide, like she can't quite believe this is happening.

I like that she isn't hiding this part of herself from me. Don't get me wrong. I'm glad that I met Laney and first got to know her without Midnight Rush factoring into the relationship. I remember questioning all the time, when the band was at its peak, if people were genuinely interested in me or just in my fame. I hated that the question ever had to be a part of making friendships or having relationships, so I was happy to leave that aspect of the band behind.

But now that I know Laney was a fan, and now that she

knows I'm Deke, I appreciate that she doesn't feel like she has to play it cool or pretend like it's no big deal.

When I was eighteen, I might have been uncomfortable dating someone who had my poster on the wall by her bed. And if Laney *still* had my poster by her bed, we might have a problem. But this far removed, it's more...*adorable*. And humbling—that someone as brilliant and amazing as Laney dedicated so much passion to the music that was such a formative part of my life.

"This place is amazing," Laney says, looking around at the farm. "It actually reminds me a little of Hope Acres. The way it's nestled into the mountains. You guys should see Adam's place. It's beautiful too."

Pride swells in my chest at her praise. I don't have the careers that any of the other guys have. I'm not making music like they are or building platforms, gaining fans. But I am proud of what I've done with my life, even if it took me a little while to get there, and it means a lot to hear Laney's words.

I press a hand to Laney's back. "Come on. We can get you settled in upstairs, then you're welcome to watch rehearsal, if you want."

I look at Freddie. "What are we working on next?"

"I want to work on 'Never Say Never,'" Leo says.

"But we should run through 'Curves Like That' one more time, now that Laney is here to watch," Jace says.

Laney gasps. "Are you doing the dance?"

"You know we have to do the dance," Freddie says.

"True," Laney says. "Fans would never forgive you."

"Meet back in five?" Jace says, and we all agree.

Goldie is stretched out on her dog bed in the corner when I carry Laney's stuff into my room.

The one downside to the farmhouse is its limited number of guest rooms. The band and other key players are staying here, and there's one more bunk house somewhere else on the property that's in use, but the largest number of people are staying at a hotel in Silver Creek and commuting back and forth to the farm. Which is fine. Not everyone needs to be here the whole two weeks, so there has already been a lot of coming and going anyway.

The point is, there isn't space at the farmhouse for Laney to have her own room, and I do not want her staying at the hotel.

So I'm giving her my room. I haven't decided where I'll sleep yet—probably on the couch in the second-floor common area where we've been hanging out every night. But I'll figure out that part later.

Laney stops in the doorway and looks around, her gaze landing on the giant king-sized bed in the middle of the room. My shoes are on the floor beside it, and a flannel is hanging on the bedpost.

"This is *your* room." She eyes me curiously. "Am I staying in your room?"

"You are, but I'm not," I say quickly. "There aren't any vacant rooms, so I thought you could stay here, and I'll crash on the couch in the living room down the hall."

She takes a deep breath, then opens her mouth like she's going to say something before closing it again. "Adam, you can't sleep on the couch."

"Sure, I can. It's not a big deal."

"But it might be a big deal if it makes people talk. I don't want to give anyone the impression we're fighting."

I think of Jace's words. Ivy's warning.

We don't need a scandal. I will never stop feeling like an idiot for getting Laney into this mess in the first place, but she's right. People *might* talk. And I'd rather my personal life not be at the center of any of those conversations.

"Only if you're sure," I say. "But I need you to know I have zero expectations here. I did not set this up expecting you to offer to share."

"I one hundred percent believe you. It's not a big deal. And it *is* a big bed. We'll be fine."

I'm tempted to ask what she means by fine.

Fine...because she plans to assemble a giant wall of pillows down the center of the bed and stay on her side of the mattress?

Fine...because she's happy to share a room and a bed and embrace wherever that takes us?

Fine...because she isn't attracted to me so it will feel like sharing a bed with her sibling?

Okay, scratch that last one. I've kissed Laney enough times to know not to worry about that.

But the truth is, I don't have a lot of experience navigating conversations like this one. I was a very young eighteen when Midnight Rush ended. Offstage, I was shy and awkward. Post-concert casual hookups never felt like the right choice for me.

Once I left the band, I was basically in hiding. I didn't date or hang out with friends. While other guys my age were attending frat parties and swiping right on dating apps, I was learning how to cook and teaching myself how to play guitar and hoping the Amazon delivery guy didn't figure out who I was.

It's not in my nature to be casual, and at some point, I'll have to talk to Laney about this. She's not casual for me—I already know that. But I still want to take things slow.

Laney lets her purse fall from her shoulder and drops it onto the chair next to Goldie's bed, then crouches down to scratch the dog's ears. "I'm glad Goldie got to come," she says easily. "Is she getting outside to enjoy the farm?"

"She tried to herd some goats yesterday," I say. "And she made friends with a basset hound named Charlie."

"Oh my gosh, I bet you loved that, Goldie." The dog rolls over to show her belly, and Laney gives her good scratches, talking to her the whole time. The diamond on Laney's finger glints in the sunlight streaming in through the window.

She's doing a lot for me this week.

She's here, for one. Taking time off work, rearranging her life so she can hang out with me, just *be here*, because I was feeling overwhelmed and thought having her around might keep me grounded.

It's already working. I need to tell her about the *TMZ* thing, about the potential for Kevin to leak a photo or *more*. But it doesn't feel as scary as it did a few minutes ago. Now that she's here, it just feels like everything will be okay.

Like she's the anchor I've always needed.

She looks up and sees me studying her, and her lips lift into a smile.

"What?" she asks.

I hold my hand and help her to her feet, then wrap my arms around her waist, tugging her against me.

I lift a hand to her cheek and press a lingering kiss to her lips. "I don't think I deserve you, Laney Lawson," I whisper against her lips.

And it feels like the truest thing I've said in a very long time.

CHAPTER NINETEEN

Laney

THE OVERSIZED DINING ROOM IN THE FARMHOUSE, WHICH I think they call the ballroom and use for indoor weddings, has been fully converted into a rehearsal space. Tables and chairs have been shifted to the back and hidden behind a wall of mirrors that reach almost to the ceiling. There's a piano, a couple of guitars, a bass leaning against an amp, and stools and microphones for each of the guys.

Adam leans over and presses a quick kiss to my lips. "Please don't laugh at my dancing."

"Why would I laugh?"

"Because I'm twenty-six doing a dance that was choreographed for a bunch of teenagers?"

"'Curves Like That' dance moves are timeless, Adam," I say in a serious tone.

"Yeah, says the person who doesn't have to do them on stage."

"I could if I had to," I say. "I know every move."

He takes a few backward steps and smirks. "You shouldn't have admitted that, Laney." He finally turns and walks to where Jace is standing in the center of the room while I find a chair near the wall. Leo and Freddie soon follow, and I have yet another *pinch me* moment. I can't even begin to explain what it feels like to see them standing together like this.

They all look older. Broader shoulders. More facial hair. But they're still Midnight Rush. Standing *right there*. It's completely surreal.

"All right, let's do this," Jace says. He looks at a sound technician across the room. "Hey, Trav, we're doing full vocal this run through. Can you bring over headsets for us?"

The tech runs over and helps them connect their mics, then they move into position, forming a diamond, Jace in the front, Leo and Freddie on either side, Adam directly behind Jace.

Adam glances my way, grinning and giving me the tiniest eye roll as he picks up his arms and positions them in front of his face for the start of the song. A tiny thrill shoots through me at the sight. I recognize this. *All of it.*

Jace nods once, then the opening notes of "Curves Like That" pipe into the room.

Before I knew he was also Deke, I'm not sure I ever would have looked at Adam in his flannel and baseball caps and thought, I bet this guy can slay on the dance floor. He's so mild mannered, it just doesn't fit the idea of him in my head.

But seeing him like this, surrounded by his bandmates, it's clear Deke is still in there. He doesn't dance as well as Jace. But he holds his own, and it's so fun to watch.

Especially because he's *watching* me watch. And he can't stop smiling at me.

They make it all the way through the song, and the eight or so people scattered around the room clap and cheer. "Sounded great, guys," Trav says.

Adam leans forward and says something to Jace, who immediately looks my way.

"All right, Laney," Jace says. "Let's see what you've got."

My eyes widen. "Um, what?"

"You know all the moves, don't you?" Adam calls. He jogs over, stopping right in front of me. "I did warn you," he says, reaching for my hand.

"Come on," Freddie adds when I hesitate. "It'll be fun."

"You are in so much trouble," I say to Adam, but I let him lead me into the middle of the room anyway. He positions me right in front of him, his hands on my hips as he leans close to my ear. "Ready?" he asks, his breath fanning across my cheek.

"Absolutely not," I say, but I'm grinning as I lift my arms, mimicking the position the other band members have already assumed.

When the music starts, muscle memory kicks in and I hit every mark through the opening sequence of moves. I am not a dancer by any stretch, but I did *this* dance a million times. Always alone, usually in my bedroom while wearing my Deke shortie pajamas. Which, I'll be honest, it kinda makes this whole moment feel full circle.

This time, when the song ends, the guys all clap for me. "You know what, you should just take my spot," Adam says.

"For real, Laney. You knew every move," Leo says.

Adam grins. "Laney might have had a tiny thing for the band when she was in high school."

Freddie gasps. "Were you a Midnighter?"

"Okay, now we're done here," I say. "Don't you guys have another song to practice?"

Adam wraps his arms around me from behind and kisses my cheek. "That was fun. Thanks for being a good sport."

I move back to my chair while the guys shift to the other end of the room. Leo sits down at the piano and Adam picks up his guitar while Freddie and Jace settle onto a couple of stools.

I am very excited about the possibility of Midnight Rush *playing* as well as singing, and I pull out my phone, turning slightly so I can take a selfie with the band in the background.

I'm about to send the picture to Percy, but then a woman with short dark curls and a stern expression drops into the chair beside me.

"So, I hate to be that person, and I totally trust *you*," she says, offering me a kind smile, "but I don't trust whomever you might want to send that selfie to, so I would super love it if you didn't share."

"Oh! Right. I totally get it." My face heats with embarrassment. I *do* trust Percy, and I doubt very seriously he'd ever send the photo to anyone, but I'm pretty new to all this. Like, less than an hour new—so what do I know? I quickly pocket my phone. "Sorry. I won't send photos to anyone."

"It's so annoying," she says. "It's just life, you know? But any little thing we can do to help them maintain their privacy is worth it." She holds out her hand to shake mine. "You're Laney, right? Deke's fiancée? I'm Freddie's assistant, Ivy."

"Adam," I correct. A fiancée would do that, right? "And yes! I am Laney. It's good to finally meet you. I feel like I already sort of know you after all the logistical texts and things you've had to send over. You are juggling a lot."

"Right! Adam. Sorry. I have to make that click in my brain."

"How long have you worked for Freddie?" I ask.

Ivy looks up at the ceiling like she's counting back in her head. She has to be close to my age. Her skin is flawless, and her eyes are big and brown. "Four years...going on four hundred?" she says, and I grin.

"That long, huh?"

She smiles. "I swear, that man has taken years off my life. I mean, don't get me wrong. He's amazing. Just completely insufferable."

"That bad, huh?"

She waves a dismissive hand. "Not really. I'm too hard on him. He's just very good at getting what he wants. The man could convince a dairy farmer to buy manure. He's that charming."

"He seems to use it for good, though." My eyes shift to Adam, who is laughing at something Freddie said. "Everyone loves him."

She turns her gaze to look at the men. "Yep. Everyone does."

Her tone makes me wonder if there's something going on between them, but then she gives her head a little shake. "Especially women. Which is why I'm so protective of his privacy. If they can find out where he is, they literally show up in packs. Ready to do or say or be anything he wants."

"Really?"

"It's the ugly side of show business," she says with a shrug. "We get annoyed when celebrities are spoiled or enti-tled, but then we obsess over their every move, give them anything they want, and demand so much that paparazzi are literally willing to ignore every ethic to steal a photo. It's a wonder anyone stays in this business."

I suddenly feel very uncomfortable with my level of devotion to Midnight Rush through my teen years. But then, my fandom was very private. I might have made one too many scrapbooks full of band memorabilia, but I wasn't lurking outside of hotel rooms.

"Sorry," Ivy says. "I probably sound so cynical. I love Freddie's fans. He couldn't do what he does without them. I've just been doing this long enough to see the downside. But enough about me! How long have you and Deke been together? Wait. Sorry. I mean Adam."

"Uhh—" I breathe out a nervous laugh as I think back to the conversation Adam and I had the night before I drove down. The plan is to keep the story simple. Be vague on timelines. Stick to the truth regarding how we met. And lie as little as possible.

I'm honestly surprised Ivy doesn't know the truth already. Adam told Freddie. Shouldn't he have told his assistant? I'm tempted to walk onto the dance floor and kick him in the shins for *not* telling her, because now I'm having to juggle uncomfortable questions with lies for answers.

"It's still pretty new," I say. That feels safe. *New* can mean all kinds of things.

Ivy studies me. "Okay, I almost buy it, but you're gonna need to deliver with a little more conviction."

I freeze. "What?"

She leans a little closer. "Freddie told me everything," she says. "Don't worry, because your secret is totally safe with me. I'm just saying, your delivery could use some work. Confidence, right? You have to talk like you don't question *at all* what you're doing here or why the two of you are together."

I huff out a laugh. "That means I would have to *not* question what I'm doing here in the first place."

"Oh, please. You're here because the guy is totally in love with you. Everyone is going to buy that part because it's true. Claiming you're a little more serious? Easy peasy," Ivy says with a casual wave of her hand.

My stomach bottoms out when Ivy says the word *love*. She's so casual about it. Like it's no big deal. Like it's how Adam *actually* feels even without our fake engagement.

It's too soon for me to believe it's true. But the hope that flares in my chest at the thought says a lot about where my feelings are headed.

"Honestly, it's a smart move strategy-wise," Ivy continues. "Some women won't care. Engaged, not engaged. They'll throw themselves at whomever like it does not matter. But most will respect the love story. I know it was all accidental, but I'm glad you're keeping it going. You'll create a little bit of a buffer for Adam, which, based on what Freddie has told me, is only going to help him."

I know Ivy is trying to be encouraging, but hearing her talk about the complications of Freddie's fame, and now, Adam's, at least until the concert is behind us, leaves me feeling queasy and unsteady on my feet.

I've thought a little about what it means to be *dating* Adam. But I haven't considered at all what it will mean if the entire world thinks I'm his fiancée. Will people know my name? See me at the concert? Will I just be some faceless, nameless *idea* of a fiancée that no one ever sees?

Keeping up the charade so industry people don't talk and start unnecessary rumors is one thing. But broadcasting the engagement to the world, to fans—is that going to happen too?

It makes sense that the information might become public. And that suddenly feels like a very big deal.

Maybe it doesn't have to be. Maybe I can just go back to Lawson Cove after this week and Adam can do the *Deke* part of his life without me. But is that what he'll want? What would be best for him?

Knowing what I know about what he's been through, I feel *very* protective of him. I want to be around because I want to make sure he's okay. I want to be able to hold his hand at the end of the night and listen if any old feelings get stirred up. I want to be a safe place for him.

I have a *very* easy time imagining myself in a relationship with Adam.

But imagining myself in a relationship with Adam when he's *Deke* feels like a different matter entirely. I am not boyband girlfriend material. I'm not sexy sweaters and thigh high boots. I'm hoodies and jeans. Even when I dress up, it's in basic wrap dresses made out of enough fabric to keep the girls and all my lady bits fully contained at all times. No accidental nip slips for me, thank you.

I don't think for a second that Adam would expect me to change to look the part.

But the court of public opinion can be brutal, and I don't think any of the guys, especially Freddie, want anything but positive press surrounding this concert.

"Freddie had the sweetest things to say about the two of you after he came home," Ivy continues. "At least he did once I murdered him for disappearing in the first place." She rolls her eyes. "The man hasn't traveled without security in *years,* and he just up and left. Drove out of Nashville like it was no big deal and left *me* to explain to his security team, his agent, his *mother*. It was a complete mess. But that's—" She pauses, her words dropping off mid-sentence. "Oh. Oh, gosh. I freaked you out, didn't I? I did. I can tell by your face."

"No, no, it's fine. I think I just hadn't thought about *everyone* believing we're engaged. Like, the *whole world* everyone."

"Ohhh. Right. Adam told you about the *TMZ* article?"

My eyes widen. "What? There's a *TMZ* article?"

Ivy clears her throat and grimaces. "Did I say *TMZ* article? I don't know what I was thinking."

"Ivy, please tell me," I say, pressing a hand to my stomach, like the gesture alone might calm my growing nausea.

She breathes out a sigh. "I'm sure Adam will mention it, but honestly, it wasn't that big a deal. It didn't mention you by name, just announced that Deke is engaged."

"Who would have leaked the news?" I ask.

"Definitely Kevin," Ivy says. She then goes on to explain the way Kevin's *PR brain* works, the way he's likely trying to build buzz before the concert news drops later this week.

Logically, I get it. It's just weird to find myself at the center of it. And it feels impossible not to worry about how my personal life would be impacted if the news of my identity *did* leak.

Pretending here, when I'm surrounded by people I don't know, doesn't feel stressful. But lying to my dad, my coworkers, clients. That feels so much worse.

Ivy loops her arm through mine like only an extrovert can. "Listen. Consumers of entertainment news are like goldfish. They gobble up what's right in front of them, and then five minutes later, they completely forget about it because they've already moved on to the next most sensational thing.

This *TMZ* thing is a tiny blip, and it doesn't say anything about you. Don't stress about it."

I smile and nod, even if I'm still dying on the inside.

"Here," Ivy says, holding out her hand. "Give me your phone. I'm going to give you my number. If you need anything or just get freaked out by any of the craziness that's going to happen the next few months, just text me."

"Thanks. I appreciate that."

"Okay, I'm off. I have to call the photographer for tomorrow's photoshoot. But I'm serious, Laney. If you need anything, I'm your girl."

I absolutely believe her. If Freddie is capable of getting everything he wants through charm, I think Ivy could probably do it through sheer force of will.

After another hour of rehearsal, I wander off in search of water bottles for the guys. I find an enormous spread of snacks and beverages in a dining area on the opposite side of the house and grab what I need, then head back into the rehearsal space just as they finish the chorus of "Memories of Yesterday."

"What if we take the harmony there up instead of down?" Adam says. "Leo, can you hit that note?"

Leo finds the note on the piano. "I think so. Let's try it."

They sing the line together, Adam taking the melody and Leo harmonizing. "That's it," Leo says. "So much better."

I hand the water bottles over one at a time, saving Adam's for last. When he takes his, I lean close, pressing a kiss to his cheek just beside his ear. "You're sexy when you talk about harmony," I say.

I move away, but he catches my hand, tugging me back for another kiss. "Hey, can you go let Goldie out for me?" he asks.

"So that's why you invited me here," I say.

He kisses me a third time. "Actually, *that's* why I invited you here."

"Okay. You like each other," Jace says dryly. "We get it."

"Be back soon," I whisper to Adam.

Goldie and I end up taking a gorgeous walk around the grounds of Stonebrook Farm. We visit goats and chickens and wander through the apple orchard and meet a golden-doodle named Toby who decides to join us for the last half of our walk, like it is his personal responsibility to show us all the best parts of his home.

By the time we make it back to the farmhouse, the guys have finished for the day, and Ivy is briefing them on what we can expect for tomorrow. Absent a band manager, it appears she has become the one in charge because no one is questioning anything she says.

"The photographer will be here at two," she says. "So that means you have to be downstairs for wardrobe and styling by noon. And Adam?" She lifts a hand to her face and strokes her chin. "It's time for the beard to go. People are going to think we replaced Deke with someone else if you don't shave."

CHAPTER TWENTY

Laney

"I PROMISE THEY'RE CLOSED," I SAY TO ADAM WHO IS currently hiding inside the bathroom.

I am, as he requested, sitting on the end of the bed, eyes closed in preparation for the big reveal.

Because Adam just shaved off his beard.

He knew better than to argue with Ivy about it, but he was grumpy through most of dinner, which I found highly entertaining and adorable. I love Adam's beard, but I'm still excited to see him without it.

The past twenty minutes of waiting have been absolute torture. Actually, torture is probably a strong word. I've been lounging in our *very* comfortable bedroom, enjoying a gorgeous view of the Blue Ridge Mountains, watching the sky turn orange and purple as the sun drops behind the horizon.

There are worse ways to wait for your not-quite boyfriend to shave. And shower, apparently. Though I did my best not to think about that one too hard. Adam, right on the other side of that door. Warm water. Suds. All that skin.

"Adam?" I call, my hands still pressed to my eyes. "Are you coming out?"

"Maybe not," he says back.

I drop my hands. "Why not?"

"Because I look like a different person."

"Come out here and let me see."

"Nope. Not happening."

I stand and move toward the door. "I'm sure you look amazing. And it's not like you can put it back—"

The door flies open, and my words stall in my throat.

Adam is...*wow.*

He does look like a different person.

He looks like Deke.

I have never seen Adam this dressed down, in dark gray joggers and a white t-shirt, and my stomach swoops as I look him over. He's still *him,* but he does look younger. And so much like the Deke of my youth.

"I look stupid," he says.

There is *nothing* stupid about him. In fact, I think I might have once described something just like this in the abysmally bad fanfiction I wrote in the tenth grade, when I briefly considered a career as a writer. Midnight Rush released their debut album that year, and my obsession was in full swing. Deke was younger than he is now, obviously, but I specifically remember a story about a freshly showered, post-concert Deke randomly encountering a fan outside his trailer and being so taken with her, he volunteers to be her first kiss.

My stories were totally innocent and sweet, but it still sends a wave of embarrassment washing over me. To think about how I thought about him *then* when he's standing right in front of me *now*.

"You do not look stupid. You look amazing."

He runs a hand down his face. "I'll probably get used to it. But I'm growing the beard back as soon as the concert is over."

"I love your beard. I would love for you to grow it back," I say. "But I love this too."

Honestly, I love his beard *more*. Maybe just because it's how I've always known him. Maybe because it works so well with the flannel he loves to wear. But you won't hear me complaining about how he looks now.

My phone buzzes with an incoming text, and I read it off my smartwatch. "Ivy says she wants proof that the deed is done."

Adam frowns. "What, like a picture?"

I shrug. "Or you could just walk down the hall. It sounds like they're all hanging out in the common area."

He sighs. "Fine. Let's just get it over with."

I am definitely a fan of this slightly grumpy version of Adam, and I happily follow him out the door and down to a comfortable seating area where Leo, Jace, Freddie and Ivy are sitting with...*Oh. My. Gosh.*

That's Flint Hawthorne.

The Flint Hawthorne. The Oscar-nominated, been in a million movies, monumentally famous Flint Hawthorne. Just hanging out like it's no big deal.

I shouldn't be that surprised.

I did some googling before I left this morning, and I learned a couple of things. One: Stonebrook Farm is owned by the Hawthornes—family of the famous actor, Flint Hawthorne, who apparently grew up in Silver Creek. Which explains how Freddie found the space. More than one online source indicated that Freddie and Flint are friends, and I easily found a dozen different photos of the two of them together at a Lakers game in LA.

I met another Hawthorne at dinner—the one currently running the farm—and remember thinking he bore a slight resemblance to his famous brother. Even *that* felt thrilling. But to actually *see* Flint here? When just last week, I watched him blow up a building in the new Agent Twelve movie?

It doesn't compute. My ability to tolerate the fantastical in my own life is maxed out. Threshold exceeded. I need at least a week of nothing but mundane, boring events in order to recover.

I'm sharing a bedroom with Adam *Deke* Driscoll, texting with Freddie Ridgefield's assistant like she's my new best friend, and Jace Campbell spent the last half of dinner showing me videos of his daughter, who is indisputably the cutest toddler I have ever seen. Now I'm supposed to hang out with Flint Hawthorne?

Cool. No problem. I am A-okay.

"Hey! Deke is back!" Freddie says to Adam. "Looking good."

"I don't know, man," Leo says. "Your beard tan is terrible."

"It's not terrible," Ivy says. "Adam, don't listen to Leo. You can barely see it."

"You're probably going to have to wear makeup tomorrow," Jace says. "The camera isn't going to like your glowing cheeks."

Adam breathes out a sigh beside me, and I loop my arm through his, giving his bicep a squeeze.

"Dude. I'm being so rude," Freddie says. "Flint, this is

Adam's...fiancée, Laney," he says, hesitating just slightly on the word *fiancée*, like he isn't quite sure how far our deception should go. Flint lifts his hand in acknowledgment. "It's nice to meet you, Laney."

I'm okay.

Just kidding.

I am not okay.

This last little bit of the impossible seems to have severely impacted my gross motor skills, because when I open my mouth to respond, no words come out. Nothing. *Nada.* Not even a grunt of acknowledgement.

Adam's hand slips behind my back and curves around my hip, giving it a gentle squeeze. I don't miss that just moments ago, I was the one comforting him, and now he's doing the same for me.

The realization is just enough to thaw my frozen vocal cords. But honestly, I might have been better off *not* talking, because I point to Adam, open my mouth, and say, "I'm Adam's vet."

It sounds just as dorky coming out as you might guess. My own version of the "I carried a watermelon" line in *Dirty Dancing.*

Flint's eyebrows lift, like my words surprise him.

"I mean, not *his* vet, obviously," I try to explain. "That would be weird because he's a human. And humans need human doctors. Not that vets aren't also humans! We're just not *doctors* for humans. We're doctors for dogs. His dogs! That's me. A doctor for Adam's dogs."

Beside me, Adam is practically vibrating, his shoulders shaking even as his grip around me tightens. Is he...is he *laughing*?

Oh, geez. That was bad. I'm absolutely positive it was bad.

"And that's basically how we met," Adam says, tucking me a little tighter against his side. He looks at Ivy. "And now that *you* have seen my face, Ms. Controlling Control Pants, we're heading to bed."

I lift a hand to wave, then let Adam tug me back down the hallway to our room.

"Thank you, Adam!" Ivy calls. "You look amazing!"

As soon as we're safely inside our bedroom, Adam dissolves into a fit of laughter that should make me feel more embarrassed, but it doesn't feel like he's laughing *at* me, so I can't really be mad.

I sit on the end of the bed and collapse onto my back. "Adam?"

"Yeah?" he says as his laughter subsides.

"Did I just monologue to Flint Hawthorne about the differences between human doctors and animal doctors?"

He sits down beside me, leaning back onto his elbows. "You did."

"Did you know he was here?"

"I met him yesterday, so I knew he was around. I didn't know he was coming over tonight."

I push up on my elbow so I'm stretched out on my side, facing him. "I've actually been pretty proud of myself today. I met Leo and Jace and hung out with all of Midnight Rush at the same time, and I didn't lose my cool."

Adam nods, his expression sober. "Flint Hawthorne was the last straw, huh? You just couldn't handle it anymore."

"It was. I already function with fewer cool cards than everyone else. This whole situation is entirely unfair."

His lips lift into an easy grin, the lamplight reflecting off his ocean blue eyes. "Cool cards? Do they hand those out in vet school?"

"Hmm. We actually have to turn them in when we *go* to vet school."

"That's how it works," he says. He holds my gaze before asking, "Do I really have a beard tan?"

There's a new vulnerability in his voice that makes my heart squeeze. He's always so confident and self-assured. It's sweet to see him feeling a little insecure.

"You can barely see it," I say. I study his face, my gaze catching on the curve of his lips. It's the same mouth I've kissed before, but I can't stop myself from wondering what it will be like to kiss it now, without the beard.

"You're staring, Laney," Adam says.

I smile. "I know."

His expression softens. "What are you thinking?"

"Just that I'm really glad I'm here."

He holds my gaze. "I'm really glad you're here too."

Warmth spreads through my chest, something that seems to happen a lot whenever I'm around Adam. But there's an added element this time. This time, it isn't just about fluttery feelings of attraction—or even hotter sparks of desire. There's a certain *rightness* to being here with him. Like I've found something I didn't know I was looking for. I'm in a room I've never been in, inside a house I've never visited. But I still feel like I'm home, because I'm with him.

He reaches over and runs his fingers down the back of my hand. We're stretched out on the bed, facing each other, propped up on our elbows with maybe a foot of space between us. It's comfortable, easy, but I am also keenly aware of how close we are. Not to mention the fact that we're on a bed—a bed we're supposed to share in a few hours. I'm not ready to stop talking, though, so I steer my thoughts back to safer waters.

"Do you think the other guys resent Freddie for being so successful?"

He shakes his head. "Nah. I think we all knew he wanted it most. Not that the other guys *don't* want it. And they deserve to be as successful. But Freddie's got that hunger, you know? He had it back then, too."

"You didn't though, did you?"

He runs a hand across his face, and I immediately miss the warmth of his touch. "I didn't, really," he says. "I mean, I thought about it. I wanted to sing. But the idea of being famous was more of a deterrent than an enticement."

"Then why did you do it? Is it okay for me to ask that?"

"I did it for my mom," he finally says.

This is the second time he's told me he made a decision for his mom, and I feel a pang of regret that I'll never meet someone who had such a profound impact on his life.

He brings his hand back to mine, and I raise my palm to meet his, threading our fingers together. This is more than holding hands. Our fingers keep moving, touching, exploring, brushing over hands and wrists and forearms.

"Your mom wanted you to sing?" I ask.

"Yes and no," Adam says. "She loved listening to me sing, but she didn't care if I ever did it in public. She never would have pressured me into that." His shoulders lift in a small shrug. "But she was sick, and we were poor. And singing felt like an easy way to make money."

My heart squeezes. Adam was young when Midnight Rush became Midnight Rush. Not even sixteen. "That's a lot of responsibility to take on as a kid."

"Yeah, it was," he says, his voice a little softer than before.

I want to know more, but I'm not sure how to ask. I already know the end of the story—he lost his mom and he left the band—and I don't want to ruin whatever is happening right now by dragging up topics that hurt.

When I don't say anything else, Adam nods toward Goldie. "Mom got her from the shelter while I was out on my first tour." Goldie, who's been sleeping on her bed since we came up after dinner, stirs and stretches, then flops back down onto her side. "I was mad at first. She was still young—less than a year—and I thought it would be too much for her to take care of a puppy in between chemo treatments. But Goldie was great. Chill and easy. Sarah used to say Goldie seemed to sense when Mom was feeling particularly bad because she always saved her troublemaking for Mom's good days."

I smile. "I'm sure she's right. Dogs realize a lot more than we give them credit for."

I find myself leaning toward him, shifting my arm out and forward, so his fingers can move up, past my elbow, sending shivers of sensation dancing over my skin.

"Did you always want to be a vet?" he asks.

The question gives me pause. Weirdly, I'm not sure anyone has ever asked me that before.

"I don't know, actually," I say. "I was always considering it, I think, because of Dad. And I've always liked animals, so...I guess I probably did?"

"Really?" he presses. "You never thought about doing anything else?"

"No," but my voice doesn't sound the least bit convincing. "I didn't. Not anything that..." My words trail off as I think about the piles and piles of journals I started filling when I was in middle school. Poems. Snatches of conversations. In high school, I started using my dad's old laptop and graduated to actual stories.

I was never quite bold enough to call myself a writer, but when the world felt scary or hard or overwhelming, writing was always the thing that made me feel better. Pouring my heart into creating something new.

"Laney, you can't *not* finish that sentence," Adam says. "Not anything that...what? What else did you think about doing?"

I groan. "No! Don't make me say it out loud. It was never anything serious. Becoming a vet was a very practical choice, and I'm very good at my job. I like animals. It makes sense."

"Okay. Good on you for making a practical choice. But what else did you *think* about doing?"

I lift my hand to cover my face. I have no idea why I'm so embarrassed about this, but then, of course I'm embarrassed. I've never actually admitted this to anyone. Honestly, I haven't thought about it in years. It was a silly daydream— never anything I took too seriously.

Adam's hand curls around my wrist, but he doesn't tug it away. He just holds it, his thumb rubbing a slow circle across the inside of my forearm. "You don't have to tell me," he says, his voice soft and gentle. "But I'd like to know."

I spread two fingers apart and peek out with one eye. "You have to promise not to laugh."

"I promise," he says without hesitation.

I finally drop my hand, but Adam doesn't let it go, instead giving me a tiny squeeze of encouragement.

"I used to write," I say.

Adam's brow furrows. "Why would I laugh at that?"

"Because I mostly just wrote fanfiction." I admit this last part without fully thinking about the consequences, but then Adam's eyes glimmer with an unspoken question, and I know before he opens his mouth what he's going to ask.

"Fanfiction, huh?"

"Did I say fanfiction? I meant just...regular fiction. About totally made-up people who only ever lived inside my brain."

"Nope. I don't think that's what you said."

I close my eyes and press my lips together. "Don't ask me, Adam. Please don't ask."

"Oh, you know I'm going to ask," he says, his smile stretching wider and wider.

I tug my hand out of his grip and shimmy backward, inching my way up the bed. "You can't make me tell you. I'll run."

He lifts an eyebrow. "Pretty sure I could catch you."

"You don't know that. Maybe I ran track in high school. Or cross country. I could be *very fast.*"

He gives me a dubious expression. "I'll take my chances."

I swear under my breath, and Adam chuckles. "Who did you write your fanfiction about, Laney?"

I quickly crawl toward the head of the bed—Adam cannot make me answer that question—but he's right behind me, wrapping an arm around my waist and tugging me against him. He's gentle—so gentle—and I'm positive I could get away from him with very little effort if I wanted to. But I love the game of him chasing me, and I let out a little squeal as he rolls me onto my back, pinning my arms over my head and holding them there with one hand. He's hovering over me now, his blue eyes flashing with heat and hunger.

"Tell me who," he says.

I bite my lip and give my head a tiny shake. "You know who," I finally whisper.

His voice is husky when he says, "Did any of your fiction ever involve a situation like this?"

"What kind of situation?"

He leans down and brushes his nose against mine. "You, me...close enough to kiss you?"

My heart practically pounds out of my chest as I close my eyes and take a long, deep breath. We've kissed before, but something about this moment feels different, like there's a new vulnerability here. There is no pretense to how Adam is looking at me right now. His feelings are written right across his face.

"Not exactly like this," I say. A twinge of compassion pulses in my chest as I think of my younger self. My awkward, insecure, lost self. "I always made up girls to put in my stories. Because something like this could never happen to someone like me."

Adam's expression darkens, the fire in his eyes turning molten. "Not until now." He leans down again, his lips grazing across the skin at the side of my mouth, his breath brushing across my cheek.

The hesitation feels intentional, like he's waiting, checking in to make sure I'm okay with where this is going.

The answer is easy. I arch up and find his lips with mine, my hands curling into fists as heat pours through my body, sensation filling me from fingertip to toe. Adam's lips are warm and soft, his touch light as he releases my wrists and moves one palm to my cheek. I wrap my arms around his shoulders, my hands against the back of his neck, and tug him toward me, wanting more of him.

He carefully lowers himself onto the bed beside me, stretching out on his side, and I roll toward him without breaking the kiss. This isn't our first kiss, but it somehow feels like it. Like we're shifting into a different gear. Like every kiss is a promise of something more to come.

A kiss on my temple and I'm hearing Adam's laughter, seeing his smile.

One on my jaw just below my ear and I'm seeing us together at the rescue, stretched out on a blanket while the dogs play around us.

On my lips, and suddenly he's holding his guitar, singing to me and only me.

On my collarbone, and I'm sucking in a breath, seeing the family we might have together one day.

The thoughts should just be snatches of possibility, but with his lips pressed against my skin, they feel more like prophecy.

Kissing has never felt like this.

This contact, *this* closeness, is unlike anything I've ever experienced before.

We kiss for a very long time. Long enough that fire builds in my body, making me desperate, aching to have as much of me touching him as possible. I love the solid feel of him under my palms, the way his muscles shift and roll as I slide my hands across his chest, over his shoulders and down the dip and curve of his bicep. I love the noise he makes when my tongue brushes against his, the way he does not hide his desire for me, but I also love that he's being so careful.

There may be fire, but it's a controlled blaze. Adam isn't pushing, he's just...*kissing.*

Realizing as much unravels a tiny knot of anxiety deep in my heart, one I didn't even know was there. I know what I want with Adam, but all of this is still so new for me, and I don't want to rush.

Adam moves his mouth to my throat, placing a line of

tender kisses along my jaw. "You stopped kissing and started thinking," he murmurs against my skin.

"Did I?"

He looks up and grins. "You did. Are you okay?"

I lift my hand to his clean-shaven jaw, still not used to seeing him like this. "Yeah, I am. I'm perfect."

He nods, his expression turning thoughtful. "Are you..." His eyes drop and he licks his lips. When he looks up again, there is an earnestness in his expression that makes my heart squeeze. "Are you okay with us going slow?" His fingers slide down my shoulder until he reaches my hand, and he presses our palms together. "I am *very* attracted to you, Laney. Insanely, *maddeningly* attracted to you. But I want to do this right, you know? Take our time."

So basically, Adam Driscoll is *perfect.*

"I want that too," I say. "That sounds perfect."

"Good." He grabs a pillow from the top of the bed and tucks it under his head, then he pulls me against him, nestling me into the crook of his arm, my cheek resting on his chest. I can hear the steady *thump-thump* of his heart under my ear.

"I bet your stories were good," he says.

I let out a little laugh. "Trust me. They really weren't. My poetry was maybe *okay.* But the fiction—it will never see the light of day, and it really shouldn't."

He lifts his hand, slowly grazing his fingers across my back and over my shoulder blades. "Poetry's cool. You never thought about writing seriously? Pursuing it?"

"Nah," I say easily. "It takes a special kind of bravery to build a career on something creative. And I definitely don't have it. I wanted safe. Reliable. People will never stop having pets, and pets will always need doctors. Job security was a very compelling motivator."

"I get that," Adam says. "And you're good at being a vet. But if writing makes you happy, you should do that too."

"Yeah? What about you? If that's your logic, you should still be making music, right?"

He's quiet for a long moment before he says, "I *do* make music. I play at home all the time."

I lift my head, propping my chin on his chest so I can look at him. "Just not where anyone can hear you?"

He runs his hand over my hair, eyes staring at the ceiling for so long, I wonder if he's going to answer. I can't fault him if he doesn't. But I want him to. I want him to let me in just a little bit more.

"I didn't like the person fame turned me into," he finally says. "I didn't think I wanted to be famous, but then we were traveling and every time we turned around, people were giving us things—anything we could possibly want. Shoes, cars, expensive clothes. A watch that cost more than the house my mom was living in back in Tennessee. The excess was..." He tenses, his words trailing off, and I slide my hand up his chest, rubbing my thumb over a spot just beside his sternum. "It was addicting," he finishes. "And I lost sight of so much. Of everything that was really important."

"Adam, you were just a kid," I say gently, but he quickly shakes his head.

"That's no excuse." His body tenses the slightest bit as he lifts his arms, running both hands through his hair.

I feel the loss of his warmth almost immediately, and a sliver of fear creeps over me. I don't want him to get up. I don't want our conversation to end. I slide my arms around him and hold on, squeezing his waist, hoping he senses that whatever he's feeling, it's okay.

It's okay, and I'm not letting go.

He relaxes under me, his arm coming down over my shoulders. "I like making music," he says, his voice steadier now. "Writing music. I'm just not sure it's worth it."

"I get that," I say. "You're older now though. More grounded. Maybe you could make music in a way that works for you *now*. Have more control over what you want your career to look like."

He leans forward and presses a quick kiss to my lips. The gesture feels familiar—like we're an actual, for real couple—and it sends an irrational pulse of happiness pushing through me. "Maybe. Or I could just keep doing what I love in Lawson Cove."

I love the sound of Adam staying in Lawson Cove, but there's a note to something in his words that makes me wonder if he's telling me the whole truth. When he and Freddie sang over FaceTime the other night, I had the very distinct impression that Adam was doing what he was meant to be doing. His guitar in his hands, his words filled with so much meaning.

Now that I know what he's capable of, it's hard to think of him giving it up.

But then, I spent a good part of today stressing over how I will handle Adam's participation in a concert that will thrust him back into the spotlight. If he went back to music full time, it would be a lot more than just one concert. It would be his entire life. A loss of privacy. Screaming fans. Paparazzi. I feel wholly unequipped to handle that kind of life. My first instinct is to run as far away from it as possible.

Life would be so much easier if Lawson Cove could be enough.

But if he wants to sing...how could I ever want anything else?

CHAPTER TWENTY-ONE

Adam

With Laney beside me, the week at Stonebrook flies by.

We are busy. Between vocal rehearsals and meetings with the creative directors and wardrobe fittings and photo shoots, there is always something else to do. But the snatches of time I get with her in between make everything seem worth it.

And our nights—those have been my favorite. I could talk to Laney for hours—I *have* talked to Laney for hours, and it's not enough. Nothing ever seems like enough. When she isn't beside me, I want her there. If I'm not kissing her, I'm imagining the next time I will be. If we aren't talking, I'm actively thinking of what I might say to her next.

I am hopelessly, *shamelessly* addicted, and I do not want to be cured.

I watch from my seat by the firepit as Laney emerges from the house wearing my flannel, the same one I gave her the night she learned that I was Deke. She must have had it this whole time, because I haven't seen it, a realization that makes me weirdly happy. It's possibly a little caveman-ish of me, but I like the thought of her having it, of her wearing it when we aren't together. As far as I'm concerned, that shirt is permanently hers.

Laney's expression is strained, and I sit up a little taller as she approaches. We aren't alone. Freddie is a few seats over, and Leo and Jace just went in search of beer, and they'll be back any minute. I'll walk away in a second if Laney would rather be somewhere else.

Ivy is right behind Laney, and she shoots me a look I can't quite read before dropping onto a bench next to Freddie. He looks at her and smiles, but when she starts talking, his face shifts, and he immediately looks up at me.

By this point, Laney has reached me, and I hold out my hand. She slips her fingers into mine as she sits down beside me. "What's wrong?" I ask. "What's going on?"

She exhales a slow breath. "Do you have your phone on you?"

I check my pockets, and I'm surprised when I don't find it. "I must have left it inside. What is it?"

She holds out her phone. "Sarah just sent this over."

There's a TikTok video pulled up on her screen, and Laney hands me an AirPod. I slide it into my ear, then push play, dread pooling in my stomach with every passing second.

The video is from someone who calls herself a celebrity cybersleuth, and what she's managed to "sleuth" is proof that something is in the works for Midnight Rush.

The first thing she shares is a photo of me and Laney, one clearly taken this week. We're standing next to the gazebo that's out past the farmhouse, arms around each other.

Goldie is visible in the background, which makes sense because that's usually where we go when Goldie needs to go out.

The ring on Laney's left hand is clearly visible, and while she's not looking at the camera, her head is turned, providing a clear shot of her face.

Just that is bad enough. Even though Ivy warned us Kevin might try to release something else, create a trail of breadcrumbs before the concert news drops, it's still incredibly disconcerting to see a picture like this after so many years of living *out* of the public eye.

This was a private moment—relevant to no one else—and someone stole it and shared it like it was nothing.

But it gets worse. The next thing the video shares is a screenshot of a reddit story from someone claiming she just saw Freddie Ridgefield in the drive thru line of the fast food restaurant where she works. And then, she shows the photo Freddie posted of himself at my house, holding up a beer from the local brewery.

With proof that Freddie was in Lawson Cove visiting "a dude with a beard," according to Reddit, the sleuth used some kind of reverse image search and found a photo of Laney on the Lawson Cove Veterinary website, comparing it side by side to the photo of the two of us, in order to confirm that the person Freddie was visiting in Lawson Cove was me.

"Freddie and Deke together again after eight years?" the creator says at the end of the video. "It has to mean something. I'm crossing my fingers and toes and everything else I can cross for a reunion concert. And I'm totally going to have a cupcake today to celebrate because hello, all my Midnighter girlies, after endless radio silence, our man Deke appears to be alive and well. I'll save the breakdown of his engagement for another video, once I've done my due diligence in learning all about his bride-to-be."

"Wow." I pull out the AirPod and look at Laney. "That's..."

"Some impressive detective work," she says. "If Kevin wanted buzz, he's got it."

"When was this posted?"

"Yesterday morning," Laney says. "But it picked up more steam today. Ivy just told me they're dropping the concert news tomorrow, so this is pretty perfectly timed."

"Who took the photo? It was, what, the first day you were here?"

"Second, I think. When we took Goldie outside after breakfast."

"But who? The farm isn't even open to the public right now."

"But there are a lot of industry people coming and going every day. And the farm has dozens of employees. It could have been anyone."

I hate the thought of it being someone who's working on the concert, but Ivy did warn me Kevin wouldn't be above putting someone up to it.

I study Laney's face and try to determine how she really feels about all of this. It has to feel weird to see her name and face blasted so publicly, and I don't love that it's happening because of me.

I know Midnight Rush fans. Someone will show up at Laney's office. They will wander around Lawson Cove, look for opportunities to talk to her. And she'll hate every second of it.

"Laney, I'm really sorry about this."

She lifts her shoulders, but her shrug isn't remotely convincing. "I'm fine."

"Don't pretend to be fine," I say. "This isn't *fine*."

"Okay. I'm not fine," she says. "I feel..." She looks up, like she's trying to figure out the right words. "Like I've got spiders crawling all over my skin. Like everyone is looking at me. Judging me."

I tug her toward me and pull her onto my lap, wrapping my arms around her. "I'm so sorry," I whisper into her hair. "I know that feeling. It's not fun."

I want to tell her it gets better. That you get used to ignoring it. But she shouldn't have to get used to it. She isn't here by choice. She's here because I was an idiot who told a lie.

She's quiet for a long moment before she sits up enough to turn and look me in the eyes. "Adam, I think I need to go to Hendersonville tomorrow."

My gut tightens at the thought of her leaving. But it's not like I can stop her. "I, uh...yeah. If you feel like you need to go."

"Not to get away from you," she says. "I just...I need to talk to my family and figure out how to handle this. What to tell people."

"You tell people the truth, Laney. You don't have to lie for me."

"It's not that easy. I can't go telling people we aren't engaged days before the concert news drops. It'll just create drama, and that's not what Midnight Rush needs."

"What about what you need?"

"I'm doing what I need by going to see my mom. I don't have any regrets here, Adam. Not about you. Not about the engagement. I just need a little bit of solitude to regroup. I know you know what that feels like."

She settles back against my chest, and I resist the urge to hold her tighter, like it might make her stay. If I'd had any forethought, I would have seen this as a possibility. I never would have invited her to come.

I close my eyes, and an image of Laney waking up this morning fills my mind. The early morning sun was streaming in through the window, casting shadows across her face and her bare shoulder. When she opened her eyes and saw me watching her, she yawned and smiled, and something clicked in my heart. She's locked in now. Whatever happens between us, whether it ends or it doesn't, there's no going back as far as my feelings are concerned.

And now I've complicated everything.

And for what?

"Hey," Laney says. She wraps her hands around my forearm, then runs her fingers over what's left of the deepest cut from when I fell in the ravine. "I can literally feel the tension growing in your body right now. Are you okay?"

I force a deep breath and will myself to relax. "Sorry. Just...sitting here worrying about you."

She holds my gaze. Light from the fire reflects in her hazel eyes, bringing out the ring of honey gold that circles her irises. "It's going to be okay," she says. "You just think about the music. We'll figure out the rest together."

I want Laney to be right, but I can't forget what I've already lost to this business. I can't lose sight of that, because I can't lose her, too.

She leans down, her lips falling on mine, and for one blissful moment, I fall into her and let myself forget to be scared.

Maybe she's right and we really will be okay.

"Hey. Knock it off or take it upstairs," Freddie yells from across the firepit.

Laney pulls back and smiles a slight smile. The sight does worlds of good for my heart, and I will myself to relax as the conversation starts up around us.

"Hey," Leo says from beside Freddie. "Does anyone remember where we started our US tour? Like, what city?"

"Our first concert?" Freddie asks. "Wasn't it in Nashville?"

"Nah, we did three or four shows before we played Nashville," Leo says. "I feel like it was something random. Like Cleveland or Des Moines."

"It was Indianapolis," Laney says.

Leo sits up a little taller and snaps his fingers. "That's it! Man, I completely forgot. That was a great venue."

It *was* a great venue. Smaller, great acoustics. "We only played it the one time, right?" I ask.

"We got too big after that," Freddie says. "Moved into arenas."

I give Laney's waist a small squeeze. "How did you even remember that?"

She huffs out a laugh. "Oh, you'd die if you knew everything I remember. Probably more than you guys do."

I chuckle. "Like what?"

"I'm not going to answer just so you can accuse me of being a Midnighter," she says.

"You already showed us your dance moves," Leo says. "We *know* you're a Midnighter just from that."

"Okay, that's fair," Laney says.

"I promise we won't make fun of you," Freddie says. "What else do you remember?"

She purses her lips to the side. "Okay, I remember that Leo's full name is Leonardo Emile LeClair."

"Emile!" Freddie says. "I forgot about that."

"And that Jace's first kiss was behind the bleachers at a middle school soccer game."

Jace lifts his beer in acknowledgement, but he doesn't say anything. He hasn't said much tonight at all. His eyes look distant, and he's frowned at his phone at least a dozen times.

"Then there's all the things I remember about *you*," Laney says. Her hand moves to the crook of my arm, where it's still wrapped around her waist, and she slides her fingers over the curve of my bicep, her touch feather soft.

If she's trying to distract me, she's doing an incredible job.

"Like what?" I ask, forcing myself to focus on her words and not just the shape of her full bottom lip as she says them.

"Like how much you love pineapple on your pizza even though it's totally gross. And that your favorite book—at least when you were sixteen—was *The Way of Kings*."

"Still is," I say. "It's a great book."

"Laney, what's your favorite Midnight Rush song?" Freddie asks from across the fire. He has his acoustic guitar in his hands and he's tuning the instrument with practiced ease.

"'The Start of Forever,'" she says without hesitation.

"Makes sense," Jace says. "That's the only one your man wrote himself."

Laney turns and looks at me. "You wrote that song? How did I not know that?"

"Because we never sang it," I say. "It wasn't very good."

"Only because it was overproduced," Leo says. "The song itself was great."

Freddie stands and moves around the fire and holds out his guitar. "Come on," he says. "Take us through it."

"Nah. You go ahead. You know it too."

He gives the guitar a little shake. "But it's your song."

Laney hops up, moving to the empty chair next to me, and I take Freddie's guitar. I strum a few chords and let the familiar notes wash over me, calm me, like they always do right before I start to sing.

"Leo's right. It was overproduced," I say. "And we sang it too fast. It's better slower. Stripped down."

The fire crackles and pops as I start to play, and an owl hoots overhead. Across the firepit, Ivy stands behind Freddie, phone in hand like she's already filming. Keeping my eyes down, I glance over at Laney, letting the warmth in her eyes ground me as I start to sing.

The lyrics are simple enough. First love, first touches, that first moment when you look at someone and wonder if they're the start of your forever. I didn't have any clue what I was talking about when I wrote it. Just vague ideas of what I thought love might feel like. But I've had a few moments like those this week, and I can't keep myself from looking at Laney when I sing about a "first kiss that leaves your heart in her hands."

The rest of the guys join in on the chorus, their voices blending as well as they always did. It's my song, so I'm biased, but we sound good. *Really good.* Good enough that at least while I'm singing, I forget this isn't what I want to do with my life.

At the end of the song, Ivy and Laney start to clap, but there are *others* clapping too. We turn to see two couples standing just beyond the fire. Flint Hawthorne has a woman I assume is his wife tucked under his arm. His brother, Perry, the one who runs the farm, is also there with his wife and their son, Jack, who designated himself as our assistant this week and has been constantly bringing water bottles and snacks into rehearsal.

"That was amazing," one of the women says.

"Sorry to interrupt," Flint says. "We were here visiting our parents, but I'm heading out of town tomorrow and wanted to say goodbye before I go."

Freddie gets up and moves toward Flint, but he pauses on his way there and looks at me across the fire.

"That was brilliant, man. We're recording it tomorrow," he says. Then he turns to give Flint a hug.

"Recording it where?" Jace asks.

"There's a studio in Silver Creek," Leo says. "I already looked into it just in case we needed one. It's nice. Mostly does folk and bluegrass. But I'm sure it'll have what we need."

"Then I'm down," Jace says. "Might be nice to release something new."

I like the idea of recording. I've thought about it a few times, especially with regard to "The Start of Forever" because the version we released ten years ago is so different from how I ever heard it in my mind. It's a little harder for me to wrap my brain around releasing it. Releasing music feels like going back. And I promised myself that would never happen. How can I even consider it in the face of what happened with Laney tonight?

I nudge Laney's knee with mine. "Want to talk to Flint again? He might have some questions about your status as an *animal* doctor."

"You shut up," she says, a teasing glint in her eye.

The Hawthornes wind up joining us around the fire, and Jack wanders over to ask about Freddie's guitar. I spend a few minutes teaching him how to hold it and how to strum while Laney moves over and sits next to Jace.

I watch her out of the corner of my eye, wondering if she also noticed how distracted he's been tonight. When she makes Jace laugh, some of the tension eases out of my shoulders.

I hope he's okay. Eight years was a long time to not be in touch with these guys, and I don't want that to happen again.

With a little bit of help, Jack manages to put his fingers in the right places to form a G chord, quite a feat considering his kid-sized hands on a full-size guitar.

He smiles wide. "I did it!"

"Yeah, you did. You're a natural."

He shifts out from under the guitar, sliding it back to me, and jumps off the bench where we've been sitting side by side, Freddie's guitar perched between us. "I'm going to go tell my mom!" he says.

I reposition the guitar, then play through the chord progressions in the bridge of "The Start of Forever." Laney looks up and smiles as the words of the song float through my mind.

But she sees you different and you realize
The forever you want—it starts in her eyes.

I don't know what's going to happen after the concert. I don't know if I'll keep singing or if I'll just do the one show then go back to Lawson Cove and run Hope Acres.

But I do know that whatever I'm doing, I want her beside me while I'm doing it.

CHAPTER TWENTY-TWO

Adam

LANEY AND I ARE STANDING OUTSIDE THE FARMHOUSE SAYING goodbye when the press release announcing the concert goes live.

Ivy has been on her phone all morning, making sure everything is set, and I'm confident that once I'm back inside, she'll fill me in on how everything goes. But for right now, I don't want to think about it.

I don't want to get out my phone or talk about it with Laney or wonder what people are saying about us.

I just want to stand here and kiss Laney goodbye without worrying about anything else.

"You know," she says as she arches her neck, revealing a stretch of smooth skin. I lean close, pressing her into the side of her car as I leave a trail of kisses from her earlobe down to her collarbone. She lets out a tiny gasp of pleasure before she finishes her sentence. "I read once that every goodbye kiss should last at least six seconds."

"Six? Why six?"

"That's how long it takes our brains to dump oxytocin into our bloodstreams. Or maybe it was about intention? A six-second kiss means you really mean it."

I lean back, shifting my hands to her jaw, my thumb sliding over a single freckle on her left cheekbone.

"Should we try it out?" she asks.

I pull her against me, my free hand moving to the small of her back. "We can try. But I can't promise I'll be able to stop at six."

According to the clock, we say goodbye approximately fifty-seven times before I step back and open Laney's car door for her. "Are you sure you don't mind taking Goldie?" I ask.

My dog has spent more time with Laney in the past week than she has with me, and since we're leaving the farm to go to the recording studio in Silver Creek, she'll be on her own all day if she stays here.

"Of course I don't mind," Laney says. "She'll love my mom's house."

"And I'll see you back in Lawson Cove on Sunday?"

She smiles. "You're cute when you're a worried dog dad."

"Sorry," I say. "I'm sure she'll be fine."

"If she isn't, I have her vet's number," Laney says with a playful smirk.

Once she's in her car and buckled in, Goldie in the back seat, she winds her window down, and I lean in to kiss her one more time.

"Stay off the internet, all right?" I say. "I've asked Ivy to monitor stuff. And Sarah already does anyway. They'll let us know if there's anything else about us."

She nods. "Call me later?"

I nod, then step back from the car, watching as she pulls away, Goldie smiling at me through the back window. I'm not sure I've ever actually let Goldie stay with anyone else. The fact that I so easily sent her with Laney is really saying something.

When I get back inside, Ivy is sitting at the table in the breakfast room, laptop open in front of her and phone in her hand.

"How's it looking?" I ask as I grab a blueberry muffin off the buffet behind her.

She looks up. "To put it mildly, the internet has lost its mind."

The rest of the guys show up for breakfast a few minutes later, and Ivy plays a couple videos of fans reacting to the news. It's only been an hour, but the responses are happening fast, and they all seem to involve some combination of crying and squealing and screaming. The Midnight Rush Instagram account, which was recently resurrected by a publicist at New Groove, posted the promo photo of the four of us together at the same time the press release went live, and it already has over ten thousand likes.

It puts us all in a good mood, so we're buzzing when we head out front to the enormous black SUV that I assume will drive us over to the studio.

"Where'd this thing come from?" Freddie says, motioning to the SUV.

Ivy is already there—the woman is somehow ten steps ahead of us at all times—climbing into the front passenger seat, and she shoots Freddie a withering look.

"She really likes to be irritated with you, doesn't she?" Leo asks.

Freddie nods. "It's her favorite hobby."

I narrow my eyes, wondering if there's something to read between the lines. "Have you guys ever...?" I ask, letting him fill in the blank, mostly so I can see how he responds.

"Me and Ivy? Nah," he says dryly. "She's like a very annoying little sister. Plus, I'm pretty sure she'd rather date Kevin, and she hates Kevin."

Freddie and Leo climb into the third row because they're a little smaller than Jace and me. "Thanks for getting us a car, Ivy," Freddie calls, and she shakes her head and smiles, giving me the sense this is some sort of game between them.

Seeing their connection makes me miss Laney, which is stupid because I shouldn't miss her when she's only been gone a few hours.

Fifteen minutes later, we pull up to Eight Fiddle Studios. Leo was right, and it's a really nice studio. Apparently, some notable folk and bluegrass albums have been recorded here.

We've got a full band with us, keys, bass, drums, and two guys on guitar, and the energy in the studio is buzzing. It feels good to be back, so after we put down "The Start of Forever," none of us really feel like stopping. We end up messing around with a couple of new songs Leo has been working on, then record one of Freddie's, with a harmony line that Leo writes on the spot.

None of it means anything. I doubt we'll do anything with any of it. It's just fun.

I forgot how fun it is.

When we get back to the farmhouse, I want dinner and then a long hot shower...and the chance to collapse into bed and call Laney. We've been texting back and forth all day, mostly with GIFS and memes. But when I was singing "The Start of Forever," all I could think about was her, and I'm anxious to hear her voice. To see how it went when she talked to her family. To make sure she's okay.

But all those hopes die when we find Kevin at the farmhouse.

He's sitting at our dinner table, an empty plate and a half-full glass of wine in front of him.

He stands as soon as we walk in and moves to greet Freddie, pulling him into a quick hug. "You're back! How was it?" He motions toward a buffet table against the wall. "Dinner's great, if you're hungry. The food here is incredible."

Leo and Jace move over to fix dinner plates, but Kevin stops me before I can do the same. He claps me on the back with a little too much enthusiasm, and I force myself to unclench my jaw.

I knew he might show up—I'm actually surprised it took him so long—and I've been anticipating the opportunity to confront him about using my engagement as fodder to build concert buzz. But the thought of having the conversation right now makes me exhausted. I just want to eat and call Laney and not deal with Kevin at all.

Mostly because I know exactly how the conversation will go. If I accuse Kevin of leaking information about my engagement to the press, he will tell me I never asked him to keep it a secret. If I bring up the photo that someone took and leaked, he'll claim ignorance, say he had nothing to do with it.

I know how Kevin operates. He pushes boundaries just enough to get what he wants without crossing any lines. He uses smooth talk and lofty promises and vague statements that he can always claim meant something else if things go south.

Freddie must still trust him, and that says a lot, so I'm

willing to be civil, if nothing else. But I don't want to have anything to do with him long term.

"Deke Driscoll," Kevin says. "Good to see you, man. You're looking good." He looks me up and down. "Bigger."

"Yeah, well. I was still a kid the last time you saw me. And it's Adam," I say. "For the third time."

"How has the week been?" he says, completely ignoring my name correction. "Feel good to be back at it? I've been hearing good things about how you sound. Let me just tell you. If you want back in"—he thumps himself on the chest with both hands—"I'm your guy."

He will definitely *not* be my guy, but I offer him a polite smile anyway.

"The week has been good," I say as I move around him and reach for a plate. I have no idea what we're eating, but it looks and smells amazing. Like some kind of beef pot pie. But honestly, I'd take the distraction of a can of Spam right now if it meant not talking to Kevin. "It went great, even. But don't get any ideas. I meant what I said about this being a one-time deal."

"Come on," Leo says as he carries his plate to the table. "Can you really say that after this week?"

Ivy suddenly appears beside Kevin and holds out her phone. "Just push play," she says. "They recorded this version at the studio today, and they've already added it to the set list."

I distract myself by heaping my plate full of pot pie, adding two enormous yeast rolls from the basket at the end of the table. I don't look up as the music starts, as everyone else quiets and Kevin turns up the volume.

"Damn," Kevin says when the song finally comes to an

end. "You guys need to release this. Release a whole new album, if you're sounding this good."

"I don't have any interest in making a *new* album," I say before anyone else can respond.

Freddie huffs out a laugh. "Man, it really is a miracle we got you to say yes to the concert."

"Actually, that's why I'm here," Kevin says. We're all at the table now, plates full in front of us, but we pause at his words, looking up as a group. He grins. "Concert is now *concerts.* Nashville, Los Angeles, and Chicago."

I put down my fork, my appetite evaporating in a second, and Freddie shoots me a concerned look before pinning his gaze back on Kevin. "What are you talking about?" he slowly asks.

"Guys, the reaction to this morning's press release has been insane. There's over a million people who entered the ticket lottery. A million! That means not even a tenth of the ones who want tickets are going to get them. This is too big an opportunity. And since Charlotte West has the vocal cord thing and had to cancel three of her shows—her loss is our gain—there are openings at Sofi in LA and United in Chicago. The tour manager is securing everything now," Kevin says. "Your reunion concert is now a three-stop tour. They sent me over to deliver the happy news."

Three shows. They want us to play *three* shows?

"Kevin, when we talked about this, you said *one show,*" Freddie says, his voice firm but steady. "When I talked to Adam, he only agreed to one show."

Kevin waves a dismissive hand. "But we knew the label might want more. Do you realize the cash cow these concerts will be? The merch alone."

"Cash cow for *them,*" Leo says calmly. "If we're Midnight

Rush, we're still under the terms of our original deal, and it's crap. You know it is."

"I'm working on that," Kevin says. "A slightly higher cut for the second and third shows." He leans onto the table. "I know this whole idea hatched because Freddie needed the good PR, but this is only going to help the rest of you."

"Sounds amazing," Jace says. "Whatever we need to do. One show, three shows, I'm in." Jace is obviously talking to Kevin, but the whole time he's speaking, his eyes are on me.

"That's what I love about you guys," Kevin says, looking around the table. "You're friends. You have each other's backs. Besides, once you've done all the work for one show, what's two more?"

Under the table, I press my palms against the tops of my thighs. I don't know how to feel right now.

Overwhelmed.

Angry.

Annoyed.

But mostly just frustrated with myself because I should have known this is how things would end up. Everything that already happened with Laney this week is just further evidence that I never should trust anything that comes out of Kevin's mouth, no matter how Freddie feels about him.

"What about the charity?" I ask. My voice is low, and it sounds menacing, and I don't even care. I *feel* menacing. I push my plate away and lean forward on my arms. "You told me we were doing this for *charity*. That it was about rehabbing Freddie's reputation, and the charity would help with that."

"You did say that," Freddie adds. "That was part of the deal."

Kevin waves a dismissive hand. "A *portion* of ticket sales

will be donated to charity," he says, like I'm a five-year-old who doesn't understand grown-up math. "Big difference."

"That's not what you said. You mentioned the Breast Cancer Foundation specifically, and you said *all ticket revenue*. Was that a lie? A ploy to get me to say yes?"

Kevin scoffs. "I would not lie to you, man. I'm sure you misheard me. New Groove lost out on a lot when you walked. They aren't giving up their shot to recoup some of their loss."

"Their loss?" Freddie asks. "They got *me*, Kevin. And I've made them plenty. Don't throw Adam under the bus for this because you stretched the truth to make him more likely to say yes."

I appreciate Freddie's defense, but Kevin's not the only one at fault here.

A wave of nausea rolls over me, and I force myself to take a deep breath.

I do *not* like how familiar this feels.

As a whole, we never had a lot of control over Midnight Rush. Mostly, we just sat around while record executives and agents told us what was happening next. We were all less than eighteen, so it was easy to let other, more experienced people call all the shots. But by the end, I felt more like a puppet than an artist.

How many *trusted adults* encouraged me to hang on just a little bit longer? To trust that Mom would make it to the end of the tour? It was easy to convince myself they were right. That I couldn't turn my back on the money, the fame, or I might risk losing it all.

But then I lost Mom instead.

"That's all water under the bridge," Kevin says. "It's behind us. What matters is that right now, we've got three amazing shows coming up, and you guys are going to kill it." He claps his hands together, like he can gaslight us into compliance with his own enthusiasm. "Who's excited? Are we excited? I'm excited." I finally turn to face Freddie. He looks...awful. Mortified. Like he had no idea this was going to happen. "You said one show," I say to Freddie. "I agreed to *one.*"

"I know. I know what I said, and I can fix this. I'll talk to the label. And the charity thing—I told them we needed ticket sales donated in order for this to work, and they said we could talk about it, so I'll make them talk. I'll call Meryl."

"What is there to talk about?" I say, anger finally creeping into my voice. "It's already done. Because just like last time, Kevin is making decisions for us without even talking to us about it."

"Let's all calm down," Kevin says, but I'm already shoving my chair back, standing up from the table.

"The thing is, it *isn't* like last time," I say. "Because I'm not a kid anymore. And people don't make decisions about my life without talking to me first."

"My back was against a wall, Adam," Freddie says. He's standing now too, shoulders squared as we face off across the table. "I might have gotten a few of the details wrong, but I was honest about why I needed you, and I hoped our friendship would be reason enough for you to say yes. Was I wrong about that part?"

"Yes to *one show,*" I repeat. "A show that, until right now, I thought would benefit cancer research. Research that might have cured my mom. Let's not forget that part. Clearly, the foundation Kevin mentioned was chosen on purpose. But three shows?" I turn on Kevin. "What else does the label have planned?"

"All the usual," Kevin says. "Half a dozen talk show appearances, mostly late night, plus *The Today Show*, Kelly Clarkson, *Saturday Night Live*. Pretty routine stuff."

I shake my head and back away from the table.

"No," I hear myself say. Because what else *can* I say? I can't do it. I can't do *any* of it.

How did I think I could ever walk back into this world and come out unscathed? *Of course* the label has everything planned. *Of course* they're taking every opportunity to milk every possible dollar from the situation.

I can't fault Freddie. I believe *he* believed what he was telling me—that he thought through determination alone, he might be able to pressure Meryl Hendrix and the rest of the New Groove executives into giving him what he wanted. What he thought I *needed* in order to participate.

But Freddie's optimism has always outpaced his reality. I don't know why I thought this situation would be any different.

"No," I repeat, a little louder this time. "I can't do it."

"Adam," Freddie says. "We can still talk about this. Let me call Meryl. You said you'd do Nashville, so we'll only do Nashville."

"Actually, the Los Angeles show is already live on the website," Ivy says from her seat beside Freddie. "No tickets on sale yet, but they've announced the date and started the lottery." She looks at Kevin. "Really? They picked a date before checking with any of the artists performing the show? Can they do that?"

"They own Midnight Rush," Leo says. "They can do whatever they want."

"They don't own *me*," I say sharply. "And I'm not letting

them call the shots like this." I hold Freddie's gaze. "I'm sorry, man. I'm out."

Freddie drops back into his chair like he knows he can't argue with me, but then Jace leans back, eyes glittering with anger. "Of course you are," he says quietly. "A quitter doing what quitters do best."

"Jace, don't," Leo says calmly.

"Why shouldn't I?" he says. "Why shouldn't I point out how much Adam screwed over all of us when he walked? When he quit and left Freddie to clean up his mess with the label? All week, we've been acting like it's no big deal. Like we're all best friends again. It's all just water under the bridge. And maybe it is for you," he says, looking at Freddie. "You've got the career you want. But you know what I have right now? A crap marriage and a dead career. And every day, I look in the mirror and wonder if it would have been different. One more album. One more tour with Midnight Rush. Would it have mattered? Given me the edge I haven't been able to find on my own?" He runs a hand through his hair, his shoulders dropping as he fixes his glare on me. "But I'll never know, will I? And that's on you, *Deke*."

CHAPTER TWENTY-THREE

Laney

I SHOULD TAKE A PICTURE OF SOPHIE'S FACE RIGHT NOW.

She's sitting at the top of my bed, her legs crossed under her, her mouth hanging open in what can only be described as absolute shock.

I just showed her the video Ivy took of Adam singing beside the campfire, the rest of Midnight Rush adding their harmony in what will always be, for the rest of eternity, one of my favorite moments of all time.

"Wait, wait," Sophie says, reaching for my phone. "Did he lean over and kiss you after he finished the song?" She tracks back about twenty seconds to watch again, then she looks up at me, eyes wide. "He did. Deke Driscoll *kissed* you right on the mouth."

"*Adam* Driscoll," I say. "It's been a long time since he's gone by Deke."

She swallows. "And you met Freddie Ridgefield," she says. "Like, he knows your name and stuff."

"Yeah. He does. He's a really nice guy, Sophie. You'd love him."

This morning, when I showed up at Mom's, Sophie was at an all-district orchestra thing. She didn't get home until this afternoon, so she's only just now getting the full story.

Miraculously, she hadn't even heard the news about the reunion show, even though it's been all over social media, and she definitely didn't see the cybersleuth video that identified me as Deke's fiancée, so she's getting all of this first-hand, directly from me.

Which, honestly, it's better that way. Now I get the joy of seeing all her reactions in real time, and after the last six hours, I'm overdue for some joy.

Dad was the first one I talked to. He called while I was en route to Hendersonville, asking why he just had a client congratulate him on his daughter's engagement. When I explained the situation, the conversation did not get better.

I don't fight with my dad. He's the easiest person on the planet to get along with. So it stung when he said, "Elena, I'm a business owner and a member of this community, and you're asking me to lie to people I care about."

"I know, Dad," I said. "And I'm sorry about the lies. But we just have to keep it up until New Year's. Once the concert happens, everything will go back to normal."

"And what do we do in the meantime? Lawson Cove is a town built on kindness. When people find out you're engaged, they want to celebrate by *helping*. Sheri Pruitt already called and offered to do your wedding cake, and her offer won't be the only one. What are you going to tell these people?"

I sighed into the phone. "That we're planning a really long engagement, and I'll keep their offer in mind?"

He was quiet for a beat before he said, "Well, I'll let *you* say that then. Because I won't cater to the idea that what people on the internet think is more important than what your neighbors think."

I hung up the phone feeling chastened but also a tiny bit indignant because the one thing Dad didn't seem to consider was how *I'm* feeling.

My conversation with Mom was a little better. She was mostly concerned about my emotional state and whether there is potential for heartbreak in my relationship with Adam. It was comforting to realize that even with everything that's happened, I'm not worried about getting my heart broken.

Adam and I feel solid in a way I've never experienced before. Which was probably the only thing that got me through all the other phone calls and conversations that consumed my afternoon.

The only one that made me smile was Percy, calling to tell me Mimi and her friends at Shady Pines want to throw me a bridal shower. Even though Mimi was in on the secret when we borrowed a ring to fake the engagement, when she came across a local entertainment news headline about the local vet engaged to a popstar, she decided fake had turned into real and shifted her brain into planning mode.

I'm not worried about Mimi, but the rest of the calls and messages made me want to chuck my phone out the window by dinnertime.

Apparently, *lots* of people saw the local news article and decided now was the time to reach out. I've gotten dozens of messages. From college friends, high school friends, even people who claimed they went to high school with me but I don't actually recognize their names. Five different people have asked me to get them tickets to the concert, one has asked if she can be a bridesmaid in my wedding, and three others have asked if I can set them up with a member of Midnight Rush.

So that's awesome.

Even though it was the thing that disappointed Dad the most, the lie doesn't bother me as much because I'm *not* lying about how I feel about Adam. I can easily imagine us dating for six months to a year, then getting engaged for real. So a *long* engagement just feels like a slight exaggeration more than an outright lie.

But having *so many people* interested in my life is completely exhausting.

I have learned to protect my social battery over the years, and today, I was completely depleted by noon. Plus, I hate disappointing my dad, and if I'm annoyed hearing from people I actually know, I can't even begin to think about the *strangers* who are talking about me without wanting to crawl out of my own skin.

I thought getting away from the hustle of concert prep at Stonebrook would help me feel better, but it's actually made me feel worse. All I want to do is wrap myself up in Adam's arms and forget that any of this craziness is happening.

If not for Sophie, I might drive back to Stonebrook right now.

My sister lifts her hands to her cheeks. "I can't even with this," she says, her voice low. "How are you breathing right now? Elena! You're freaking engaged to Deke Driscoll! I mean, sort of engaged to Deke Driscoll. But still! That kiss was real!"

I laugh, and it feels so good to focus on the happy, even just for a second. "Pretty wild, right?"

She grabs a pillow from behind her and squeals into it, then seems to realize exactly *what* is on the front. It's the kind with sequins that push both ways, either hiding or revealing a picture depending on which way each individual sequin is flipped. Adam's face is on the front, and Sophie spends a minute brushing all the sequins to reveal the entire photo. She holds it up. "Laney, it's your *boyfriend*. His face is on a freaking pillow!"

Ha. On the pillow...and on the wall in three different places and all over the memory board that's hanging above my bed. My high school bedroom is basically a time capsule. I have no idea why Mom hasn't turned this room into a gym or an art studio or even just a normal guestroom. But she hasn't touched a thing since I moved out. Maybe she's waiting for me to do it? Actually, that's probably a reasonable assumption. It's my stuff. I probably *should* do it.

In fact, I should do it sooner than later before Adam comes to meet my family. I can just imagine Sophie leading him upstairs to see my childhood bedroom.

"Are you hungry?" Sophie asks. "I want snacks."

"Sure. But then you have to update me on *your* love life. What ever happened to the guy you texted me about?"

Sophie's cheeks flush a deep pink as she smiles wide. "He's a *very* good kisser."

"Sophie!" I grab the Deke pillow out of her lap and toss it back at her face. "Why didn't you say anything?!"

"Oh, I don't know. Maybe because you were busy telling me about your new boyband BFFs." She stands. "You want a soda too? I think Mom has some of that zero crap you like."

"No caffeine for me this late. I'll never sleep."

Sophie rolls her eyes. "You're so old."

My phone vibrates against the desk as Sophie disappears

into the hallway, but it's a number I don't recognize, so I ignore it and pull up Instagram before leaning back on my bed. But then a text pops up that has me sitting back up again, heart pounding in my chest.

The text reads: *Laney? It's Freddie. Can you answer?*

The phone immediately starts to ring again.

"Freddie? What's wrong?" I say as soon as the call connects. "Is Adam okay?"

"Hey," he says. "Sorry to scare you. He's fine. As far as I know. But...he's gone."

"What?"

"He left. Left Stonebrook. Backed out of the concert."

I press a hand to my chest. "Freddie, what happened?"

He spends the next five minutes walking me through the argument that broke out when Kevin showed up at the farm and unceremoniously announced their one-time reunion show was now three shows.

At some point, Sophie comes back in with soda and popcorn and Twizzlers, but she must sense something is happening because she sets everything down, then slowly backs out of the room.

"It's my fault," Freddie says. "Or Kevin's fault, mostly. But Kevin is *my* agent, so I still feel responsible. But I swear, Laney, I didn't know they were going to book more shows. They said they might, but I thought we would have the chance to talk about it first. That I could convince Adam—"

"Freddie, you know how big it is that he agreed in the first place."

"I know. But I just thought once we started singing again, he would realize how much he loves it. He's so good at it. Why is he so against it?"

I hesitate before answering. Adam and I have talked

around the issue enough that I feel like I have a pretty good idea. On the surface, it's easy. He doesn't love the attention. But in ordinary circumstances, I think he'd deal with that to be able to sing. He loves the music enough that he would. But as long as he blames the fame for keeping him away from his mom, he won't want to. I'm not sure if it's fear or resentment, but I'm sure the feelings are deep and tangled and more complicated than either Freddie or I can sort out in one phone call. "Freddie, he lost his mom. You know that's a part of what's going on."

"I know. *Geez.* I know you're right. But if I could have just talked to him before Kevin showed up. Tried to explain."

"Did he leave in his car? Or did he just walk off into the woods?" The question sounds stupid when I say it out loud, but given Adam's track record, it feels like something I have to ask.

"No, he drove. Packed up all his stuff and just...left."

I sigh. "I hope he's okay."

"Jace said some stuff," Freddie says, his voice softer now. "He's clearly going through some stuff with his marriage, but...it wasn't good, Laney. I doubt he meant everything that came out of his mouth. I have to hope he didn't. But I'm not surprised it made Adam run."

From the floor beside the bed, Goldie perks up, ears lifted as she stands and turns toward the door.

Voices sound on the stairs, my mom's, then a deeper one I immediately recognize.

"Freddie, I have to go. I'll call you back."

I hang up just seconds before my mom knocks once, then swings open my bedroom door. "Hey," she says, eyes wide. "You have a visitor."

Adam comes into the room, and Goldie rushes over to

him, tail wagging. He crouches down to greet her. When he stands and finally looks over at me, I have no idea what to say. How to act. Should I tell him Freddie called? Should I act like nothing happened?

No. I can't do that. I can't lie.

Behind Adam, Mom slowly closes the door, leaving us alone in my bedroom.

I swallow against the knot in my throat. "Adam, what happened?"

He doesn't say anything, he just moves across the room and drops onto the end of the bed, leaning forward so his elbows are propped on his knees.

"Did someone call you?" he eventually asks.

"Freddie. Just now. He didn't say much. Just that you… left."

He nods, but he doesn't look up. "Sorry to show up like this," he says.

I scoot closer on the bed and lift a hand to his shoulders. "It's fine. Of course it's fine. Actually…how did you find me?" He knew I was in Hendersonville, but I didn't give him an address.

He tilts his head toward Goldie. "She has an AirTag on her collar. I can trace it with my phone."

Huh. I guess that's one way to find me.

"I would have given you the address," I say.

"No, I know. I was just kind of in a panic and wasn't thinking right." He presses his forehead into the palm of his hand. "I'm still not thinking right, actually. I just came to pick up Goldie so I can go home."

My heart sinks. So he tracked Goldie instead of calling because he didn't come here to see me. He only came here for *her.*

When I don't respond, Adam finally looks over. I'm not sure what he can see on my face. Fear? Confusion? Uncertainty? Maybe all three? Whatever it is, it prompts him to reach over and pull me into a hug. I sink into his embrace, but there's a stiffness to it that feels different. He's hugging me because he realizes he should, but he isn't *present*. It feels like his mind is a million miles away.

When he leans back from the hug, he looks around the room, as if realizing where he is for the first time.

"This was your bedroom," he says, a statement, not a question, as his eyes move from one wall to the next.

A wave of embarrassment washes over me, which is silly. I've never hidden my fandom from Adam. I told him I wrote *fanfiction* and admitted to kissing his poster before I went to bed every night. Nothing in this room should surprise him.

Still, imagining what it must feel like for him to see it like this all at once, in all its pink and sparkly glory, makes me feel foolish in a way I never have before.

"I know it's a lot," I say.

"It's definitely *something*."

"I'm going to tell my mom she needs to redecorate," I say. "She can turn the room into an office or something."

He nods. "Good idea." His expression shifts the slightest bit. "Pack up the past for good."

His words give me pause. What does that mean? Pack up the past for good? And what on earth happened in the past twelve hours to shift his thinking so completely?

"Adam, please tell me what happened," I say.

He shakes his head. "I just need to get home. Clear my head."

I want to protest, to beg him to stay with me, but I would

be asking him to stay *for me,* and I'm not sure that's what he needs. It's definitely not what he *wants.*

So I swallow my protests and nod. "Okay. If you're sure you'll be okay."

"It's going to be better now," he says. "The drama, the attention. We won't have to deal with that anymore. No more feeling like spiders are crawling all over your skin."

Even though I've been stressing about the attention all day long, his words don't bring the relief I think he wants them to. Not if saying them means he's quitting.

But I know Adam well enough to realize we aren't going to get anywhere trying to have this conversation tonight, so when he stands and holds out his hand, I let him pull me to my feet, then I gather up Goldie's things.

Sophie and Mom stand side by side in the kitchen, backs to the refrigerator as we walk through to get Goldie's food and bowl. I load everything into the bag Adam packed it in this morning—was it really just this morning?—and hand it to him before crouching down to say goodbye to Goldie.

A beat of awkward silence passes before he takes a hesitant step toward the door. He pauses and looks over at my family. "Sorry to come and go like this," he says. "It's nice to meet you both."

Mom manages a tight smile and Sophie blinks and nods, but neither of them say anything.

I follow Adam to the front door and out to his SUV. He opens the back door for Goldie, who jumps right in, then turns to face me, hands tucked into his back pockets.

"When are you coming home?" he asks.

"Tomorrow? I think? I have to work on Monday."

Adam nods, then holds my gaze before lifting a hand to

my face. "Six seconds," he whispers, then he presses a lingering kiss to my lips.

As soon as he pulls back, he lets me go, then climbs into his car and drives off into the darkness.

I sigh and sink onto Mom's front stoop. His six-second goodbye kiss was a gift after everything else—a message that says he's still in this with me.

But I still don't like feeling so helpless. Whatever is hurting him, I want to help. I want to make this better for him.

I pull out my phone and text Freddie.

> LANEY
>
> Sorry to hang up so quickly. Adam actually showed up here.

> FREDDIE
>
> For real? Did you talk to him?

> LANEY
>
> Not really. He just wanted to pick up Goldie, and he definitely didn't want to talk.

> FREDDIE
>
> What do I do here, Laney?

I tap my phone against my palm. The problem is, I don't actually know the right move. On the one hand, I know how much Adam loves to sing, how important music is to him. But he shouldn't be forced to play more shows than he wants or feel manipulated because Freddie's agent seems to lack even a modicum of human decency.

Actually, maybe *that* is something Freddie can do.

I'm not sure I can suggest it. I only know of Kevin what Adam has told me, so I'm chasing a gut feeling more than anything. But Freddie *did* ask.

I close out my message thread with Freddie and find Ivy's contact.

> **LANEY**
>
> Hey. Honest reaction. Is Kevin a good person?

IVY

He's toxic on every level. Freddie is loyal by nature and assumes the best in people and thinks Kevin is great at contract negotiation. Which, fine. He's good at that one thing. But he only has dollar signs where he should have integrity.

Why?

> **LANEY**
>
> Just checking to see if my intuition was right.

IVY

Was it?

> **LANEY**
>
> Dead on.

I switch back to my message thread with Freddie, which has lengthened in the time I was talking to Ivy.

FREDDIE

I need you to believe me, Laney. I didn't trick Adam on purpose.

I really did think I could work all of this out.

I thought I had more time.

> **LANEY**
>
> I believe you.

> But Freddie, your agent is screwing you over, and now he's taking advantage of your friends.

> If you want to do something for Adam, start there.

It takes Freddie a very long time to reply and involves countless dots appearing and disappearing and reappearing before a single word pops up.

FREDDIE

> Noted.

A second message follows a few minutes later.

FREDDIE

> Watch out for him for me?

I drop my phone into my lap and lean forward, resting my elbows on my knees.

I would love nothing more than to watch out for Adam.

I just hope he'll let me.

CHAPTER TWENTY-FOUR

Laney

IF I WANTED SOMETHING TO GROUND ME BACK IN REALITY after a week hanging out with Midnight Rush, Fifi's anal glands will definitely do it.

I hold up the tiny chihuahua and look him dead in the eye. "You only exist to torture me," I say.

Fifi snarls in response and lets out a low growl. Honestly, I feel bad for the little guy. It must be so stressful to be so angry all the time.

"Talk about a rude welcome back to the real world," Percy says from behind me.

"Says the guy who just gave a cat a flea bath."

He holds up his arms. "And has the battle scars to prove it. I still wouldn't trade if it meant dealing with Fifi."

The rest of my afternoon is blissfully low key. I even get to leave an hour early due to a last-minute cancellation, so I'm home and showered and wearing leggings and my favorite hoodie by six o'clock.

I'm pulling the plastic off a freezer pizza when Percy knocks, then opens my front door. "I'm coming in!" he calls. I have no idea when we transitioned from regular friends to the kind of friends who let themselves into each other's houses, but here we are. "Don't put that in the oven," Percy says as he heaves a to-go bag onto the counter. "I brought Chinese."

"Have I told you how much I love you, Percy?"

"Not today, so tell me again."

"What's the occasion?" I ask as I pull containers out of the bag. "If you're here to make me talk about Adam, then I'm eating all the egg rolls *and* the crab rangoon without sharing."

Percy rolls his eyes. "Calm down. I have zero Adam-related agenda, though my opinions on the subject haven't changed."

I gave Percy a quick debriefing when he stopped by for coffee on the way to work this morning. At the time, I'd texted Adam, letting him know I was back in town, and I hadn't heard back from him yet.

Twelve hours later, nothing has changed. It's only been twenty-four hours, which doesn't seem *too* alarming?

Or, I don't know. Maybe it does. I don't have enough relationship experience to know one way or the other.

Adam probably just wanted time to regroup. For all I know, he's camping on the ridge behind the rescue, meditating and doing sunrise yoga every morning and will be in touch next week when he feels like rejoining civilization.

To be fair, I have no idea if Adam camps or does yoga or meditates. Which just goes to show: I barely know this man.

We had an intense week. An *amazing* week. But it's only

been a month since our first date. A month is a very tiny blip of time.

I want to see him. Talk to him. Hug him and ask him if he's okay.

But unless I'm going to strap on my hiking boots and go find him, I don't know what else to do but *wait*.

Percy, on the other hand, thinks I should be camped out on his porch demanding he talk to me.

"It hasn't even been twenty-four hours, Percy."

"Girl. You're in a relationship. Twenty-four hours is a long time to go without answering a text."

"I'm *barely* in a relationship that we never actually defined with any official labels," I say. But it's a lie. I am *absolutely* in a relationship with Adam. Heart, mind, body, all of it. I'm invested. I care. And it's killing me that he hasn't texted back yet.

"Can we please talk about something else now? What's going on with *you*?"

He points an eggroll at me and opens his mouth to respond, but then a knock sounds on my front door.

"You expecting company?"

I shrug and dig into my orange chicken. "It's probably the neighbor kid. She's saving up for a bike and keeps stopping by to ask if I have any yard work she can do. If I don't answer, she'll go away."

"You just ignore her?"

"Last time she was here, I paid her ten dollars to rake my mulch. You can't make me feel guilty about this."

He rolls his eyes and goes to answer the door.

When he comes back a minute later, his eyes are wide. "Definitely *not* your neighbor," he says under his breath.

I put down my fork, my skin prickling with awareness,

and point at Percy. "Don't say a word," I say to his knowing grin. "Not a single word."

When I round the corner into the living room, I stop in my tracks.

Adam is standing near the front door, looking handsome as ever. His hair looks a little shorter, and I wonder if he got it cut today, but his stubble is longer, not quite a beard, but close, making him more Adam and less Deke.

But it isn't Adam's hair or his beard that stops me. It's Ringo, sitting in Adam's arms with a big red bow around his neck.

"Oh my gosh," I whisper as Adam walks toward me, Ringo tucked closely against his chest. The hopeful look in Adam's eyes makes the anxiety coiled in my belly snap and dissipate.

"Hi, baby," I say as Adam lowers the puppy into my arms. "My sweet boy. I missed you!"

Ringo wiggles and squirms until his tiny paws are on my chest and he's licking my chin with a determination only matched by his enthusiasm.

"If you aren't ready for him, I can take him back," Adam says. "Keep him until—"

"No, this is perfect," I say. "I'm ready."

Adam lets out a breath as he nods. "Good. I'm really glad." He looks over my shoulder, then clears his throat. "I, uh...sorry for interrupting your evening."

I look over my shoulder to see Percy leaning against the kitchen door frame, arms folded across his chest. "Don't apologize," Percy says. "We're just hanging out. There's plenty of food if you're hungry."

"Thanks, but I have an early morning tomorrow," Adam says. "And still lots to do at the rescue beforehand."

I frown at the thought of Adam leaving so soon. Now that he's standing in front of me, I feel an intense need to wrap my arms around him, to breathe him in and hold him close, but I still have no idea what's going on inside his head, so I settle for hugging Ringo a little tighter. And shooting Percy a glare that says he'd better get back in the kitchen.

If I only have minutes before Adam leaves, I'd rather they not happen with Percy watching.

Percy must get the hint because he heads back to the kitchen after offering Adam a wave and a, "Nice to see you, Adam."

"How are you?" I ask once we're alone.

Adam's expression shifts the slightest bit, like he just pulled a layer of protection around himself. "Good. Great."

"Really?"

"Yeah. Things have been really busy at the rescue, so I'm tackling paperwork, trying to get caught up. I'm actually heading to Georgia first thing tomorrow to pick up five new dogs from a kill shelter in Rabun County."

I have no idea what's happening here. Adam is talking like everything is fine. Like last week didn't happen at all and there's nothing for us to discuss.

But I was *there.*

We can't pretend like nothing happened if we were both *there.*

But I don't know how to say any of that, so I just nod and say, "Lucky dogs."

"That's what I'm doing tonight, actually. Cleaning the barn. Getting everything ready for intake. Otherwise, I'd love to stay."

There is a warmth to his words that tells me they're true, and it helps to soothe my still slightly anxious heart. But something still isn't right. He's here and he's fine and he's happy, but there is a giant boyband-shaped elephant standing directly between us.

"I should be back by midafternoon tomorrow," Adam says. "Do you want to come over for dinner? I'll cook, then we can watch a movie, maybe?"

Adam asking me to come over is a good thing. Of course it's a good thing. So why doesn't it *feel* like it?

I must be wearing my feelings on my face because Adam frowns.

"Or...maybe you don't want to come over?" he says.

"No!" I say quickly. "I would love to come. That's not it. I just..." I bite my lip, hesitating. "Are we just going to pretend like last week didn't happen?"

"I don't understand what you mean."

Okay, what? Am I being an idiot here?

"Adam. The stuff with the band. With *you*. The last time I saw you, you were not okay."

He lifts his shoulders in an easy shrug, looking perfectly unbelievably indifferent. "It happened. I changed my mind. I'm moving on. It's not a big deal."

"Did you talk to Freddie?"

He sighs and moves a hand to the back of his neck. "I appreciate that you're concerned, but it's not an issue. It isn't something you need to worry about."

It very much feels like something I need to worry about, because more and more, *he* is someone I worry about, and I'm pretty sure he's lying.

And not just to me. To himself.

"What about the engagement? People have been asking questions all day."

"Just tell people the truth. We're dating, but the media

turned it into something it wasn't. Since I won't be at the concert, it won't take long for people to forget they care."

So that's it then? We're really just forgetting any of it ever happened?

Adam tilts his head toward the door. "Want to walk me out? I have a few things for Ringo in the car."

I don't want him to go without talking about this, but I also don't want to *make* him talk. So I just say, "Sure," and follow him outside.

He opens the hatch of his SUV and pulls out a tote bag stitched with the Hope Acres rescue logo.

He holds it open. "Food, his favorite toy, new collar, new leash." He loops the bag over his shoulder and turns back to his car and slides a smallish dog crate forward. "Plus the crate he's been using—Sarah started him on his crate training last week—and another bed he's been using for spot training." He pulls a dog bed forward and sets it on top of the crate.

"You give all of this to every person who adopts?"

He shrugs, his expression sheepish. "I hate the idea of people starting out at a disadvantage because they can't cover the basics."

"Adam. This is way more than what your adoption fee covers."

"It's not a big deal. The rescue has the funds to cover it." He makes quick work of unloading everything and leaving it on my front porch right by the door. "Thank you," I say. "This will definitely make things easier."

"No problem." He reaches forward and scratches Ringo's ears. "He's been such an easy puppy. I don't think he'll give you any trouble."

"Can I bring him with me tomorrow night?"

"Sure. He can hang out with Goldie. Come over at seven?"

"Okay."

Adam steps closer and settles his hands on either side of my waist, gently tugging me against his chest, Ringo perched between us.

"It's good to see you," he says.

I look up to meet his eyes, and he bends down, pausing for the briefest second before pressing his mouth to mine in a lingering kiss. His lips are soft and warm and intoxicating, and I feel myself leaning in, forgetting my earlier anxiety because *gah,* it feels so good, so *right* to be in his arms like this. We hit six seconds and keep kissing, melting my fears and worries one by one.

Adam lifts a hand to my cheek, brushing his thumb over my jaw and triggering a wave of goosebumps across my skin.

"See you tomorrow?" he says, his voice low.

I nod. "I'll be there."

Five minutes later, Percy finds me in the living room, sitting stone still on the couch, Ringo curled up on my lap.

"What happened to you?" he says. "I didn't even hear you come back in."

"Adam brought me my puppy," I say.

"I see that."

"And he kissed me and invited me over for dinner tomorrow night."

"Okay, and why don't we sound happy about that?" He drops into the chair across from me and pulls a yellow-fringed throw pillow onto his lap.

"I *am* happy about that, but also...I don't know. I'm worried about him."

"Why?"

"Because he clearly doesn't want to talk about what happened with the band. It's like he just locked it all up inside. He said he changed his mind, but I don't know, Percy. I think he's hiding from how he really feels."

"Which is how? What do you think he's feeling that he isn't saying?" Percy asks.

"I think he wants to sing," I say.

Percy leans forward, his brow furrowed. "Okay. But does that mean he *has* to do the concert? Because Freddie's agent sounds pretty terrible."

"His agent *is* terrible. But Midnight Rush isn't. I saw them together. I just hate the idea of him throwing everything away."

"Are you sure that's what he's doing?"

"I'm not sure about anything. I only know what Freddie told me, because Adam won't talk to me about it."

"Okay. New question." Percy says. "Are you sure you don't just want him to do the concert because then you'd get to be *Deke's* girlfriend?"

"One thousand percent—that is *not* it," I say. "I would never pressure him into something like this for my sake. Honestly, it's the opposite. My life would be easier if I didn't have to share Adam with the world. I would love not to worry about stupid *TMZ* articles and TikTok videos."

"I can't blame you there," Percy says. "The comment section on that one video was brutal."

"What? Are you for real?"

Percy's eyes widen. "No! I was just...guessing that it might be. I didn't see anything."

"Percy."

He winces. "Fine. Yes. Definitely don't read the comments."

I groan, and Ringo lets out a tiny bark.

Stupid Kevin.

Stupid jerkface Kevin who ruined everything.

"Maybe it really is for the better," Percy says. "You and Adam could have a good life in Lawson Cove. Without having to deal with all of that mess." He reaches over and scoops Ringo from my lap. "Now give me this cute baby." He leans back in his chair and plops the puppy on his chest. "I'm going to be a very good friend and hold this precious puppy while you finish your dinner."

I think about Percy's words for the rest of the night. While I'm eating. While Percy tells me about a cute new administrator at Shady Pines named Jamal. While we watch two episodes of *Schitt's Creek* and cry through the "Simply the Best" episode.

By the time Percy goes home and I'm standing in the front yard waiting for Ringo to pee for the fifteenth time, I'm almost convinced.

Maybe I can just let it go.

Maybe I can have a relationship with Adam, and it will be enough.

Maybe we can both forget that once upon a time, he was in a boyband.

CHAPTER TWENTY-FIVE

Adam

IT'S BEEN A WHILE SINCE I'VE MADE A MEAL THIS EXTENSIVE.

Short ribs. Roasted carrots. Homemade angel biscuits. But I'm going for broke tonight.

Last week was more like a fantasy than real life. Laney and I were together almost nonstop. Even when I was doing stuff with the band, she was right there on the sidelines, watching, cheering me on.

But that *isn't* what my life is like normally.

And I want her to know that *this* life, my Lawson Cove life, is good too.

It's stupid to think that I'm in competition with myself, but her childhood bedroom made it clear how much she loves Deke. I don't want her to be disappointed that she's dating Adam instead, because I can't be Deke.

Not anymore. Not ever again.

I spent a long time up on the ridge over the weekend,

avoiding the ravine that practically killed me, and thinking through everything that happened over the past week.

One thing became perfectly clear.

I never should have gone back. Never should have said yes to Freddie in the first place.

In the weeks right before my mom died, she called me every day.

And every day, she told me how much she wanted to see me. I hadn't been home in months, but I was in Europe on tour, and we had shows too frequently for me to just jump on a plane and leave.

I couldn't go see her without disrupting the entire tour.

So I didn't go.

I listened to her tell me she was dying, and I convinced myself I had time.

I let *Kevin* convince me I had time. I prioritized money and fame and fan expectations over my own life—over my *mother's* life.

And I disappointed the one person who deserved it least.

I missed years that I could have spent with her so I could sing for everyone else.

It doesn't matter how much I loved making music then or how much I love making it now.

I won't make the same mistake again.

Which is why I have to make *this life* really count.

Laney knocks on the door right on time, and she looks *beautiful*. Casual, in jeans and a soft green sweater that's loose and hanging off one shoulder.

I feel a sudden impulse to *kiss* that shoulder, to press my lips to the hollow right above her collarbone and breathe in the scent of her.

Fortunately, I'm not an animal lacking all self-control, so I say hello instead.

"You look amazing," I add. "Thanks for coming."

Ringo is at her feet, holding his sit like a very good boy, and I lean down to give him a treat.

"Did you seriously just pull a random dog treat out of your pocket?" Laney asks as she comes inside.

"Hazards of the job," I say. "Are you hungry?"

"Hungrier now. It smells amazing." She takes Ringo off his leash, and he runs into the living room where Goldie is lounging on her dog bed.

Laney steps close, one hand lifting to my shoulder as she leans up and kisses me, lingering just long enough for this to be *more* than a hello kiss.

"You look good too," she says, her voice soft. "Now feed me. I'm hungry enough to eat my arm."

Heat spreads through my chest and something like relief washes over me. I worried it would be weird tonight, that we might not find our footing after everything that's happened.

Seeing her last night helped, but this—this gives me the hope I need.

We're going to be okay.

And we *are* okay.

Dinner is easy. The short ribs turned out perfectly, the wine compliments the meal just like I hoped it would, and the yeasted angel biscuits are the best batch I've ever made. By the end of the meal, I'm buzzed on good conversation and good wine and a growing certainty that this is exactly what I want my life to be.

There may still be a niggling sense of doubt at the back of my mind.

But it's only a matter of time. The doubts will fade.

They did before. They will again.

"Okay. You have to tell me where you learned to cook like this," Laney says as she helps herself to a second serving of white cheddar grits. "I've never thought about serving short ribs over grits, but this is unbelievable." She cocks her head to the side. "Actually, I've never made short ribs. But if I *had*, this combination wouldn't have occurred to me."

"Mom taught me the basics," I say as I grab another biscuit. "But I mostly learned through trial and error. When we were still living together in Knoxville, Sarah would do all the shopping, so I did all the cooking."

"Did either of you go to college?" Laney asks.

Her question is curious, but not judgmental, so it's easy to answer honestly. "Sarah has a marketing degree she did online. But I didn't. At the time, it felt too risky to put myself out there in such a public way."

She puts her fork down on top of her empty plate and slides it forward. "That must have been a weird time. Right after. What did you do to stay busy?"

"I cooked," I say. "I taught myself how to play guitar. I worked out a lot."

"The muscles are finally explained," she says through a grin. "And Sarah was with you the whole time?"

"She spent three months in foster care right after Mom died, but as soon as she was eighteen, she moved in with me, and we were together until we moved here and she wanted to get her own place."

"You were just kids," Laney says. "I can't imagine living on my own at eighteen. I mean, college didn't really count for me because my parents still gave me so much support."

"We definitely floundered for a while. But we figured it out. Mostly thanks to Sarah. She did pretty much everything that required face-to-face interaction. Attorneys, real-estate agents. She handled it all."

"Sarah was a big part of why you left in the first place, wasn't she?" Laney says. "With your mom gone, you only had each other."

I stand and grab our empty plates, then carry them into the kitchen. "Yeah. She was."

Laney follows me into the kitchen with the platter of short ribs and sets it on the counter. She holds the sides of the platter for a long moment without moving, her face pensive.

"You okay?" I ask.

"Yeah," she says, but then she turns away. "I'm gonna go check on Ringo."

She disappears into the living room while I finish clearing the table and top off our wine glasses. When I go in search of her, the dogs are alone in the living room. Ringo is conked out in the center of Goldie's bed while Goldie is stretched out on the floor, giving me a look like I should be proud of how patient she's being with her guest.

I finally find Laney in the music room, standing beside the piano, her eyes fixed on the empty bookshelf in front of her.

Two boxes sit on the floor, both filled with music.

I hold out her wine glass, but she shakes her head, so I set it on the back of the piano.

"Adam, what are you doing?" she asks, and I breathe out a sigh.

"What does it look like?"

She huffs. "*Why* are you packing up all your music? Where are your guitars?"

"Put away."

"Why?" she repeats.

I drain my wine and walk back to the kitchen, but she follows after me. "Please answer my question." The pleading tone of her voice makes my heart tighten painfully.

I don't want to argue with her about this, but there's only one way I can answer her question, and she isn't going to like it.

I turn and lean against the counter, hands pushed into my pockets. "Because I'm not going to play anymore."

"Why?" she says, her voice practically a whisper.

"Because it's not worth it."

"That doesn't make any sense."

"It makes sense to me," I say.

She shakes her head and steps toward me. "Adam, if we're going to be together, then I need to understand how you're feeling. Explain it to me."

I lift a hand to the back of my neck. "There's nothing to explain. I just don't want to sing anymore."

"I don't believe you," she quickly says. "Do you know what I listened to on the way over tonight? I listened to 'The Start of Forever.' The version you did in the studio, and Adam, I've never heard anything like it."

I close my eyes. I worked hard over the last few days to construct a reality in my mind where all of this was going to be okay. I still have Hope Acres, I still have Laney, my life can still be everything I want it to be *without* Midnight Rush.

But I must have been building with popsicle sticks and Elmer's glue, because that reality is crumbling now, my control crumbling right along with it.

"How did you even hear it?" I ask darkly, but even as I ask the question, I know the answer. It was Freddie who called her the night I left Silver Creek. It was probably Freddie who sent it to her.

Sure enough, she crosses her arms over her chest and says, "Freddie sent it to me."

I don't know why it irritates me—probably for stupid and irrational reasons that have everything to do with my heightened emotional state—but arguing about this would be easier than arguing about why I'm not going to sing anymore, so I dig in.

"Freddie, huh?"

It's mean and spiteful to even imply she's texting Freddie for anything but the most benign reasons. I don't mean it at all, but the only part of my brain that's functioning right now is the part that wants this conversation to end.

Laney's jaw clenches the slightest bit, but then her gaze softens. "Don't do that," she says gently. *Too* gently. "Don't sabotage this conversation by accusing me of something you know full well would never be true. Freddie only texts *me* because he's concerned about *you*. He sent me the song because he knows how I feel about *you*."

"I'm not sabotaging anything."

"You are," she snaps back. "And I think you're doing it because you don't want to be honest with me."

"Honest about what? What do you want to know? You asked me where I put my guitars. I told you I put them up. I told you I'm not going to sing anymore. I'm being honest about that."

"But you aren't being honest about why."

"Why doesn't matter."

"Of course it matters," she says.

She doesn't get it. She *can't* get it.

"Adam, I want you to answer one question...not unlike the one you asked me."

I lift my eyes to meet hers, hands propped on my hips.

"If you took away everything else. Kevin. Your mom's death. All of it. All the conditions and circumstances and crappy things that have happened in your life. Take it all away."

She pauses and tucks a strand of hair behind her ear. Her hand is trembling, and I have to clench my hands into fists to keep from going to her, pulling her against my chest.

"What would you do with your life?" she finishes. "Would you sing?"

Yes.

I don't even have to think about the answer. It's just there, solid and certain in my mind. Not that it matters. There's no point in even asking the question because I *can't* change what happened. I can't fix what I screwed up. I can't bring my mom back.

"It doesn't matter," I say.

"What you want always matters," she says.

I grip the edge of the counter. "What *I* want? The last three months of my mother's life, she called and called and begged for me to come home. That's what she wanted. And I didn't do it. There was too much at stake. I couldn't risk the tour. My contract wouldn't allow it. And a dozen other BS reasons Kevin gave me. I hadn't seen my mother in over a year. And then she died."

Laney's eyes close, her voice quivering as she asks, "You didn't get to see her?"

My shoulders drop, some of the fire draining out of me. There's been an ache in my chest for eight years, right between my ribs. Sometimes it dulls to the point that I can forget it's there, but it only takes a word, a look, a random thought for it to flare to life, reminding me all over again what I've lost.

The ache is more like a volcano right now, hot pulsing pain, but it eases the slightest bit for having been spoken out loud. For having admitted things—feelings—that I've never admitted to anyone else. "I was on stage in London when she died."

Laney holds my gaze for a long moment before she crosses the kitchen and wraps her arms around my waist, squeezing until I lift my arms and let them fall around her shoulders. Her hands slide up and down my back for a solid minute, maybe two, while we just stand there.

I breathe in the scent of her hair, savor the feel of her pressed against me. But even this feels like too much. She shouldn't be here with me. I thought I could compartmentalize, build a life apart from my past.

But then I let Freddie in, and it ruined everything.

Maybe it's going to ruin this, too.

"Laney, I can't sing anymore because I stood on my mother's grave and promised her I wouldn't. I can't because after what I did, after the way I disappointed her, I don't deserve the chance. I don't deserve any of it."

CHAPTER TWENTY-SIX

Laney

ADAM HOLDS ONTO ME FOR A LONG MOMENT AFTER HE SAYS the words, then he presses a kiss to my temple, murmurs an "I'm sorry" into my hair, and turns and walks out the back door.

I know, instinctively, that I shouldn't follow him. Adam has shown me that he needs solitude and time to process his emotions, and I get the sense he just admitted something to me that he's never admitted to anyone before.

So I let him go.

When he's halfway across the field beside the barn, I call Goldie and send her outside after him, watching until she reaches his side, and his hand falls to her head.

At least he won't be completely alone.

It feels wrong to just leave, and I cling to the hope that Adam might return, so I do the dinner dishes while I wait. I package up the leftovers and put them in the fridge. I load the dishwasher. I hand wash our wine glasses and leave them on the counter to dry.

But that only takes twenty minutes, and there's still no sign of Adam.

I don't know what else to do but leave, so I scoop Ringo up from where he's been sniffing at my feet and go home.

There are so many things I want to say to Adam.

Starting with I love you.

That became perfectly clear when we were standing in his kitchen, and I wished with my whole entire soul that I could hug the hurt right out of him.

But I also want to tell him he's wrong—that he deserves every happiness. I recognize why he blames himself, but he was just a kid. A kid dealing with a lot of pressure, surrounded by a lot of adults who did not have his best interest at heart. If I were making the call, I would lay the blame squarely at Kevin's feet. But I'm not the one who lost my mom, so my feelings aren't nearly as tangled as Adam's.

When I get home, I send Adam a text asking him to let me know when he gets home safe.

I type out and delete a hundred more messages, but it doesn't feel right to send any of them. Adam doesn't need *my* reassurances, he needs his mom's. And I can't give him that. No one can.

An hour later, Adam finally responds.

ADAM
Home safe.

A few minutes later, another pops up.

ADAM
Thank you, Laney.

LANEY

Thank you for telling me.

I'm here, okay? Whatever you need.

I send the message hoping he'll respond, but nothing comes through.

So I wait.

And wait.

Tuesday night turns into Wednesday, then bleeds into Thursday, and soon, it's the weekend, I haven't talked to Adam in five horrible days, and I'm beginning to think I might completely lose my mind.

Right before Adam walked out of his kitchen, when he said he didn't think he deserved *any of it,* I assumed he was talking about fame. But the longer we go without talking, the more I'm starting to wonder if he was also talking about *me.*

If he's convinced himself that his past actions somehow negate him from experiencing *any* happiness.

It doesn't make any sense. But grief doesn't always play by the rules. And while I'm definitely not an expert on these things, I'm pretty sure Adam is still grieving.

Percy is over, and we've just finished Saturday morning yoga at my neighbor's studio, but I'm about as zen as a sugar-hyped preschooler in Chuck E. Cheese. I can't relax. Can't focus on anything but my all-consuming worry for Adam.

I've texted him two more times in the past week. Once to send a picture of Ringo, who, as fully expected, is the sweetest boy on the planet. And a second time to ask him if he's doing okay.

He hearted the photo of Ringo, but he didn't answer my question.

Finally, on Thursday, I texted Sarah just to make sure he

was still alive and eating and taking care of himself, but she couldn't offer much by way of encouragement. She'd been out of town since Sunday visiting a friend in Tennessee and won't be back until Friday morning.

She could at least guarantee he was alive because they'd texted multiple times about rescue business, but he hadn't mentioned our conversation at all.

"Are you googling Midnight Rush again?" Percy asks from the couch beside me.

"Obsessively," I answer, not even trying to hide my phone.

When Freddie texted me the final cut of "The Start of Forever," we texted back and forth enough for me to know they have no choice but to go forward with the concert in Nashville, as well as the two in Los Angeles and Chicago, even without Adam, and promotion is in full swing.

It's possible reading every scrap of news is my coping mechanism for *not* talking to Adam.

Freddie, Leo, and Jace have all made individual appearances on various talk shows, but so far, they haven't made any together, a strategy that likely has everything to do with Adam's absence. Ticket sales open any day now, so I'm surprised they still haven't mentioned that Adam won't be there. That feels like something fans need to know before they decide to go. But knowing Freddie and his perpetual optimism, he's likely hoping Adam will change his mind.

I've been careful not to let my love for Midnight Rush influence my feelings, but I can't help but wish for the same thing.

Especially when I listen to "The Start of Forever."

The song sounds like Midnight Rush, but better. Mature. Grounded, somehow. And Adam's voice—it was amazing when he was singing around the fire, smiling at me whenever he caught my eye. But on the track, the rich tone of his voice comes through loud and clear.

According to Freddie, they won't keep the song in the setlist without Adam, and they won't release it, either. I recognize Freddie trying to do the right thing, and it means a lot. But it still kills me to think that no one will ever hear this song but me.

"Anything new?" Percy asks.

"Freddie was on Jimmy Kimmel," I say. "But that's it."

"It's starting to look funny that they aren't doing any appearances together," Percy says, and I breathe out a sigh.

"I know."

"I'm not saying I blame him. But shouldn't the three of them at least show up somewhere?"

"Unfortunately, no one is consulting *me* about their marketing decisions," I say. I toss my phone onto the coffee table and groan, tossing my arms over my face. "Yoga didn't work, Percy. I don't know what to do."

Percy's quiet for a second before he says, "Laney, just go over there."

I drop my hands and look at him. "To the rescue?"

"No, to the auto parts store."

"What? Why would I go—"

"Of course to the rescue," he says, cutting me off. "Go see him. Be there for him."

I shake my head. "I don't know how."

"Nobody *ever* knows how. Sometimes we just have to act. Are you in love with him?"

I don't even hesitate before nodding my head yes.

"Then go tell him," Percy says. "Make him talk to you."

I'm tempted. *Really* tempted.

But then Sarah shows up on my front porch.

"Oh good, you're here," she says when I open my front door. "We definitely need to talk."

I invite Percy to stay—he's earned the right with how much he's listened to my whining all week—and the three of us settle in my living room, Percy and me on the couch, and Sarah in the chair across from us.

"Okay, things are bad," Sarah says. "I didn't know just how bad until I got home, but yeah. It's not good."

She goes down a list, checking things off on her fingers while she talks. The music room is totally packed up now, guitars gone and piano closed up. His hygiene is suffering—he smells worse than the kennels on cleanout day—and the house is a mess. Only the dogs are in good shape, because Adam has apparently thrown himself into running the rescue with single-minded determination.

When Sarah finishes, I give them a rundown of the last conversation Adam and I had, sharing everything but what he said right before he left. That feels too personal to repeat, but I don't have to, because Sarah seems to understand exactly how her brother feels.

"He blamed himself," she says. "And honestly, I blamed him too. At least, at first. I felt like he left me to handle everything on my own, but that's not really fair, because he was the only reason Mom still had her house. She couldn't work for the last two years of her life, so we had no other income but Adam's. Midnight Rush might have kept him from us, but it also sustained us."

"Which is a hard burden to carry when you're only eighteen," Percy says, and Sarah nods.

"It's always been Adam's nature to take care of people. Which is amazing. But I'm sure he felt a lot of pressure. And

Kevin—I didn't realize how terrible he was until I interacted with him at Mom's funeral. With Kevin pushing the way he did, it's a wonder Adam didn't crack sooner. He was juggling a lot of people's expectations." She breathes out a sniffly sigh. "All that to say, I forgave him a long time ago for not being there when Mom died. But I don't think he's ever forgiven himself."

"How did your mom feel about Adam being in Midnight Rush?" I ask.

Sarah wrinkles her forehead as she thinks. "I mean, she missed him. And there at the end, I think she was concerned *for him*. About how he would feel if he didn't see her before she..." Her words trail off, and she lifts her hand to a silver flower pendant hanging around her neck. "But I know she was proud of him. She actually moderated a fan group on Friendly Fans so she could talk about the band. The group was small, only like a hundred people or something, but they had their own fan name, and they had watch parties for media appearances, stuff like that. No one knew she was Adam's mom, but she liked being in charge because then she could keep it a safe space where stuff stayed age-appropriate, and it gave *her* a place to talk about what Adam was up to with people who were as excited as she was. She tried to get me involved a few times, but I was a teenager and thought people fangirling over my brother was weird, so I was never very interested." Sarah lets out a little chuckle. "Gosh, I haven't thought about that in so long. I'm not even sure I ever told Adam about it."

"Wait, wait," I say, sitting up a little taller. "Do you remember what the group's name was? Was it the Night Riders?"

My heart is in my throat, because *I* was in that group.

And the moderator was amazing. She was basically like a mom to all of us. Giving us advice on high school and boys and friends. I mean, there were *a lot* of Midnight Rush groups on Friendly Fans. The whole point of the website was to create small communities within a larger one to foster friendships and more personal connections. But what are the odds the random group I was in was the same one Adam's mother ran?

"I don't remember," Sarah says. "It definitely could have been."

"What about your mom's username?"

"Are you thinking you were in her group or something?" Percy says.

"I might have been."

Sarah sits up a little taller, brow furrowed. "I don't know it off the top of my head, but I can guess. My mom's name was Dahlia, but she was just Dolly to her friends, because of how much she loved Dolly Parton. Probably something with Dolly in it?"

I shake my head and start to laugh. "Something like DollyDaeDreams? But day was spelled differently. D-A-E."

Sarah grins. "Dae was Mom's middle name. So you *were* in her group?"

"We talked all the time," I say. "She gave me some of the best advice when I was dealing with my parents' divorce. And she had this thing she always said..." I close my eyes trying to remember. "Something about worry."

"All worry does is give a small thing a big shadow," Sarah says.

"Yes! That's it!"

Tears spring into Sarah's eyes. "I don't know why that makes me so emotional, to think you got to know her."

It makes *me* emotional, too.

I knew Adam's mom.

We may not have met in person, but for almost three years, we chatted multiple times a week. Even today, I can hardly think of Midnight Rush without thinking of Dolly-DaeDreams. It's incredibly surreal to think that I knew her then, and I know Adam now.

Like somehow, this was always meant to happen. We were always meant to be together.

"She was amazing," I say to Sarah. "Truly. She was like a second mom. Half the time, we weren't even talking about Midnight Rush. She was just checking in on us. Making sure everyone was okay. She always seemed to know what the band was up to, which makes so much sense now, so we relied on her to keep us in the loop. She made the group what it was."

Sarah shakes her head. "I had no idea her group actually mattered to people. I always thought it was kind of silly."

"Parts of it were silly," I say. "But she made a real difference in my life."

Sarah wipes at her eyes. "If I had no idea, then Adam *definitely* had no idea. He would love this though. It would probably mean so much for him to see what Mom was doing. Is the website still up?"

"Not anymore, but that might not matter." I stand and pace across the room, hands propped on my hips as an idea hatches in my brain. If Adam's mother had been disappointed in him, she wouldn't have run a fan group for his band. She wouldn't have posted pictures and talked about his music and mentored his fans.

In Adam's mind, his mother only looked at him through one lens. But if we can show him a different one, if we can show him how much she supported him in the only way her illness allowed, maybe he'll change his mind.

I turn and look at my friends.

"Who's in the mood for a road trip?" I say. "I know how to help Adam, but we've gotta drive to do it."

FOUR HOURS LATER, after Percy calls Mimi and reschedules a visit and Sarah delays her afternoon date with Jake and Ringo pees on my hoodie, then again on my shoe, the three of us, four including my very naughty puppy, pull into the driveway of my mom's house in Hendersonville.

"I'm just warning you," I say as we climb out of the car. "My bedroom might scare you a little. Mom hasn't changed it at all, so just...prepare yourself for a lot of Midnight Rush."

"Please tell me you had one of those sequin face pillows," Percy says. "I love those things."

I unlock my mom's front door with the same key that's been on my keychain since I lived here in high school. She and Sophie are shopping in Asheville this afternoon, so they aren't around, but honestly, it's probably better this way. I don't want to waste time visiting when what I really want to do is grab what I need, then race back to Lawson Cove to see Adam.

"One for every member of the band," I answer. "But only Deke's pillow lived on my bed."

"Gross," Sarah says.

"Trust me, the pillow should be the least of your concerns."

I leave them gawking at the sheer number of times Deke's face adorns my bedroom walls while I dig into my closet, pulling three enormous scrapbooks from the top shelf. I cough from the dust I disturb and cover my mouth as I use the sleeve of my hoodie to wipe them off.

"I might have underestimated the extent of your fandom," Percy says as I drop the books on the bed.

"Don't judge," I say. "I turned out normal."

Percy lifts an eyebrow. "Can we compromise and say normal-ish?"

I scowl in his direction. "The only reason I'm not elbowing you in the ribs right now is because you're holding my dog."

Sarah is already flipping through the first scrapbook. An enormous Midnight Rush band logo in navy blue and yellow is stuck to the front cover as well as the words, written in my lovely teenage handwriting, *Year One*. Inside, we find everything you might expect. Pictures of the band. Tour schedules. Magazine spreads. But it's more than that, too. It's a history of the Night Riders fan group. It's printed out screenshots of our conversations. Copies of the photos we all uploaded of our matching Midnight Rush socks. Concert photos people shared. Lists of our favorite songs. Our favorite song lyrics.

Dolly's comments show up a lot, and I watch as Sarah runs her fingers over each one as she reads.

@DollyDaeDreams: Just listened to the new single. Did anyone else notice how much stronger their vocals are on this one? They're all getting better, but Deke especially seems to be coming into his own.

@DollyDaeDreams: Just read the article in People magazine, and I'm just saying, I think the reporter could have

been a little more gracious when he talked about what happened outside the arena on Friday night. These boys are working so hard. They don't need judgment and criticism. They need homemade soup and chocolate chip cookies and a night off.

"Was this about the fans who complained when the guys wouldn't get off the tour bus to say hello?" Sarah asks.

"Sounds like it," I say, reading over her shoulder.

@DollyDaeDreams: Thought you all might like to see a photo from backstage at the Chicago show. Was anyone there? I would love to hear all about it if you were!

"She asked about concerts a lot," I say. "I remember that specifically. She wanted to know everything. What the vibe was like. How fans reacted." I look at Sarah. "Did she ever get to see him perform?"

Sarah shakes her head. "Not in person. She was always too sick. She'd already started chemo by the time Midnight Rush was a thing, and she couldn't handle the crowds. Her immune system was too weak."

We spend a few more minutes reading through the entries in the first book. If I were Sarah, I would want to sit here all night just reading her mother's words. But I'm also anxious to get these to Adam.

I don't know much about what it feels like to be a mom. But I do know what it feels like to love someone. And I'd be willing to bet everything that Adam's mom loved him just as much as he loved her. That she was *so proud* of him.

Maybe it won't do any good. Maybe he still won't want to sing.

And I'll have to be okay with that.

But Adam deserves to know how his mom really felt.

And he has to know that whether he thinks he deserves it or not, I'm not going anywhere. Maybe I've always taken the path of least resistance, made the choices that are safe and practical. But Adam is worth fighting for. I'm not giving up.

And I'm not letting him give up either.

CHAPTER TWENTY-SEVEN

Adam

DOLLY IS NOT GOING TO BE ADOPTED THROUGH HOPE ACRES.

I think I probably knew when I named the chocolate lab who was dumped at Laney's office that she would end up being mine. Sarah picked her up and got her settled while I was in Silver Creek. But as soon as I found her in the barn, I brought her inside, and she's been my shadow ever since.

Goldie took to her right away. She seems content to let the younger dog do the heavy lifting of keeping me company while she stretches out on the porch in the patches of fall sunshine filtering through the trees.

Dolly's energy has been good for me. She's always up for a walk to the ridgeline or a game of fetch—she'll bring a ball back five hundred times if I'll throw it for her.

But by Saturday night, a week after I walked out on Midnight Rush for the second time, five days after I last saw Laney, even Dolly can't pull me out of my funk.

I realize that *I* am the problem here. I am the one who

hasn't texted Laney back. I'm the one who has thrown myself into work, ignored Freddie's texts, ignored Jace's apology.

If someone were to type in my story to one of those "Am I the Asshole" threads on Reddit, where strangers get to weigh in on your behavior, I have no doubt the answer would be *yes: YTA.*

I turned my back on my friends.

I'm ignoring my girlfriend.

I'm hiding from everyone.

But every time I think about responding, about texting, about reaching out myself, I feel sick. Like there's something physically restraining me, filling me with this overwhelming sense of dread.

Somewhere in the logical part of my brain, I know that I need to move past this. That hiding from everyone who is important to me isn't the answer.

I have also begun to doubt that hiding from *music* is the answer.

When Freddie sent over the final cut of "The Start of Forever," I couldn't believe how good it sounded. That is a song I would *love* to release.

I just don't know how.

Probably therapy.

A knock sounds on my door, and Dolly stands, ears perking up as she looks at me, like she's asking if this is something that should alarm her.

I don't feel alarm—but I do feel hope. It feels shameful to admit it after how I've been acting, but I really want Laney to be standing on my porch.

It *is* Laney, and as soon as I open the door, it's all I can do not to immediately pull her into my arms. I have no idea how I walked away from her on Tuesday night, but I never want to walk away from her again. This feeling—it's not just a craving. It's a *need*, deep in my bones.

For a long moment, I just stand there, taking her in. There's an uncertainty to her posture, like she's unsure of how I will respond to her being here. But there's a determination in her eyes that makes up for it, like she has a purpose and she's prepared to hold her ground.

"Hey," I finally say.

"Hey. Can I come in?"

"Of course." I step back, making room for her to pass me, then I close the door behind her and follow her into the living room.

She pauses when she sees Dolly stretched out next to Goldie in front of the fireplace. "You're keeping her," she says.

"Yeah."

She smiles at Dolly as she crouches down to say hello. "That's why you named her Dolly," she says. "You already knew she'd wind up being yours."

I narrow my eyes at Laney. It's too early in our relationship for her to be reading my mind.

She sets a Lawson Cove Library tote bag on the coffee table and nudges it toward me. "These are for you. But I need to tell you about them first."

I still have no idea what's in the bag, but I let Laney tug me onto the couch anyway. We're sitting side by side, knees angled in so we can still face each other.

Laney reaches over and takes both of my hands in hers.

"This is going to sound a little absurd, so brace yourself," she says, "but this morning, Sarah and I figured out that I knew your mom."

I frown. "You—*what*?"

"Not in person," she quickly qualifies. "But I knew her online. She moderated a fan group that I was a part of, and we talked all the time. Weekly, at least, sometimes even daily. I didn't know she was your mom, obviously, but I do remember how much she loved Midnight Rush."

I don't even know how to begin to process what she's telling me. Laney knowing my mother is hard enough. But Mom moderating a fan group? I had no idea she ever did *anything* like that.

"Are you sure?" I ask, because how do you even figure out something like that?

"Absolutely sure," Laney says. "Your mom's username was @DollyDaeDreams. Dae, spelled D-A-E."

"Her middle name," I say, and Laney nods.

"And it was what? A fan group?"

I listen closely as Laney walks me through it. Explains the website. The concept of small group communities inside a larger fanbase. Then she details all the ways my mom followed my career and celebrated what I was doing with other fans.

It doesn't add up. It's not that Mom wasn't supportive of Midnight Rush. She always encouraged Sarah and I to forge our own path and do what made us happy. But the year before her death, our relationship was strained. She wanted me home and grew frustrated when I didn't seem to have the power or freedom to make that happen.

I could have. I *should* have. I should have walked sooner, made demands, put pressure on the label to pause the tour long enough for me to be with her when she passed.

How could Mom *not* be frustrated when my priorities were so far off what they should have been?

"Did you—" My voice breaks, and I clear my throat and

try again. "Did you know when she died? Did the group know?"

Laney shakes her head, sadness filling her eyes. "Two or three months before the band broke up, she stepped down as moderator, said she was going through something personal and she needed to focus on her family. There were only twenty of us who were still active by that point, and she wrote personal notes to each of us as a goodbye. Then she signed off, and we never heard from her again."

"You got a personal note from my mom," I say.

"I did," she says. "And lucky for you, I was a highly devoted, borderline creepy, extreme Midnight Rush fan. So I documented my years in your mom's fan group by making a series of scrapbooks." She tilts her head toward the bag on the coffee table. "The note from your mom is in the middle one with your second album cover on the front. And other comments she made are woven through all three. Please don't judge me for how much glitter I used. Also don't laugh at all the different MASH games. I saved every one that resulted in me marrying you."

"I don't understand. You saved her comments?"

"It's more like I saved *everyone's* comments. I'd print out screenshots of our conversations. Not all of them. Just the fun ones. Lists of our favorite songs, favorite lyrics. Stories we told about concerts we attended. There were also pictures and ticket stubs and magazine articles. All kinds of stuff. But if you look for your mom, you'll find her in there."

I reach for the bag and pull out the top album. It's navy blue, with the Midnight Rush logo across the front in bright yellow.

"I can't believe you made these."

"I know it's a lot. But that group of fans—they were friends when I didn't really have them anywhere else."

"No, I'm not judging," I say quickly. "This is amazing. And my mom is in here?"

Her expression softens. "Yeah. She is. And *she* was amazing." She reaches over and squeezes my knee, then stands up.

"Wait, where are you going?"

"I left Percy at my house with Ringo. And Sarah will be here any minute. I thought you guys might like to read through them together."

"Sarah knows about these?"

She nods. "She actually drove with me to Hendersonville to pick them up. She looked through a little, but then decided she wanted to wait for you."

I hate to see Laney go, but I also understand why she wants to give this moment to Sarah.

I walk her out to her car, but Sarah is already pulling up, and she looks like she's been crying, so Laney and I don't have much time to say goodbye.

"Thanks for bringing them over," I say. "I still can't wrap my head around it."

"Yeah, it's pretty wild."

I hold her gaze for a long moment. "Laney, I'm sorry about this week. That I've been so...absent."

"You kinda do that," she says. Her tone is gentle, but I still sense the censure in her words. "But you can talk to me about stuff. I know you like to process on your own, and I get that. But if we're going to do this, you have to answer my texts. You have to let me in."

She's right. I know she's right, but it still takes all my willpower to keep my feet planted, to stay right here with her. I don't know why I always feel the impulse to flee. But if there was ever a good reason to break the habit, it's Laney.

"I just get scared," I say. "And then I think I don't deserve you, and then the longer I wait, the worse that feeling gets, and then I just spiral."

She steps forward and lifts her hands to my chest, and I wrap my arms around her waist. "You deserve to be happy," she says. "You're telling yourself you can't have a life when your mom is not here because of the choices you made when she was. But that isn't how life works."

I drop my eyes, shame washing over me, but Laney moves her hands to my face, her thumbs brushing over my beard. "Look at me," she says gently.

I force a breath in through my nose and out through my mouth. I don't want to look, but I want to ignore her even less, so I force my gaze to hers.

Her warm hazel eyes are full of love and compassion and understanding, and suddenly my heart is too big for my chest and emotion is climbing my throat with a ferocity that makes me want to punch something and cry at the same time.

"You deserve to be happy," Laney repeats. "You deserve to have a music career if you want a music career. Or a dog rescue if you want a dog rescue. Or both if you want both. You deserve to love and have people who love you. That's what your mom would want for you. I know that's true."

I pull her against me and bury my face in her hair, letting her words sink in. She smells so good. Familiar and safe and like everything I want in my life. I don't want to let her go, but Sarah is waiting, and Laney is right. There's a part of this my sister and I should do together.

And another part I have to figure out on my own.

SARAH and I are up for hours.

It's weird seeing a catalog of my Midnight Rush years through the eyes of a fan. Even weirder to see Mom's commentary. But it's mostly just amazing. She's funny and encouraging and interested in how the other group members feel about songs and concerts and music videos.

She doesn't mention me by name very often, which was probably intentional on her part. But in the note she wrote to Laney, she *does* mention me.

> *@DollyDaeDreams: To @Laneyfeelstherush—you, my dear, are going places! I have loved catching glimpses of you growing up over the past three years. You have matured into a lovely, thoughtful young woman. You'll be a great vet one day, and I appreciate all the advice about my Marigold! She's a rotten puppy, but you've given me hope she won't be forever. I know you probably won't ever meet Deke for real, but I bet if you did, he'd love you just as much as I do.*

"For real," Sarah says as she reads the note over my shoulder. "It's like she was predicting the freaking future."

"I can't believe you didn't know she was doing any of this," I say as I turn the page to find a two-page spread from *Seventeen* magazine featuring the four of us looking broody and serious and absolutely ridiculous.

There's a message board exchange cut out and included at the bottom of the page.

> *@DollyDaeDreams: Honestly, couldn't they just photo-*

graph these boys looking like boys? Smiling normally?
Like they're happy to be making music every day? Why
so serious?

@laneyfeelstherush: FOR THE SMOLDER. WE NEED
THE SMOLDERS!

"I did know," Sarah says. "I just didn't know it was such a big deal. She tried to get me to join, but I couldn't think of anything worse than watching other teenagers fangirl over my brother."

"Okay, that's fair."

It takes me a long time to work up the courage to ask Sarah my next question. In eight years, I've never asked. Because I believed I already knew the answer, and I didn't want Sarah to prove me wrong. Staying angry at myself was easier because anger was better than sadness—than grief.

"Sarah, was Mom really mad when I didn't come home?"

She takes a deep breath, studying my face. "It's not like she knew when she was gonna die. Like you'd missed the deadline or something. She was just trying to hang on long enough for you to make it."

I shake my head. "I've relived those last couple of months so many times. Gone over the conversations I had with Kevin, with the label. I just kept saying over and over that I needed to go, that she was sick, that she might not make it. And they all just kept reassuring me, telling me everything was going to be fine. That *she* would be fine. And I think I believed them because it was easier than believing I'd lose her."

"I know," Sarah says. "I was mad at you for a really long time. But I get it. We were both just kids, Adam. We weren't supposed to navigate stuff like that by ourselves." She nudges my knee with her toe from where she's sitting on the opposite end of the couch. "You have to let it go now."

"What does that mean?"

"It means stop beating yourself up. Forgive yourself, already. Go be in your stupid boyband and love your freaking amazing girlfriend and *be happy*."

Her words trigger a reaction deep in my gut, something swirling and light that lifts and pushes up, but then a familiar sense of panic quickly stomps it back down again. "I can't, Sarah. I can't let Kevin push me around like he did. I can't go back to other people making choices for me."

"Okay," she says dryly, like I'm missing something incredibly obvious. "So get a different agent who represents *your* best interests. Or, I don't know, just be a grownup and advocate for yourself. Set your terms. Tell them what you're willing to do, and then don't budge. It doesn't have to be one extreme or the other. Be your own boss. Make your own destiny! Captain your own ship!"

"I got it. Stop with the metaphors."

"Good. Cause I couldn't really think of a fitting fourth one." She tosses the throw pillow she's been holding at my head and stands. "I've got to go home. This was fun. Please tell Laney you love her so she'll stay with us forever."

"I'll get right on that," I say.

"So, just in case you really might think about it," Sarah says from the door where she's slipping on her shoes. "Midnight Rush has not announced that you *won't* be at the concert. As far as everyone knows, you'll still be there."

"But the schedule—they've already started doing press."

"And so far, they've done it all individually." She shrugs.

"You know Freddie. With his optimism, he's probably holding out hope you'll still change your mind."

That *does* sound like Freddie.

The big idiot. He really does have a way of getting what he wants.

But maybe this time, it will be what I want too.

CHAPTER TWENTY-EIGHT

Laney

I DON'T KNOW IF ADAM IS THE ONE WHO PREPROGRAMMED MY puppy to wake up at six forty-five every single morning, even on weekends, but I could set my watch by this puppy's schedule. So far, we're twelve for twelve. Twelve mornings at my house. Twelve wake-ups at six forty-five from Ringo's tiny bark, at which time he wants to cuddle and eat breakfast and pee and chew on my underwear all at the same time.

"You're killing me here, Ringo," I say as I roll out of bed and crawl toward his crate. "Why so early, huh?"

He answers with a tiny yip and a tail wag, which, on Ringo, is more like a whole butt wag.

"Fine. You're adorable," I say. "I forgive you."

I unlatch his crate and scoop him up so we can race outside. I still don't trust him enough not to squat the second he's loose, but I do trust him not to pee in my arms.

As soon as we're out the back door, I plop him in the grass, then cheer like only a proud dog mom can when he immediately squats and pees. He runs back to me, little butt wiggling again, and I give him all the praises and hugs and cuddles for being the very best boy.

I feel a sudden impulse to text Adam and tell him how well Ringo is doing sleeping through the night, but I swallow it down. It's been almost a week since I dropped off my Midnight Rush scrapbooks at his house, and I haven't heard from him since.

Well, that's not entirely true. He texted me the morning after, thanking me again, and said he was going to take a few days to work through some things, and he didn't want me to worry if I didn't hear from him.

I haven't worried.

Not really.

But I have been anxious to know how he's doing.

I'm debating the merits of crawling back in bed and taking Ringo with me to grab another hour of sleep. I don't see patients until eleven today, so I technically could. But I do have a couple of post-op patients I could check on, and Dad has been hounding me to click through a QuickBooks tutorial for small business owners for weeks, claiming he can't fully retire until I know how to be both a vet *and* a business owner.

Things have been tenser than normal between my dad and me since the news of the engagement broke. We're mostly okay. Things died down after a few days, and I've successfully managed to field all wedding-related comments and inquiries before any more of them reach Dad.

But I could still use the brownie points. And I *am* already awake.

I breathe out a sigh, then pick Ringo up and look into his

big brown eyes. "You're going to turn me into a workaholic," I say.

In the end, I only arrive at work a little bit early because Ringo chewed through my shoelaces while I was drying my hair, and I had to stop at CVS on my way in to buy some replacements.

When I carry Ringo through the employee entrance, I find Percy and Patty and two other vet techs all standing in a line outside Dad's office, staring at the closed door.

"Um, what's happening here?" I ask.

Percy spins around, eyes wide, and lifts his finger to his lips to shush me. He grabs my elbow and hauls me around the corner into a treatment room. "You aren't supposed to be here until eleven," he whisper-yells.

"I wanted to check on my post-op patients. Where's Dad? Is he okay? Why is everyone staring at his door?"

Percy frowns. "Because he's in there talking to Adam. Who came to the office right now on purpose because *you* aren't supposed to be here yet."

My heart climbs into my throat. Adam is *here*?

Knowing he's so close cracks something open in my chest, and it's all I can do not to burst into Dad's office and throw myself into his arms. I hope he's done needing space because I really don't think I can give him anymore.

Except, *wait*. There's another important part to this equation.

"Why does he need to talk to Dad?" I ask. "What are they talking about?"

"No clue," Percy says. "But girl, wait until you see him. This is a version of Adam I have *never* seen before."

Dad's office door swings open, and I hear Adam's voice. "Yes, sir. I agree," he says.

I step around the corner, heart pounding, and Adam turns.

We make eye contact, and I know exactly what Percy meant.

Adam looks like he just stepped off a movie set. He's wearing black jeans, a black button-down with enough buttons undone to reveal a very pretty stretch of skin at his chest, and a gray leather jacket. The last time I saw him, his beard had mostly grown back—it's been almost three weeks since he shaved in Silver Creek—but he's clean shaven now. Combined with his *very solid* wardrobe choices, he looks like a Deke/Adam hybrid, the two sides of him melded into an improved grownup version of who he used to be.

Incredible. Good enough to eat. Sexy as all get out.

But it's more than that, too, and my brain finally lands on the description that fits best.

Adam looks like *a star.*

Dad steps out of the office behind Adam and claps him once on the back, then he walks over to me. He puts his hands on my shoulders and gives them a quick squeeze. "I like him, Elena," he says softly enough that only I can hear. Then he reaches for Ringo. "Now let me spend some time with my grand dog."

Adam walks toward me, pausing a few feet away. "Maybe we can talk outside?"

I swallow and nod, my brain still trying to come up with a reasonable explanation for Adam talking to my dad. I mean, there is one very obvious reason, but we've only been dating *a month.* It's way too soon for that. Plus, we're kind of going through something else right now.

When I don't move my feet, Percy, who is still standing beside me, nudges me forward until I'm close enough for

Adam to take my hand. He leads me outside to a picnic table that's sitting in the grass behind the office. When the weather's nice, I usually take my lunch breaks out here. I sit down, but Adam stays on his feet, and I get the sense that he's nervous about something.

"Sorry to surprise you," he says. "I was actually going to leave here and come straight to your house."

"You were?"

He nods. "Percy told me you start later on Fridays."

"Yeah, I usually do. But Ringo's been waking me up early."

"Ah. Yeah. Puppies make good alarm clocks."

A chilly October wind lifts the leaves collecting at the edges of the lawn, and I tug down the sleeves of the thermal I'm wearing under my scrubs.

"Do you want to tell me why you were talking to my dad?" I ask.

He looks a little sheepish. "A couple of reasons."

"Okay."

"Patty mentioned he was kinda hard on you about the whole engagement thing."

"You talked to Patty?" I ask.

"Just about vet records for the rescue. But then she brought up the engagement and...yeah. It's hard *not* to talk to Patty once she gets started."

"Very true," I say.

"I thought it might help if I explained to your dad how I actually feel about you. If he knew that I'm not playing games. And that even if we aren't technically engaged *yet,* I think we both know that's where this relationship is headed."

I press my lips together. "You said all of that to him?"

He nods. "I also told him that I am really, *really* in love with you."

I suck in a breath.

"I maybe should have saved that part so I could tell you first."

I practically fly off the bench and throw myself into his arms. He chuckles as he catches me, stumbling a few steps backward as his arms come around me and I bury myself in his chest.

He smells so good. Manly and clean, like leather and soap and sandalwood and Adam and I don't want to ever let him go.

I lean back, keeping my arms around him as I look into his impossibly blue eyes. "I love you too," I say. "So much."

He presses his lips to mine, and all of the doubt and worry that's plagued me the past week fizzles away. There are so many things we still need to talk about. And I'm sure we eventually will. But right now, knowing that we love each other is enough.

I lift my hand to Adam's jaw--his *very smooth* jaw.

Okay, maybe there's *one* thing we need to talk about right now.

I tap my thumb against his cheek. "So...can we talk about this?" I slide my other hand over the shoulder of his *very soft* leather jacket. "And also your incredible wardrobe choices this morning?"

"Actually, that has to do with the *other* reason I came to see your dad."

"Yeah? How so?"

"I figured if I was taking you to New York with me, he'd need to know you weren't coming into work today."

I freeze. "New York?"

He nods. "Midnight Rush is doing an interview on *The Tonight Show*. First one with all four of us present."

It takes my brain a few extra seconds to process what he's telling me.

"*The Tonight Show*," I repeat. "Are you...does that mean...?"

"Yes, and yes," he says, glancing at his watch. "I'm catching a plane in just a few hours." He lifts his lips into a sly half grin. "Want to come?"

"You want me to go to New York with you?"

He shrugs. "I want you to go everywhere with me."

If our last kiss was a warmup, this one is the main event. My emotions feel too big for my chest, too big for the entire freaking world. I'm so proud of him, so happy that *he's* happy.

Adam's hands slide up to my face as he breaks the kiss, but he doesn't pull back. He keeps his face close, his forehead pressed to mine.

"I know it's a lot to ask when you didn't sign up for this, for any of the weird fame stuff. To pull you into this world with fans and paparazzi and invasive questions. But I promise, Laney, I'll do whatever it takes to protect your privacy. To protect *you*."

"I know. I know you will."

His thumb slides across my cheek, and his expression shifts, revealing a new vulnerability. "I still have no idea what I want to do after the concerts," he says. "If I'll want to keep singing or...I don't know. There's so much I don't know."

"Whatever you decide, I'll be right here," I say. "You don't have to know everything right now."

He nods, hesitating for a beat before he says, "I probably need some grief counseling."

My heart squeezes. "I think we all need counseling in one way or another. That's a great idea."

"And I promise I'm going to work on talking instead of running. You helped me recognize how important that is. How much it can help."

"I want you to talk to me about everything, Adam."

"I want that, too."

My gaze catches on a silver pendant hanging around his neck and tucked inside his shirt. I reach for it, lifting it gently. It's a smooth matte silver, with the shape of a flower etched into the top. I've never cared much about whether a man wears jewelry, but this looks good on Adam. Masculine and intentional and sexy, but still subtle. It's not blingy at all. The fact that he's wearing it against his skin so it only peeks out when he moves certain ways makes it seem like he's wearing it for him, and not for his outfit.

Except, *wait*. This isn't just any flower. It's a dahlia.

"Adam," I say, the pendant still in my hand.

"Sarah got it for me this week," he says.

Tears spring to my eyes. "It's a perfect way to keep her with you."

"I think so too." He settles his arms at the small of my back, and I lean into him. "You know, I've thought more than once that my mom would love you. It was nice to learn that she actually did."

I sniff and smile. "I loved her too."

"So what do you say? Want to come to New York? I hate to pressure you, but..." He glances at his watch one more time. "If you're coming, we kind of need to hurry."

"I don't have to worry about work?"

He shakes his head. "Your dad said he's happy to cover for you. And we'll be back before Monday."

"What about Ringo?"

"Your dad's going to watch him."

"Did you think of everything?" I ask.

"I definitely tried."

———

THE NEXT TWELVE hours go by in a blur.

We race home long enough for me to pack, then head to the airport in Asheville to catch our direct flight to New York. As we drive, Adam fills me in on the many, *many* conversations he had over the past week.

With Sarah. Who loves him and had a lot to tell him about what life was *really* like while he was on tour with the band.

With Freddie. Who fired his agent, apologized profusely, and admitted that he always knew, and this part is a direct quote, Adam "couldn't actually live without him."

With Jace. Who learned, the day Adam walked out on the band, that his wife is filing for divorce even though she's currently pregnant with their second child.

Adam seems anxious to see them again, which makes me love him more. These men are a part of his heart. It will be good for all of them to be back together.

We're in Asheville, in line at airport security, the first time I *feel* someone figure out who Adam is. My skin prickles with a strange sense of awareness, then I look up and see a couple of women who look to be about my age staring directly at us.

I squeeze Adam's hand. "Hey. Um, pretty sure those

women recognize you." I tilt my head in the direction of the two women, and Adam turns to look.

"It appears they do," he says.

"So what do we do?"

"Nothing."

"We just ignore them?"

"We do."

"What if they try to talk to you?"

"Then I'll say hello and pose for a picture and send them on their way."

He makes it sound so easy, but once we reach our gate, that's exactly what happens, and it isn't all that bad. Adam introduces me as his fiancée, we all shake hands, I take a picture of the three of them, they tell him how excited they are about the reunion tour and they're hoping to get tickets, then they leave us alone.

Easy.

We're on the plane and settling into our seats when I ask Adam, "Hey, did it bother you that they called you Deke?"

He shakes his head. "Nah. I'm happy to be Deke to them." He leans over and presses a quick kiss to my lips. "As long as I'm always Adam to you."

"I actually know a thing or two about being in love with *Deke*," I say. "And it was pretty fun. But I don't need you to be Deke." The thought fills me with a sudden urgency to make sure he understands, so I turn in my seat and reach over, wrapping both hands around his forearm. "Actually, it's important to me that you know that. If you do these concerts, then decide you never want to leave Lawson Cove again, that would be okay with me. I fell in love with *Adam*. That's the only person I need you to be."

His expression softens, and he leans over and kisses me

one more time. But then he grins. "I don't know, Laney. Those scrapbooks were pretty telling."

My eyes widen. "You are not allowed to make fun of those. It was an act of kindness to share them. You can't laugh!"

"The MASH games were my favorite," he says. "But I veto us living in an apartment when I already own a house. And six kids, Laney? That feels like a lot."

"Please stop," I say, lifting my hands to cover my face. "I can't handle this kind of embarrassment."

"I particularly loved the fanfiction at the back of Year Three," he says.

I drop my hands. "What? There was *not* fanfiction in there."

"Oh, there totally was," he says. "A beach vacation. The band playing a venue nearby. Deke, out for a walk on the beach..."

I reach over and press a hand to his mouth. "Please stop talking. Never *ever* talk about this again."

He wraps his hand around my wrist and pulls my hand away before pressing a kiss to the pad of my thumb. "The writing was actually pretty decent. I think you could do something with this talent of yours."

I drop my face onto my knees and wrap my arms around my head, letting out a low groan. "I can't believe you read that," I say. "I can't believe I gave it to you!"

He chuckles as he drops a hand to my back, rubbing slow circles across my shoulder blades. "I'm glad you did," he says, and I sit back up. "But I'm glad you like the Hope Acres side of me more."

I will always like the Hope Acres side of Adam best.

But it *is* fun to see him reunite with his band in the green room of *The Tonight Show*. It's fun to see them perform live for the first time in eight years. Fun to hear the fans cheering, screaming when the guys walk out and sit on the interview couch.

And I won't lie. It's also pretty fun to have everyone on set treat me like I'm someone special too, simply because I'm here with him.

I can't even begin to wrap my head around where life is going to take us. What it will look like if Midnight Rush becomes a more permanent part of Adam's life. But there's a strong, peaceful certainty deep in my heart that whatever happens, together, we'll be strong enough to handle it.

On stage, Jimmy Fallon congratulates Adam on his recent engagement and asks him to tell the story of how we met.

Adam smiles, thanks him, then jumps right into explaining how he locked himself out of his car and I came to his rescue. "She'll kill me for not leaving this part out of the story," he says, "but when she turned on her car, there was a Midnight Rush song *blasting* through her speakers."

Oh, I am going to kill him.

Except, maybe not. Because the next thing Adam says is, "That was the moment I knew I was going to fall in love with her. And that's exactly what I did."

EPILOGUE

Laney

AND THAT'S THE WHOLE STORY OF HOW I ACCIDENTALLY FELL in love with a popstar.

Sometimes, I still don't believe it myself. But I have a feeling it's going to feel much more real after tonight.

The Ben King Arena in Nashville is packed—the show sold out in less than six hours--and the energy among the fans is everything I expected and more.

The last three months have been bliss--a whirlwind of press events and Midnight Rush rehearsals punctuated with luxurious weeks in Lawson Cove hanging out with the dogs, catching up on work, and enjoying time where we can simply be together. Just the two of us.

But tonight—the concert is what we've been waiting for —planning for.

The guys are ready. Their last week of rehearsal went great, and when I left them in the green room, they were buzzed and happy and excited to be performing again.

Ivy gave me the option to watch the concert from backstage, but I want the full experience, so I've got seats in the front row with Sophie, Sarah and Jake, Percy, and his new boyfriend, Jamal. I might sneak backstage before the end of the show, but for now, there's nowhere else I'd rather be.

The lights dim, strobe lights flashing around the arena, and the crowd goes wild. Sophie jumps up and down beside me, grabbing my hands. "Are you losing your mind right now?"

I smile and laugh. It *is* pretty surreal. Similar in so many ways to the first Midnight Rush concert I attended, when I was only a little bit younger than Sophie. But this concert is different, too. I'm older now, more grounded, more sure of myself.

I know my own worth, what kind of love I deserve, and I've found a person who makes me feel like the very best version of myself. That doesn't have anything to do with the fact that he moonlights as a popstar.

Though, it is a *very delicious* bonus.

The lights on the stage go black and a hush falls over the arena. When they come on again, Midnight Rush has taken the stage and the opening notes of "Curves Like That" blast through the arena.

Adam hits every dance move perfectly, but I don't miss the relief on his face when the song ends, and the crowd erupts into another round of cheers. Song after song, the guys are *on*. They sound amazing, they look amazing, the energy in the crowd is amazing.

I'm going to lose my voice if I don't stop screaming, but I don't even care. It is *so much fun* to watch Adam on stage, especially knowing what it took for him to get here.

During the chorus of "Never Say Never," the four of them

spread out across the stage, reaching down and touching hands, interacting with the fans.

Adam comes over and reaches for my hand. When he lifts it and presses a kiss to my knuckles, the crowd goes wild, and Adam smiles and lets me go, but he keeps his eyes on me as he touches his palm to his chest just over his heart.

The mood settles for the next song, the guys lining up on stools, and Adam retrieves his guitar from backstage.

"So, this next song is about what it feels like to fall in love," Adam says as he sits next to his bandmates. "The trouble is, I wrote it before I'd ever experienced it for myself." He looks over at me and smiles. "But now I do know, so we've reworked the song a bit, and we hope you like it. This is 'The Start of Forever.'"

"Oh my gosh," Sophie says from beside me. "You are living the plot of a romance novel."

As Adam sings the words that were seared into my heart three months ago, I actually disagree with my little sister.

This is better than a romance novel.

Because it's real.

The last three months have not been perfect.

I had my first real panic attack when a very enthusiastic Midnight Rush fan showed up at work with a dog she "borrowed" from a friend so she could get close to me and ask a million questions about the band.

Adam and I had our first very stupid fight about communication and timing and responding to texts when he's on the other side of the country.

And we've both struggled to keep up with work at the rescue and my responsibilities at my father's practice without taking advantage of the people who pick up the slack when we run off to do Midnight Rush things.

But through all the ups and downs, we've only grown closer. We've learned how to communicate, how to fight in a way that makes it very easy to make up after. And we're stronger for having worked through the hard *and* the easy.

Hours later, when the concert is over and the arena is empty, Adam and I are alone in our hotel room, but we're too buzzed on adrenaline, and for him, the high of performing, to actually fall asleep.

We're stretched out on the bed, my head propped on his shoulder, and I'm scrolling through all the Midnight Rush posts on Instagram. The general consensus seems to be that the band sounds better than ever, the concert was a magical experience, and can they *please* release a new album so the Midnight Rush magic can last forever.

Adam says they've talked about a new album, but who knows if it will ever be more than talk. Freddie has a solo album dropping next month, and Leo isn't sure he actually *wants* to be on stage when he loves being in the production studio so much more. But there's still time to figure all that out.

"I want to ask you something," Adam says.

I put down my phone and roll onto my side to face him. "Okay."

He pushes up on his elbow, mirroring my position. I see the scar from his fall into the ravine, the first time I saw him run away from something. "I don't want you to freak out."

I narrow my eyes. "Okay."

"Because it's fast."

My heart starts to beat a little faster.

Then Adam pulls a ring out of his pocket and sets it on the bed between us.

"Maybe because we've been pretending all this time, I

have a pretty good idea of what it feels like to be engaged to you, and I *really* like it. So I thought...maybe we could make it official."

I pick up the diamond with trembling hands. It's beautiful—an oval stone set in a circle of tiny sapphires.

"It's my mother's ring," he says softly. "I talked it over with Sarah, and we decided Mom would want you to have it."

I close my eyes, and tears slide down my cheeks.

"Will you marry me, Laney?"

I lean over and kiss him, ring clutched in my fist, and he lifts his hand to my cheek, wiping away my tears.

"Of course I'll marry you."

I open my palm, and he picks up the ring, slowly sliding it onto my ring finger.

As fate would have it, it's a perfect fit.

Adam kisses me again, and I lean back onto the bed, pulling him down with me.

We've kissed countless times in the past three months. Six-second kisses. *Much longer* kisses. But this one feels different. This one feels like a beginning.

It's the early hours of the morning, the sun turning the sky purple and orange as it rises above the Nashville skyline, before we're finally ready to sleep.

My head is on Adam's shoulder, my eyes getting heavier and heavier when he murmurs, "The forever I want really did start in your eyes."

I lift my head and prop it on his chest. "Are you seriously quoting your own lyrics to me?"

He grins without opening his eyes. "I probably need some new material, don't I?"

"Yes, please," I say as I settle back down. "An entire album of love songs."

"Done," he says. "I've got all the inspiration I need right here."

I chuckle. "That was cheesy, Adam."

"You're cheesy."

It's the last thing he says before he finally drifts off to sleep.

The truth is, *we're* both pretty cheesy. At least when we're talking about each other.

But love can do that to you.

And I wouldn't have it any other way.

For a Once Upon a Boyband Bonus Epilogue, please visit www.jennyproctor.com and click on Bonus Content.

ACKNOWLEDGMENTS

My first ever concert was New Kids on the Block. I was twelve years old, and I had a New Kids sleeping bag, and a poster on my wall, so I was, as much as I could be at twelve, a dedicated fan. Of course, this was just the beginning. I eventually fell in love with the Backstreet Boys and NSYNC and was exposed to the magic of One Direction when my daughter became mildly obsessed with Harry Styles. These bands and many others contributed to an incredible playlist that accompanied the writing of this book. So I must be grateful to all the boybands who ever decided to make music. Trust me when I say we are ALL eternally grateful.

To my lovely niece, Elena, thank you for letting me borrow your name! I thought of you every time I sat down to write.

To all the amazing people who help me do what I do, thank you from the bottom of my heart. From my cover designer to my critique partner to my agent to my social media manager to my accountant, there is a whole team of people who keep me afloat, and I would be lost without them. Lucy, Kiki, Emily, Kim, Marie, Cathy...and so many others, thank you, thank you.

Josh, you're the greatest influence in every love story I write. Twenty-five years in, thanks for still making me swoon. Love you.

ABOUT THE AUTHOR

Jenny Proctor is an award-winning author of more than fourteen romantic comedies and an Amazon bestseller.

She began her career in publishing in 2013; her writing has been a constant since then and is now her full-time focus, but in the past, she spent several years as the owner and managing editor of Midnight Owl Editors and as the chair of the Storymakers Conference.

Wired for relationships, Jenny loves public speaking, teaching, and building lasting connections.

Jenny was born in the mountains of Western North Carolina, a place she considers one of the loveliest on earth. She loves to hike with her family and spend time outdoors, but she also adores lounging around her home, reading great books or watching great movies and, when she's lucky, eating delicious food she did not have to prepare herself.

Jenny currently resides with her husband and children in the Charleston, South Carolina area. To learn more, find Jenny online at www.jennyproctor.com.

ALSO BY JENNY PROCTOR

The Some Kind of Love Series

Love Redesigned

Love Unexpected

Love Off-Limits

Love in Bloom

How to Kiss a Hawthorne Brother Series

How to Kiss Your Best Friend

How to Kiss Your Grumpy Boss

How to Kiss Your Enemy

How to Kiss a Movie Star

The Oakley Island Romcom Series

Eloise and the Grump Next Door

Merritt and Her Childhood Crush

Sadie and the Badboy Billionaire

The Appies Hockey Romance Series

Absolutely Not in Love

Romancing the Grump

Other Novels

The Christmas Letters

Her Last First Date

Just One Chance

Love at First Note

Wrong For You

Mountains Between Us

The House at Rose Creek

Made in the USA
Columbia, SC
26 November 2024